Barrie Seppings spent his early career in advertising, moving between Australia and South East Asia. He now lives in Sydney with his family.

ShelfLife

Barrie Seppings

First published by Rubber/Road in 2017
This edition published in 2017 by Rubber/Road

Copyright © Barrie Seppings 2017

https://twitter.com/BarrieSeppings

ShelfLife

EPUB format: 9781925579482
Print on Demand format: 9781925579499

Cover design by Red Tally Studios

Publishing services provided by Critical Mass
www.critmassconsulting.com

Contents

For Sharon, Della & Izzy.

Crash cart

Trent knew if he hesitated any longer the blood-spattered man on the gurney would become a blood-spattered corpse. And it would all be his fault.

'I could just leave him here,' Trent thought. 'The nurses will probably handle it.' A sharp, rattling intake of breath focused his attention. He lifted the plastic oxygen mask from the man's face. Glistening and pulpy, the face made a noise somewhere between a gurgle and a cough. 'OK, let's think this through,' he spoke to himself, a calming technique he'd learned from a yoga teacher he dated briefly. 'That didn't sound too good. Probably blood pooling in the trachea. Time to go, buddy.'

He took a deep breath and pushed the gurney through the doors.

'What is that man doing here?'

'Sir, you cannot go that way!'

'The bleeding's internal, we need to address that first.'

'What's her insurance status? Does she have a next of kin listed?'

Some of the faces in the emergency room turned to look as Trent surged into the searing fluorescent light. Snatches of shouted instruction whizzed past his ears like tracer fire. Coats flapped as they trailed behind nurses and orderlies. Trent could barely focus. His heart snapped at his ribcage.

'I asked you,' said a female voice, 'what have we got?'

The face loomed closer and came into focus. Her skin was lightly freckled, blonde hair pulled into a severe ponytail, as if sailing into a headwind. 'Please don't make me ask you again.'

Trent blinked, struggling to reconcile the aggressive tone with the child-like face. Since when did they let teenagers run emergency rooms?

The nurse reached across, flipped the badge on Trent's coat and recoiled. 'So sorry, doctor. I've just started residency here and it's been one of those shifts. Can I have the patient's status, please?'

What had he overheard the paramedic say only a moment ago in the receiving dock? 'Asian male, mid thirties. Assault victim. Multiple facial lacerations, multiple contusions, possible internal bleeding. Pressure is ninety over fifty, falling fast. They used the paddles on him twice in the bus and administered ten ampules of morph, thirty of adrenaline. And I think...'

The admissions nurse looked up from her clipboard. 'Yes, doctor?'

Trent swallowed hard. 'I think he has fluid on the lungs. Blood. Probably need to drain the cavity before we attempt re-sus.'

The nurse reached for the mask and lifted it off the man's face. The body convulsed and started coughing. A small, ragged fountain of blood shot into the air. Trent jumped back. The nurse returned to the clipboard and made a new set of scribbles.

'Correct you are, doctor. I could get him into OR twelve in the next slot if we hustle,' she said, glancing at her watch, 'but I just don't have anyone to get him to the prep area right now.'

'I can take him.' Trent volunteered.

The nurse looked directly at him. 'But you're a doctor, right?'

'I was just on my break, trying to clear my head,' Trent threw a thumb over his shoulder at the scrum of nurses working the ER. 'And you guys seem pretty busy in here.'

'You're sure?' The walkie-talkie on her belt crackled into life and she reached for it, fiddling with its dial.

'There's nothing wrong with helping each other out once in a while, is there?' Trent smiled.

Her face relaxed and she returned the smile. 'If you say so, Doctor…?' she hunted for his name badge.

'Oh, I'm Doctor, umm, just, you know, helping out…'

A violent spluttering erupted on the gurney and the nurse snapped back into action. 'Okay, Doctor "Helping Out", get him down to prep area B. I'll call ahead and let 'em know the cavalry's coming.'

'Umm. Can you point me in the right direction?'

The nurse paused to stare at him, eyes narrowing.

'I'm new. Here, at this hospital. Probably why we haven't seen each other. Around. Yet.'

'Yeah, that must be why,' she said, hooking a single, errant strand of hair behind her ear. 'Take the elevator on your left. Go down to B2. Straight, then right. Swiftly, doctor.' She jabbed her clipboard at the body on the gurney. 'I think this one's on the way out.'

Trent pushed the gurney into the lift. The floor numbers seemed to move about at will. He blinked several times before finding B2, stabbing it repeatedly. He flipped his name badge back around to conceal the ID, smoothed his hair and leaned in to check his reflection in the lift doors. Trent straightened up immediately once he noticed the surveillance camera mounted on the ceiling and tried to check his watch casually yet professionally.

His breathing echoed in the metal confines of the lift, reminding him of the man on the gurney. Trent lifted the patient's mask. No movement. The 'ding' of the lift sent him jumping backwards and the mask snapped back onto the patient's bloodied face, provoking another desperate, liquid intake of breath.

The operating level was coated in polished steel, bathed in a soft blue glow and seemed almost deserted. Trent could hear the murmur of voices, low and measured, as he straightened up, assembled his serious face and strode along the corridor, looking for OR twelve.

He rounded a corner and discovered a small person waiting for him in a pool of light. It was difficult to tell the gender beneath the gown, cap and gloves. Trent almost turned and ran, but took the last few steps with as much purpose as he could muster. This was dangerously close to actual surgery and he was very far from being an actual surgeon.

'You must be the amazing Doctor Helpful,' the tiny doctor said.

Trent thought the voice sounded more female than male.

'Kelly said you were the third amazing thing she's seen this afternoon.'

'I'm only third?'

'Don't worry, the other two were amazingly bad,' she said, removing the breathing mask, cutting the clothing away and feeling her way slowly along the patient's torso. 'Help out in ER on your break often, doctor?'

'I help when I can,' Trent's smile widened as he hovered near the gurney. He didn't want to end his incredible run of being viewed as gallant and helpful, but also didn't want to do any actual helping. 'I should get back to my –'

The patient's eyes bulged open. The body convulsed, sending charts and equipment to the floor.

'Get me some tylenphosol and mediprosen.' She pointed at a large cabinet behind him. 'Then secure the restraints.'

Trent stared at the patient, thrashing, sputtering blood and turning purple.

'Behind you, doctor.' The woman raised her voice but remained calm.

Trent spun around and scanned the shelves, pronouncing the name of each chemical under his breath as he read it. He plucked two bottles and delivered them to the woman, who palmed them without looking up.

'If you could secure the restraints as I asked, please doctor, I would appreciate it,' she said, prepping the syringes and flinging the used bottles at a bin.

Trent reached under the gurney and used his body weight to contain the thrashing patient while he tensioned the straps.

'Careful, doctor! We don't want to break anything that's not already broken, do we?' she said.

He loosened the straps a fraction and stood back.

'You're welcome to join us, doctor, but I'm sure you have more urgent matters to attend to.' Her voice softened as she looked up at him. 'But seriously, thanks for being the hero on this one. I wish we had more doctors like you around here.'

Trent started in on his 'no need to thank me' speech but the nurse had already spun the gurney and sailed it into the blinding light of the operating room. The doors swung closed behind her.

In the sudden quiet of the prep area he heard the pounding of his own pulse in his ears. He placed a hand on his chest to help slow his breathing but felt something warm and moist. A red smear oozed from one side of his pale blue coat to the other. He didn't want this little act to end, but he knew he should get off the stage. 'Time to go,' Trent thought. 'Before I do any real damage.'

As the doors of the elevator opened to the intake area Trent felt like a diver returning to the surface. He loitered on the threshold and looked around for Kelly, the admitting nurse who had dubbed him 'third most amazing', but found no sign of her. He wondered if she might be in the admin section, and under what pretence he might be able to extract her phone number. Patient follow-up? Quarterly performance review? Situational de-brief?

He glanced at his watch and decided not chance his arm any further. Besides, Robert would be pissed at having to wait so long for him. Trent strode across the ER, nodded at a couple of orderlies who were arguing over paperwork and pushed through the swing doors back to the receiving dock. Only twenty minutes earlier he had been sniffing about, nosing through the racks of equipment when the ambulance lurched to a halt and the harried paramedics spilled out. Desperate to unload their cargo and respond to a fresh catastrophe, they had wheeled the gurney to the edge of the dock, spotted Trent in his borrowed lab coat, barked a quick set of instructions and left the bleeding man in his care. What was he supposed to have done? With his medical experience, didn't he have some kind of duty to step in and help? The delivery dock was quiet now, almost deserted. Trent looked back at the doors leading to the intake area. A fresh commotion broke out on the other side. He exhaled, smiled to himself and walked on.

* * *

'Where the fuck have you been? You said you were just going to leave the brochure at the procurement manager's office,' Robert snarled without looking up from his phone. Despite being naturally heavyset, with an additional layer that had settled over his beltline, Robert always looked like he'd just showered and changed, even in the middle of the day. He pushed himself off the wall and fell into step alongside Trent. 'I have to be at General Mercy by three, remember? Some of us actually need to make our sales targets if we want to keep our jobs.'

'Don't be a dick, Robert. We'll get there in time,' said Trent. He didn't naturally dislike his colleague, but the barbs about his position in the company made it easier to get there.

Robert looked across at Trent's chest and grimaced. 'Jesus, did you just do open heart surgery or something?' He reached into his pocket, exchanged his phone for car keys.

Trent looked down, saw the smear of blood. His hands trembled as he unbuttoned the lab coat, the adrenaline already receding as he recalled the thrill of walking the hospital corridors, the orderlies giving him nods and the nurses giving him shy half-smiles. 'Just some nurse, bumped into me while she was carrying a stack of plasma packs,' he lied. 'Must have burst one open.'

Immediately Trent started to think of a way to go back, to stay longer, but without the fear of being caught. He wanted it to be legitimate.

'I swear. Is there anything you won't do to get a girl's phone number?' Robert shook his head. 'Except to ask?'

'Seriously, I was just trying to get a look at what other brands they were stocking in the ER,' Trent protested, balling up the lab coat and dumping it in an open laundry hamper. They walked out of the main entrance of the hospital and made their way toward the car park. 'You ever heard of industrial espionage?'

'You ever heard of due process? Why don't you just put an information request through admin, like I do? It's a non-profit hospital, they actually have to disclose how they spend their money.'

'If I did everything the way you did it, then I'd be doing everything the hard way,' Trent said as they approached Robert's car. The sun was high overhead and the silver Lexus dazzled in the blinding light, chirping as the door locks released. 'And where would be the fun in that?'

Keep Austin wired

Shanti made a show of checking her watch as she resisted the charms of a pod of Colombian art directors at the bar, but not to the extent they were dissuaded from buying her another drink. The low cut of her white tank top against her caramel skin kept catching eyes and detaining glances, leaving her free to choose her rate of engagement. The main lounge of The Driskill was swimming in deep leather Chesterfield couches and oil paintings of hunting scenes. The stuffed head of a longhorn steer stared balefully at the crowd as they high-fived each other and barked into their phones. Considering it was the last night of the most popular week of one of the most over-subscribed conference-cum-festivals on the tech industry calendar, the scene wasn't quite as bad as she had expected. However, considering it was her last night before returning home to face the uncertain politics of work and the relentless pressure of family, she had been hoping for more.

If it weren't for Trent, she would probably have fled across town to the strip of whiskey bars and music joints where, according to Thrillist, the Austin locals went to escape the 'insufferable hordes' of South By SouthWest. Bumping into him last night had triggered a flurry of memories from her time in London and she was keen for a proper rewind.

Trent waded through the crowd, trailing a compact stack of executive luggage on wheels. He wore a white business shirt untucked and open at the collar beneath a tailored charcoal jacket. 'See, I told you the 'Skill would be fine. It's so great to see you again.'

He leant down and embraced Shanti, kissing her on the cheek. Her thick, black bob swayed as she moved to kiss his other cheek, but he had already pulled away and they wavered awkwardly for a moment.

'I forgot, you Euros with your double cheek-pecks.' Laughing away the embarrassment he eased himself on to the barstool Shanti had been saving. 'That was so funny when we saw each other last night, wasn't it?'

'Too funny. I'm standing in the queue and then I see you in another queue going past me in the opposite direction and I'm thinking –'

'This is a scene out of a late 90s rom-com.'

'Exactly,' Trent slapped his thigh. 'You should have given me your number on a slip of paper, then it would have blown away and I would have spent the rest of the night on a madcap adventure trying to find you again.'

'I guess the net killed off that whole genre of Hollywood storylines, didn't it?' Shanti swizzled her drink. 'Anyway, I'm glad you're here. It's good to see you again.'

'You too. God, it's been, what? Almost two years since we worked together in London?'

'Longer. That company was total chaos.'

'Like the world needed another share trading platform,' Trent shook his head. 'Too much money, not enough clues.

Segways in the office. Massages and koi ponds. All those parties. Spending money like it was going out of fashion.'

'Maybe that's why the mood at Southby seems so familiar. I remember you enjoyed yourself though,' Shanti smiled and finished her drink. 'How many receptionists did you end up going through at that place?'

'You should talk,' Trent gave her arm a light slap. 'Every week there was another poor little coder who'd never been that close to a girl he hadn't downloaded, crying in the HR manager's office because you couldn't quite remember his name in the morning.'

'You are such a bitch,' Shanti returned a playful slap on the shoulder. 'I wasn't that bad, was I?'

'Well, not every week, but it did seem like you were on some sort of a mission.'

'First time away from home, in a big city, earning my own money. You can't blame a girl for wanting to make up for lost time.'

'Speaking of…' Trent swivelled on his stool, hoping to snag the eye of the bartender. 'What have you been doing with your time since London? Still in *Cher*-many, working for your university pals?'

'Yes to Munich, no to the university pals.'

'Did they implode like our London comrades?'

'Quite the opposite. Started getting successful, brought in some Swedish management consultants who pushed them out and took control. Changed their name to Opod. Heading for IPO, apparently.'

'Seriously? It's just a hotel room aggregator, isn't it?' Trent brushed his lapel.

'Started that way, but then the Swedes went all Pac-man, gobbled up a bundle of specialist travel sites. Yours truly had to figure out how to migrate each one of them onto the existing platform in literally a week.'

'Which is why they pay you the medium-sized bucks, no doubt.'

'Hardly,' Shanti snorted. 'I guess the money isn't too bad, and I rent a place from my uncle, so it's affordable, but I was really pushing for some equity.'

'And did you get some?'

'Nope. They sent me here to Southby as kind of a consolation prize. I wasn't going to turn that down, was I?' Shanti smiled and finished her drink. 'What about you, still working for your parents?'

'Ha,' Trent grimaced. 'Well, yes, but it sounds much better the way I say it.'

'Which is how?'

'I'm a VP of Strategy and Biz Dev for a med tech company based in New York,' Trent announced, shooting his shirtsleeves out from the ends of his jacket and sitting a little more upright.

Shanti laughed. 'And how has that line been working for you this week?'

'Truthfully, I think I'm ready to move on to the next phase of my career.' Trent smiled and sat back. 'And when I do, I want you to come and work for me.'

'Oh dear, I'm going to need another drink before I hear this one,' Shanti raised an eyebrow and the bartender sailed over. 'I'll have a vodka lime and my friend here, if I remember correctly, will have a scotch rocks.'

Trent nodded.

'Same drink, same schtick. Reminds me of London. Every week in you'd swing by my desk and go: "Shanti! Shanti! I've got a killer idea for an app. Buy me a drink and I'll tell you about it." Remember?'

'You have to admit, some of those ideas were borderline genius,' said Trent.

'What? Like the dating app for dogs?'

'You laugh, but I saw some guys pitch basically the same idea on a VC stage here this week.'

'Always were a man ahead of your time, Trent.'

'You mock, but this time I've got something that's truly life-changing,' Trent took a sip and stared at Shanti. Shanti returned the stare with a side order of sly smile.

'Dammit Shanti, aren't you going to ask me about my idea?'

'Tell me about your idea, Trent,' Shanti smirked.

'Forget it. You're not going to take it seriously.'

'Oh, come on Trent, look around,' Shanti waved at the lounge full of conference goers talking at each other at maximum volume, lanyards swaying. 'These big tech conferences are like an evangelical church. The preacher gets up on stage to deliver an uplifting keynote, saying all you have to do is believe in yourself, believe in your idea, hire an IP lawyer, let the angels find you and take you up to IPO heaven.' She had risen from her seat, hands clenched, arms outstretched, eyes shut.

'That's pretty good,' Trent laughed. 'The bit about angels especially. But listen, this idea is important to me. I had an experience – '

'Religious? Out of body?' Shanti grinned as she regained her perch on the barstool.

'Way better,' Trent paused for effect. 'I became someone else.'

'What do you mean?'

'A couple of weeks ago, I accidentally became a surgeon. It didn't last long, but it was absolutely amazing,' he rose from his seat and placed his palms together under his chin.

'I've been trying to figure out a way to make it happen again and yesterday, while I was sitting in one of these conference sessions, it came to me.'

'You're going back to med school?'

'God no. Who has time for that? What I'm talking about is harnessing the power of the shared economy, removing friction from the transaction and satisfying un-met demand. I've got an idea that will change people's lives.'

'You sound like one of these wannabe startup douches,' she took a sip. 'Except maybe worse.'

'Okay, let me run a demonstration for you,' Trent looked around the crowded bar. 'Pick someone.'

'Like who?' Shanti furrowed her brow.

'Someone old. Someone blue. Someone in a fedora. Doesn't matter.'

'Someone cute?'

'As you wish. Say you're doing a short survey about a new product. Offer them a free drink for five minutes of their time,' he motioned for her to leave. 'Quick, my flight is in a couple of hours. Go find someone. Bring them here. I'll ask a bunch of questions. You'll see the idea and it will blow your mind. Promise.'

'Oh, Trent, you really haven't changed,' Shanti slid off her barstool, straightened her skirt and made her way into the crowd, scanning faces as she moved. She had missed being around people like Trent. People with the energy and confidence to treat life as one big game. No wonder he was good at sales. Trent had been one of the best in the highly competitive team in the London office when they worked together, despite his heart never really appearing to be in it. A lot of people sniped that Trent had the safety net of his parents' wealth to fall back on, but Shanti couldn't help but wonder what he might achieve if he really had to fight for it. *Just because you're good at doing something doesn't mean that's the thing you should be doing* he had often counselled in the dying days of London as she searched frantically for another coding job, hoping to avoid a forced return home to Munich. Like most people, Trent underperformed when it came taking his own advice.

She rounded a column to find a group of women in pantsuits and pearls, cackling over bellinis and twirling their lanyards. Nope. Trent would just start flirting with them and she'd never get to hear about his idea. A little deeper into the crowd she spotted a man staring into his phone, with broad shoulders and v-shaped swimmer's torso, something she admired greatly in men, far less so in women. He stood a little taller than she did and his thinning hair had been clipped to about the same length as his stubble. Luckily, he had a fairly regular-shaped head. Not all men were so blessed. Shanti found it an altogether appealing package, although she wanted to deduct a few points for the checked shirt draped over a faded graphic t-shirt (a print she was certain she'd seen on Threadless the previous summer), paired with lightly distressed jeans and an undoubtedly limited edition pair of sneakers. Honestly, it was like a global uniform for pixel pushers. This would be easy, she thought to herself.

'Enjoying the conference?' Shanti breezed into his personal space.

'Thanks,' he said without glancing up from his phone. 'But I'm trying to not take any more flyers. It's all just landfill.'

Shanti took a half step backwards, but quickly regrouped for a more targeted approach.

'Oh, I'm so sorry. I was actually looking for some design expertise,' she waited a moment while the lure flashed in the water. 'We have a new product in beta and we're running some one-on-one focus groups with leaders from the design industry.'

'One-on-one focus groups?' he looked up from his phone with a raised eyebrow. The eyebrow was joined by its twin as he took in Shanti's face. 'I mean, if that's what you're doing, that's fine, I guess. What's the product?'

'It's in early design stage,' she pushed her hair back and patted the bob into place. 'Just a few minutes of your time. I'd love to borrow your expertise, if you don't mind?'

Shanti broke out a smile and let her gaze drift downwards.

'Sure. Why not? Happy to help,' he returned the smile and pocketed his phone.

'Fantastic. I'm Shanti,' she extended her hand. 'Come and meet my colleague.

He'll take you through the questions.'

'Okay,' his smile slipped a little.

They shook hands slowly and he paused a moment to take her in as she turned to weave through the crowd.

'I didn't catch your name,' she called over her shoulder as she led the way back to the bar.

'Gavin. Is this your first Southby?'

'It is.'

'How did you find it?'

'Way bigger than I expected, but the energy of the place just keeps you going, right?'

'True. But lots of people seem like they're just drinking the kool-aid. I suppose some of them are genuine, right?'

'A little of column A, a little of column B.' Shanti came to a halt by the bar where Trent was in animated conversation with one of the pearl and pantsuits crew. She didn't wait for a break in the conversation.

'This is my colleague, Trent Carlisle. He'll be running the survey. Trent, this is Gavin.'

Trent wavered for a moment before excusing himself. He stood and offered a hand.

'I want to thank you for helping us out, Gavin. Should take five, ten minutes tops. Take a seat. What are you drinking?'

'I wasn't, but I'll take a rum and coke. What are you developing?' Gavin hopped up on to a barstool. 'Your lovely colleague here's a little short on detail.'

'Still in early development.' Trent waved the bartender over. 'Before we get started, we just need a bit of background on you first. If that's okay?'

'Sure,' Gavin shrugged. 'I'm an open book.'

'Fantastic. Here's the first question.' Trent stared into Gavin's eyes, allowing the drama to flow into the silence. 'Are you happy?'

'Ah-ha, yeah, I guess,' Gavin stifled a laugh. He glanced toward Shanti, as if seeking explanation.

'Now that this conference is almost over, we all have to go home, back to our regular lives,' Trent waved grandly around the bar. 'But what if you could go anywhere and be anyone?'

Gavin blinked. Then again.

'Where would you go? What would you do? Who would you be?' Trent leaned in even closer.

'Can I think about that for a moment?' Gavin turned fully to Shanti and leant towards her, placed a hand by the side of his face to create a small moment of privacy. 'Is this how you normally do your product surveys?' he asked in a loud whisper.

'Actually, yes,' she laughed and pulled back, 'Our methods may seem unconventional, but it's all part of the process.'

'Okay.' Gavin turned back to Trent. 'I'd probably go and be Marty.'

'Marty? Who's Marty?' asked Trent.

'Mate of mine. Deckhand on a yacht.'

'Oooh, nice! Where's the yacht?'

'In the Mentawis.'

Trent stared back, raising his eyebrows to ask for clarification.

'Off the coast of Sumatra.'

More eyebrows.

'Indonesia. It's a surf boat. He's a deckhand and a surf guide. Takes groups of surfers around tropical islands and shows them perfect waves.'

'That. Is. Fantastic!' Trent leapt to his feet and put his hand up for a high five. Gavin sat, confused for a moment, but felt compelled to return the palm slap. Shanti smiled, watching Trent's performance as the drinks arrived.

'I don't get it. Why does he think that's fantastic?' asked Gavin, looking to Shanti again.

'Okay. Now what is it that you do, Gavin?' Trent continued.

'I'm a designer with an ad agency in Melbourne. The one in Australia,' answered Gavin.

'Melbourne's cool. I love Melbourne. Keep it flowing, man.' Trent rolled his hand in encouragement. 'Where do you live?'

'Umm, well I'm in a share house right now, with three friends.'

'Girlfriend?'

'No, they're all just friends, flatmates, the usual,' Gavin checked Shanti's reaction, but she gave none.

'I meant: do you have a girlfriend?' Trent clarified.

'Not, um, currently,' he checked again, and Shanti checked him checking.

'OK, nice and simple,' Trent clapped his hands. 'So here we have a cool design guy, sharing a house with cool friends in one of the world's least-visited cool cities. I love you, Gav, and I love your surfing mate. I have one more question: have you ever wanted to trade places with Marty?'

'All the freaking time!' said Gavin, 'Do you know how cold it gets in Melbourne in winter?'

'Try Munich,' challenged Shanti.

'Don't worry my dear, we'll get to you in a moment.' Trent placed a hand on her shoulder but kept his gaze locked on Gavin. 'Do you think Marty would want to trade places with you?'

'Probably.' Gavin sat back. 'He crashes on our couch sometimes and hangs with us when he's on a break. He comes into my work, we go crate digging, see bands, watch girls walk past. So, yeah, I guess.'

'You see that, Shanti? That's the demonstration,' said Trent clapping his hands together again. 'We all want to trade places sometimes. Some of us do it already. It's actually an unspoken social norm, just waiting to be codified and scaled.' Trent was up and talking with his hands.

'And monetised,' said Gavin.

'Yes, exactly. My god, Gavin, you're right there, you've got it already,' Trent placed a hand on his shoulder.

'Is that your product?' Shanti crossed her arms and frowned. 'A job swap platform?'

'I think he's talking about swapping lives,' said Gavin. 'Aren't you, Trent?'

'Neither of you is exactly right, but Gavin is less wrong.' Trent placed his finger in the air as he took a drink. 'I *am* talking about changing lives, but there's no money in swap platforms. This is about product. Inventory. Rental revenue.'

'Holy shit, Trent, do you want people to rent out their lives? To other people? For money?' asked Shanti.

'You got it in one,' Trent winked at her. 'Welcome aboard.'

'That's pretty crazy,' Gavin laughed and took a sip. 'I mean, cool idea, but functionally it would never work.'

'Where do you see the issue?' asked Trent.

'I'm not sure how you'd be able to structure the search algorithm to deliver meaningful results against such fuzzy criteria,' Gavin said.

'You structure algorithms for a living, do you?' Shanti crossed her arms.

'I mean, well, I don't create the algorithms, if that's specifically what you're asking,' Gavin rubbed the stubble on his scalp.

'That was what I was specifically asking, yes,' Shanti smirked.

'Easy tiger. Shanti here is something of a legend in German e-commerce and trading platforms, I'll have you know,' said Trent, placing an arm around her shoulder. 'One of the smartest coders I know.'

'Oh, shut up. You don't know anything about code either. But I appreciate the compliment,' she brushed Trent's arm away. 'What sort of design do you do back in Melbourne?'

'Front end. User experience. Experimental interfaces,' he took a drink and shrugged his shoulders.

'You design websites?' asked Shanti.

'Hey look, if that's the end of the survey then thank you for the drink and good luck with everything.' Gavin pushed himself off his barstool.

'Oh, come on, buddy,' Trent protested.

'I'm sorry,' Shanti placed a hand on his bicep and gave it a squeeze. 'I didn't mean that. It was rude and I shouldn't have said it.'

'Did I tell you that Shanti can be a bit of a bitch, sometimes?' Trent offered. 'Jesus, Trent, I'm trying to apologise, here,' said Shanti, still holding Gavin's arm. The shape of it pleased her. 'He's right, I can be. But mostly I'm not. Back me up here, Trent.'

'I'd say 49 per cent bitch, weighted average.'

Gavin laughed, breaking the tension. 'You guys are kinda odd, you know that? Cool, but odd.'

'I'll take that as a compliment,' Shanti smiled and patted his arm once more. 'Did you meet many other cool, odd people here this week?'

'Y'know, I came here expecting the whole town to be full of wankers, but I got that wrong.'

'You sound disappointed,' said Trent, pulling out his phone and waving it. 'Sorry, I just need to book a cab to the airport.'

'I kind of *am* disappointed, but mainly in myself. A lot of the people here are talking about inventing stuff, doing deals, launching companies, changing the world. Kind of like you guys. But then I think about what I'll be doing when I get home – pushing pixels around a screen, doing whatever the client tells me. I just feel…'

'So what do you want to do instead?' Trent glanced up from his phone. 'Go and be your friend Marty on the surf boat?'

'I wanted to become a war photographer,' said Gavin.

'Serious?' Shanti leaned in closer.

'Totally serious. I applied for a course in Spain. Super intense, they only take eight students a year. But it turns out you have to already be a legit news photographer. So they didn't let me in.'

'This world can be so cruel to amateurs. Hey, bingo, I have a ride,' Trent pocketed his phone and spread his arms. 'Shanti,

I hate to love you and leave you like this, but my plane is leaving. We've got a lot more to talk about, you realise.'

'You've always got more to talk about,' Shanti stood on the rung of her barstool to give Trent a hug, but still only came up to his chest. 'So good to see you again. I mean that.'

'I know you do,' he took both her hands in his. 'Now, I know I've said this before, but I'm very excited about this idea.'

'You're right, I have heard you say that before,' she laughed.

'Okay, you know what? I'm not going to say anything more about it, I'm just going to go ahead and get it started,' he straightened his collar and buttoned his cuffs. 'So when I call you in a couple of weeks, be ready.'

'Sure thing, Trent,' Shanti shook her head. 'I'll be waiting by the phone.'

'That's my girl.' Trent slapped a few bills on the bar. 'Gavin, really great to meet you, man. You seem very switched on. Will you leave your deets with Shanti, so I can get in touch?'

'I guess so,' Gavin met Trent's outstretched hand. 'Are you planning another survey?'

'No. So I can find you and kill you if you try and steal my idea,' Trent stared directly at Gavin, holding his grip but not shaking it. Several moments passed.

'Ha! I'm just fucking with you, Gavin,' laughed Trent. Gavin exhaled and held his chest in relief. 'As if I'd kill you myself.'

Trent paused for a moment and broke into a fresh round of laughter. Gavin held his palms up. 'Like I said, you guys are odd.'

'And you seem cool, too, my friend,' Trent pulled him in for a bro hug, followed by a brief round of enthusiastic back slapping. 'Hope we get to talk again soon.'

Trent bowed to them both, shuffled his luggage stack out from under the bar and disappeared through the crowd.

'You okay?' Shanti placed a hand on Gavin's thigh as he regained his seat. 'Trent can be a real scene-stealer when he's on a roll. Always talking a big game. I kinda miss him, though.'

'You two used to date?' asked Gavin, looking around for his drink.

'He's not really my type for that sort of activity.' She curled the corner of her mouth, in exactly the way she knew men liked. 'We met at this really intense finance startup in London a couple of years back and just kind of bonded. Felt like we were in a secret club – the only people in the whole company who weren't completely insane.'

'Been to that movie,' said Gavin. 'Good to have those people around.'

'You two probably have a lot in common.'

'How so?' asked Gavin, straightening and inflating himself a little.

'I think you're both secretly worried that you're already coming up on thirty and your job isn't important enough. That you'll spend your lives working for undeserving douches.'

Gavin threw his head back and laughed. 'Isn't that everybody our age?'

'Not everybody. That's why a conference like this gets people like Trent so worked up. You're looking at these muppets up on stage, talking nonsense and bigging themselves up, while everyone applauds and throws cash. And you sit there thinking "These guys aren't that clever. I could do what they're doing."'

'So do you think he'll actually do anything with that idea?'

'I doubt it,' said Shanti. 'He's living in New York. Has a really cushy sales job with a medical company, owned by his parents. Probably on a respectable salary. Plus he'll inherit a fortune eventually. Why would you trade that life to struggle in a startup? Even for a week?'

'Then what about you? If you've got "leet skills" as a coder, there's almost nothing stopping you from doing your own thing, right?'

'Yeah, well, I've got my own douchebags to worry about.' She looked down and swirled her glass. She didn't want to dwell on her homecoming just yet, there were still a few hours of freedom to be had. 'You flying out tonight as well?'

Gavin shook his head and smiled. 'Morning.'

'Same here,' she raised a corner of her smile to underline the point. 'Are you looking forward to getting back to your cool life, doing cool design in cool Melbourne?'

'For cool douchebags?' Gavin laughed. 'That's going to be hard to take after this week. Every time someone got up on stage to talk about how they had seen the future of something, someone else got up and read the eulogy: the web is dead, apps are dead, brands are dead, agencies are dead, design is dead, ideas are dead. I don't know what to believe. I just know I can't go back to do corporate web design forever.'

'Sounds like you've got some bad FOMO going on there,' Shanti offered, draining the last of her drink. 'You're becoming paralysed by a surplus of opportunity. You won't commit to anything, because you want to stay open to the next thing, which you also won't commit to, so you can continue to remain open to a rolling future of endless opportunities, none of which you will embrace fully.'

Gavin sat back and stared at her. 'Are you a psychologist?'

'No, I heard it from one on a panel yesterday. She believes the technology we love so much, like phones and apps and social platforms and all that stuff, is making this noncommittal behaviour worse. Made me realise I've been doing the same thing all week.'

'Did the psychologist offer any solutions?'

'She did, actually,' Shanti placed her hand on Gavin's leg. 'Stop thinking about what you're not doing and start deciding on what you will.'

She felt his thigh tense just a little under the palm of her hand, then waited for him to step through the door she'd just opened.

All your surveillance tape are belong to us

The turbulence shook Trent awake. His mouth was dry and his thoughts scrambled for traction. The cabin of the Airbus was dim and most of his fellow passengers were still sleeping. He pushed himself up in his seat and massaged his face, rolling his shoulders to get the circulation moving again. Some people considered business class on domestic to be an extravagance. Those people were generally below six foot one.

'Never a pleasant wake-up call, is it?' The man in the next seat had the infrastructure of a rugby player and the upholstery of a restaurant critic. He used his sheaf of papers to gesture at Trent's laptop, perched on the edge of his tray table. 'You might want to grab that before it hits the floor.'

Trent blinked a couple of times before reaching for his computer. 'Thanks for that. I must have completely passed out.'

'The moment the wheels came up. A week at Southby can do that to you,' his girth lending a deep resonance to his clipped British accent. 'What did you think of it this year?'

'It might have finally jumped the shark. Too big, too commercial,' said Trent, summarising the view of a *Guardian* journalist he had befriended at a bar during the week. 'Was that your experience?'

'Yes and no. This year was too crowded, but it wasn't nearly commercial enough, in the truest sense of the word,' he said, placing the printouts on the tray table and resting his hands on his belly. Trent couldn't help noticing the Panerai on the man's wrist. His jowly face was slightly flushed and his thick grey hair stood to attention, trimmed to disguise the beginnings of a retreat. 'Plenty of ideas on sale, but everything was very US-centric. Nothing looked ready for market. All a bit frustrating, really. What were you looking for?'

'General research. I'm in strategy and business development,' Trent unrolled a shirt cuff. 'Medtech is our core focus, but we're always looking to diversify. We have a few ideas currently in development. One or two of them are very promising.'

'Sounds like you're warming up for a pitch,' the older man laughed.

'Well, no, we're not looking for funding –'

'Oh, trust me. Everyone's looking for funding, only most people don't realise it yet. Sooner or later, you learn the only way to bring something new to market is with OPM.'

'OPM?' Trent shook his head.

'Other People's Money.' The cabin lights started to brighten and the flight attendants began bustling behind the galley curtain. 'If you don't mind, old chap, I'll visit the little boys' room before we get told to strap in for landing.'

Trent stashed his laptop, swung his tray into the armrest and stood in the aisle as the older man wedged himself out.

'Might have overdone it on those Texan Ribs,' he patted his sides as he turned and shuffled past Trent, 'but they were so very tasty.'

Trent considered pulling out his laptop to finesse his presentation. If the fat man was right about scaling with Other People's Money then Trent would need to revise his ask upwards. And while his father was a soft touch and would probably approve the funding straight off the bat, his billfold was limited. If Trent wanted more, and he realised now he probably did, he'd have to take the proposal to his mother, who controlled all the major decisions – and the major money – but was far less inclined to indulge him. To the point of basically not at all.

He had been with Mediclinical for almost two years now, in a sales and development role hastily arranged by his father and grudgingly approved by his mother to cushion his return from London. He had arrived on their doorstep, yet again, with precious little in the way of entrepreneurial success or financial stability. His parents had been rescuing him from unemployment ever since he left med school minus a degree but with the makings of a crushing student debt.

Susan and James Carlisle owned most of Mediclinical through their holding company, but had little to do with the day-to-day operations of the business. As far as Trent could tell, James no longer had much to do with the day-to-day operations of his marriage to Susan, either. She had an appetite for detail that simply could not be satisfied, wearing out several CFOs in the first few years of the business before finding one with the stamina of an oil rig and the soul of a calculator. They made beautiful finance together. His father was far more interested in making speeches and handshakes, spending his time on hospital boards, chairing advisory committees, consulting to university research projects and drinking Scotch. Trent was always going to find it difficult to measure up to his mother's idea of success. Thanks to his two much older and more successful sisters, both in medicine, the bar was now set to stratospheric.

'That's a weight off, thanks old chap,' Trent's window-seat companion returned, looking fresher. 'Made any progress on your pitch deck?'

Trent pulled up short for a minute, wondering if he'd been thinking aloud. Or maybe talking in his sleep.

'Didn't mean to pry, but it was up on your screen when you passed out. I closed it down for you. To save the battery, of course,' he landed heavily in his seat and began to re-cuff his sleeves. 'It's also a matter of professional interest. Charles Archer-Ellis. I connect inspiration with liquidity to create opportunity.'

Charles extended a newly-cuffed hand and Trent grasped it in return.

'Trent Carlisle, VP at Mediclinical.'

'Don't worry, I didn't see anything of material import on your screen,' said Charles, settling back in. 'Even if I did, the idea's not really the valuable thing, you know.'

'It's not?'

'Ideas are everywhere. In fact, the market is entering an ideas surplus. What we're short of is people.'

'Why aren't there enough people?' Trent asked, trying to appear interested rather than out of the loop.

'When I say not enough people, I mean not enough of the right people. It's not difficult to get ideas off the ground if you have the classic startup trio.'

An attendant advised that they'd be starting their descent soon and offered a final refreshment. Trent ordered an Evian and Charles requested a glass of champagne.

'Been up all night. Need something to put a spring in my step,' Charles winked.

'Whatever works for you, Charles. What's your take on the trio? Do you favour the "operational pillar" model?

'The operational stuff is boring. Even worse, it's hard work. I recommend you outsource anything that's uninteresting or difficult immediately.'

'You don't think I should keep those things core?'

'Trust me, I've made a career out of avoiding the heavy lifting. The trio everyone's looking for now are the three H's: the hustler, the hacker and the hipster. Ah, breakfast. Thank you, my dear,' Charles smiled at the attendant as she poured the champagne. 'The hustler is someone with vision, plenty of chutzpah and an eye for a shortcut. They may or may not have had the idea themselves, but the hustler always leads the deal and puts the team together. The next person you need is a hacker, someone who understands the technology and isn't afraid of hard work. Which is crucial, because they'll be doing most of it.'

Trent nodded, making a mental shortlist. 'And the hipster? What does he do?'

'Well he could be a she, you know. It's far too easy to get yourself branded as sexist in this day and age. Ok, the hipster is someone who really understands what's cool. They don't have to have the full single-origin beard themselves, especially if they are a girl,' Charles laughed, 'but they need to understand that scene. Or whatever scene went viral in the four hours since we boarded. You see, your product has got to pass the cool test when you launch, and you only get one shot at that. Just look at what happened to Hometown last year.' Charles knocked back the remainder of his glass.

'Not sure I've ever heard of Hometown,' admitted Trent.

'My point exactly. So your hipster, for want of a better handle, makes sure your product looks and feels cool enough to be considered completely cool by all the cool little people who run around deciding what's cool this week. It's like fashion: incredibly arbitrary, mostly tedious and absolutely vital.'

'And that's it? That's the team?'

'As far as leadership goes, yes. Everyone below that is basically interchangeable. Even better if they are outsourceable. Honestly, any half-decent idea can get funding with a rock star trio at the helm. Venture capitalists don't invest in ideas, they invest in people.'

'Is that how you invest?' asked Trent.

'Absolutely I would,' Charles raised an eyebrow. 'If I were a VC myself. I'm more of a facilitator. An agent, if you will.'

Trent looked past Charles to the small slice of the horizon offered by the aircraft window. The wing dipped slightly to reveal the lights of New York City, shimmering like glitter in a carpet of dusty ink.

'I heard the VC money was getting a lot more cautious. At least that's what my friends in the valley are telling me,' Trent lied as he started collecting his things from the seat pocket.

'The only people still talking about the valley are the guys who've never left it. The real opportunity is in the east.'

'Is that why you're based in New York?' Trent nodded out the window.

'Far East, old chap. This is all very nice,' Charles gestured out the window as the plane descended, 'but Manhattan is no longer the centre of the universe. There's more money in Shanghai, or Singapore for that matter. The deal flow in Jakarta has to be seen to be believed. There's an extraordinary amount of wealth chasing a limited number of legitimate opportunities. I'm just catching up with an old friend in New

York to help with his book launch. He's written a how-to guide for startups. *Zero to Launch in 30 Days*. Terrific book. I even gave him some of the ideas in there. I'm going to a couple of launch events, a few parties, then I'm off home.'

'And where's home for you?'

'Hong Kong. Amazing place. You should come have a look sometime, Trent. It's all happening. Incubators, tax breaks, investors, great talent and so much cheaper than anywhere in the west.'

'Maybe I will,' said Trent.

'I mean it. I'm going to give you my card, which I only do if I expect the recipient to use it,' said Charles, lifting a thick, linen-textured business card from his jacket pocket. 'Want to know why I'm prepared to give you my card?'

'I do.'

'You ask questions and you listen to the answers.' Charles gripped the armrests as the tyres kissed the runway. 'But the thing that impressed me the most? You didn't try and pitch me straight away. You've got a bit of class, Trent, and that's also in short supply.'

Trent afforded himself a little smile. During the entire descent he had ignored the little voice in his head screaming at him to pitch his brilliant life-swap idea and ask for funding. The only way he could stop himself was to fall back on his sales training – ask open-ended questions, nod encouragement and let the target do the talking.

'Thanks, Charles, I really appreciate your insight.' Trent studied the card briefly then made a show of putting it in his pocket, patting it for safety.

'If you do find yourself with a team and a pitch deck to go with that idea of yours,' Charles winked and put his hand out, 'do me a favour, will you? Please get in touch.'

The business class cabin devolved into a scrum of passive-aggressive jacket straightening and aggressive-aggressive luggage swinging. Trent stepped into the aisle and was swept along by the crush. They stampeded the aerobridge like wounded bison and rushed the luggage carousel like rhinos to a waterhole, only to find it turning gently, completely barren of luggage. The assembled passengers then fished phones from pockets, bent heads and began scrolling.

Trent nodded as he spotted Charles strolling past with his carry-on. The older man gave a half salute and disappeared through the exit. Trent could feel only admiration for a man who could survive over a week on the road with just the contents of a regulation cabin bag to sustain him. To be fair, though, Charles' roll-on looked a couple of sizes beyond regulation. Much like Charles himself.

The contents of cattle class began to fill the spaces around the carousel as Trent scrolled his phone. A bunch of emails, a few @ mentions, some likes, several swipes and a text from his father: *Heads up. Your mother is looking for you. Call me.*

'Dad, what's up?' Trent held the phone with his chin as he unwrapped a stick of gum.

'Oh Trent, good morning. How was your trip?'

'Really good. I've something to talk to you about. And mother. I've got some plans. An idea I want to pursue. Could be great timing.'

'I'm not sure it is, Trent.'

'What do you mean?'

'I really should let her talk to you first, but she's unhappy with your sales technique.'

'Don't worry about it, Dad, I'm not in sales anymore. I have a plan that I think you guys are really going to like.'

'Trent, I'm happy to hear you're figuring out what you want to do. Trust me when I tell you that you don't want to be working for your mother your whole life. But I'm also telling you she's not in a receptive mood right now.'

A buzzer spat and the carousel lurched into action, inciting the crowd, now six deep on all sides, to move as a pack. Trent spotted his luggage as it tumbled out the chute.

'Seriously, when is she ever? Hey listen, Dad, good to speak but I gotta go. Talk soon.'

***

The cab wound its way towards the city as the rain fell and traffic thickened. Trent watched as early-morning commuters and contractors argued with the radio, sipped coffee and sent texts. Maybe it was time to get out of Manhattan for a while. Take the funding from his parents, move to San Francisco, set up the office in a converted warehouse space and find a couple of co-founders. Maybe live in an Airstream for a while. If what Charles had told him on the plane was true, he'd probably be spending half his time in Asia. So a West Coast base would make more sense anyway.

Trent's phone chirped with an email. Meeting request from one of his mother's assistants: 8:30 at the Vandten offices in Midtown. He sent back a counter for 12.

Moments later his phone rang.

'Mr Carlisle, it's Jennifer from Susan Carlisle's office.'
'Jennifer, how are you on this lovely New York morning?'
Trent had never met this particular Jennifer, but he imagined she was similar to the rest of them. Long straight hair, serious glasses, a hint of a dimple and well-defined calves.

'I'm afraid we can't accommodate you today at twelve.'

Perhaps she'd be friendlier in person. Probably had Susan prowling nearby and needed to demonstrate her ruthless corporate efficiency, something Susan valued greatly in her assistants.

'Well, maybe something a little later in the afternoon? Actually, tomorrow would work better for me. Anything after ten.'

'Mrs Carlisle has requested that you make the meeting as originally scheduled.'

'Well, I've just landed from a red-eye, Jennifer, so although I'm still handsome, I really do need to freshen up,' Trent wafted his collar. 'I smell more like Texas than is reasonable right now.'

'Are you still in the terminal?'

'Just coming in through Brooklyn, thank God,' said Trent.

'I'll let Mrs Carlisle know you're on your way directly. We'll see you at eight-thirty as scheduled, Mr Carlisle.'

Trent slumped as the cab rumbled onto the Manhattan Bridge, rain blowing across the windshield in weak squalls kicked up by the passing trucks. He considered standing in the rain a few minutes before going upstairs to the meeting, just to make a point of how inconvenient the schedule was for him, then thought better of it. His mother was rarely moved by his plights, particularly when they were manufactured.

Trent tapped on the partition. 'Driver, take me to 48 and Park, thanks.'

'Thought you wanted the Village?'

'It's not about what I want,' said Trent.

'Ain't that the truth,' said the driver, changing lanes to make the northbound exit.

* * *

Trent found himself sizing up the receptionists (there were two, but neither was Jennifer), trying to decide which one he would ask out if only they didn't work for his mother. After a couple of emotional on-premises showdowns his mother had issued an edict – and had it written into the boilerplate of his employment contract – that Trent was forbidden to dip his quill in the company ink.

It was only when he was ushered into the company boardroom, rather than Susan's personal office, that he started to wonder what this meeting was about. To be honest, he hadn't talked with his mother much at all lately, so he didn't have much to go on.

The receptionist pushed against the heavy boardroom door and gestured for Trent to follow. The enormous room was brightly lit and empty, save for Jeffrey Small, a short and conservative man who was also Vandten's long-term Head of Regulatory and Legal Affairs.

'Ah, Jeffrey, I wasn't expecting to see you here this morning,' said Trent, unbuttoning his jacket and taking a seat at the expansive boardroom table a few places along from the older man.

'A pleasure to see you again, too, Trent,' he replied with a thin smile, getting up to pour himself a glass of water from the carafe on the credenza. Jeffrey chose a new seat, directly across the table from Trent.

'Are we waiting for Madam President?' asked Trent.

'I want to show you something,' said Jeffrey, clicking a small remote control.

The upholstered wall of the conference room slid back to reveal a mammoth flat panel display, which showed a black and white image of a corridor, seen from several different angles in a split-screen arrangement. A small line of numbers tumbled over at the base of the screen.

Trent struggled to make sense of the video until he saw a familiar figure stroll into view in the bottom right hand frame. He was watching himself, via security camera, wearing a long lab coat and wheeling a gurney.

Trent's glance flitted to Jeffrey, who had not bothered to watch the screen. Presumably because he was already familiar with the footage. Trent watched himself talk to the nurse holding the clipboard. Even in the jaws of imminent professional disaster, to be dispensed by his parents' highly compensated litigator, Trent couldn't help but admire himself in action. Jeffrey stabbed the remote again, freezing the onscreen Trent just as he was sticking his onscreen chest out to allow the nurse to inspect his onscreen badge.

'Can you tell me, Mr Carlisle, what is the nurse looking at in this frame?'

'She's admiring my pecs, I believe.'

'The correct answer is: the hospital identification badge belonging to a Dr Shane Robertson,' Jeffrey tapped the remote on the table. 'A face reconstruction specialist at Stamford Hospital. Can you explain to me how Dr Robertson's badge came to be attached to your lab coat?'

'Before we go on, I'd just like to state for the record,' Trent leaned forward and pointed at the screen, 'that is not my lab coat.'

Another stab of the remote shut the flat-screen down and closed the panelling. Jeffrey took a large envelope from his compendium and slid it across the boardroom table.

'What's this?' Trent asked, placing a hand on the envelope, as if trying to stop its advance.

'Your termination notice.'

'Termination? From what?'

'From Mediclinical and from all other companies and entities associated with The Vandten Corporation. Effective immediately.'

'Oh, come on, Jeffrey– '

'You're lucky you aren't terminated from the Carlisle family as well.'

'That's ridiculous. You can't fire someone from their own family.' The lawyer allowed himself the faintest of smiles and raised an eyebrow.

'That's legal?' asked Trent.

'Perhaps you should apply yourself to the study of law if you are so interested in its reach, Mr Carlisle.'

'I think it might be best if I spoke directly with Susan on this matter.' Trent started to wave Jeffrey off as he opened the envelope and flipped through the pages.

'I assure you, I have Mrs Carlisle's complete authority to execute her instructions.'

'You're enjoying this aren't you, Jeffrey?' said Trent.

'I assure you there's very little enjoyment to be had when the largest public healthcare network on the East Coast is threatening a complete ban from their procurement process for up to two years,' Jeffrey tapped the remote on the table to underline his point. 'You don't seem to appreciate the situation you've placed us in. And we're extremely fortunate they've decided not to press charges.'

Trent slumped back into his seat. 'They were going to charge me?'

'You? I have no idea,' Jeffrey placed his hands together underneath his chin. 'It's entirely possible they will pursue criminal charges against you as an individual. I happen to know the lead counsel for the healthcare network in question, who has given me her assurance that Mediclinical will be in the clear, once we've established that you were not an employee at the time of the offence.'

'Oh, but I was,' Trent scrambled for a defensive foothold. 'The security footage proves it.'

'The security footage proves only that you were at the scene of the offence.' Jeffrey removed an expensive pen from the breast pocket of his suit jacket, studied it for a moment and then returned it. 'This termination agreement, however, is dated prior to the incident you are referring to. I strongly recommend you sign it.'

'I'd love to, Jeffrey,' Trent patted his pockets. 'But it seems I've misplaced my pen.'

'Allow me to do you the favour of translating the offer into terms you can understand: your resignation will apply from the third of the month, the day before this recording. You will not set foot in any healthcare facility, nor any property owned or operated by the Vandten Corporation or its subsidiaries. In return, you will receive a lump sum of forty thousand US dollars and a week to vacate your parents' apartment in the West Village. We will also take steps to ensure formal criminal charges are not brought against you.' Jeffrey straightened his suit as he stood. 'I recommend you locate a pen, Mr Carlisle.'

Trent sat in the enormous boardroom, tapping his fingertips together and breathing deeply. He thought about watching more of himself on the security footage. Then he thought about hurling one of the leather-lined chairs at the screen. Then he considered his mother was watching on closed-circuit. The door opened once more and the receptionist poked her head in. 'I'm very sorry, but I need to reset the room for the next meeting.'

Trent looked around at the rows of perfectly aligned chairs, the clutch of glasses on the credenza, the orderly row of whiteboard markers and eraser beneath the recessed whiteboard. Apart from the glass of water that Jeffrey had poured and then abandoned, the only thing that needed resetting, evidently, was him.

Trent smiled at the receptionist. 'Do you have a pen that I might be able to borrow?'

Girl, I'll haus you

'I know you've all worked very hard to get us to where we are today and I want to thank you for that. Sincerely, I do.'

There was no response from the crowd of young tech workers pressed into the large meeting room.

'As some of you may have heard, thanks to reports in the business press this morning,' said the tall, lean Swede as he adjusted his designer eyewear, 'all that hard work has not gone unnoticed. They say that imitation is the most sincere form of flattery, but I'm here to tell you that it isn't.'

The Swede smiled and made deliberate eye contact with people in at least three different parts of the room. 'In this business, *acquisition* is the most sincere form of flattery. Our main competitor likes what we've built here at Opod. They like it so much, they've decided to buy us.'

He spread his palms wide as if delivering great bounty, but encountered only stony faces and crossed arms. He wavered for a moment until a solid-set balding man in blue chambray and khaki chinos stepped in to rescue him.

'Yes, hi. My name is Matt. You'll be seeing more of me around the place in the coming weeks so don't be shy,' he made a small wave. 'I think what Lars here is trying to say is that we have an exciting new chapter of growth ahead of us at Opod and we think you're going to be, ah, excited by what's ahead.'

'Yes! Exciting stuff! For all of you,' the Swede added.

'For most of you,' said Chambray Shirt, with far less enthusiasm. 'Are there any questions at this time?'

'Who are you?' a voice came from the back of the room. Shanti turned to see it was one of her coding team, Paul, a younger guy who wore his hair in a perfect London punk-era mohawk. She made a zipping motion across her lips. It was too late.

'Excuse me?' said Matt, blinking and cupping his ear.

'You said we would be seeing more of you in the office. Why? Who are you?' said Paul, turning a simple question into a threat. Shanti covered her eyes and tried to shrink. She'd been criticised about her team's immaturity before. Paul was not helping the cause.

'Okay, well, valid question, I suppose. So let me start by asking you a question.

How long have you been at Opod?'

'Three months. Going on four,' Paul folded his arms.

Matt nodded at Sven and made a writing motion with his hand. Sven blinked and then scurried off to locate a notebook.

'OK, great chat there,' Matt offered a thumbs-up to the back of the room and turned to the crowd. 'Sorry we don't have more time, but you know my door is always open.'

* * *

Paul wasn't the only coder in Shanti's team to return to his desk and discover their login was no longer valid. Hands were thrown up, moans uttered and threats to head to the pub were made. Calls to IT rang out. Around ten minutes later, building security arrived and the full picture emerged.

A couple of people cried; a few were angry. Paul muttered something about reaping and sowing. Shanti asked everyone to calm down while she went in search of answers. Matt's door, contrary to his earlier proclamation, was well and truly closed. She could see through the frosting that he was keeping company with at least two of the Swedes. She could tell by listening that they were also keeping company with several bottles of champagne. Matt's PA asked her to come back later in the afternoon.

'Can you believe this?' Shanti found the CFO trotting for the fire stairs, phone in one hand and a pack of cigarettes in the other. 'And since when were you a smoker?'

'Shanti, I know you're a bright kid,' said the greying man as he rushed through the door. 'Just keep your head down, don't say anything dumb and you should be fine.'

She shook her head and power-walked back to her department. Paul and the others were already gone.

'Five minutes,' a pimply teen sniffled. 'That's how much time security gave them. No backups, no goodbyes, nothing. Told them to pack their stuff and go.'

'That's outrageous,' Shanti placed her hands on her hips and looked around the department: eight desks, jammed together and sectioned off from the rest of the floor by a low partition. 'How are we going to get the commerce engine from Flightenator patched in?'

'Is that all you're worried about? The patch?' The teen wiped his face and stood up. 'What about Paul and Gretchen and Tran? They're all out of a job. Don't you care about them?'

'Of course I do, Herman.'

'Herbert.'

'Herbert, shit, I'm sorry. I'm just trying to figure this out. Where are you going?'

'I'm going to the bar with everyone else,' Herbert said, slinging his messenger bag. 'You should come and talk to them. You hired us all, remember?'

'I will, but we have to sort out this migration first,' Shanti tapped her keyboard to wake the screen and started scanning her emails. 'Otherwise we could wind up in a real shit storm real quick.'

'You're a really awesome coder, Shanti. We all learned a lot from you,' said Herbert, taking his coat from the back of his chair. 'But what's the point of working so hard if these guys are just going to throw us away?'

Shanti watched Herbert walk out of the cubicle. How could she help Paul and the others if she herself didn't know what was going on? If they didn't deliver the migration on time, as promised, she could very easily wind up boxed as well. And then what help would she be? It frustrated her how illogical people became when faced with uncertainty. Start by working on the parts of the problem you understand. Simple logic, really.

'Umm, Shanti?' came a small voice from the corner of the office. 'Do you still want me to compile those tables?'

She turned to see the only non-drinker of her team, another young Indian coder who had worked with her in London. Shanti had been able to bring him across to Munich to help scale Opod's commerce platform.

'Excellent. Yes please, Krishnan. See if you can get all those query terms matching up by this afternoon.' At least someone in her team was still thinking straight. 'I'm going to find HR. See if we can get some freelancers in here.'

* * *

'What are you going to do?' asked Shanti's cousin. 'Will you lose your job, too?'

They sat on boxes of produce in the restaurant's cool room. The back door hung open onto the laneway, the afternoon light fading and the temperature of the Munich air starting to fall.

'Oh god no,' replied Shanti, toying with the swing top on an empty beer bottle. 'They're just shuffling things around, trying to reduce the head count before they take the business public. Bosses do that sometimes to show that they're in charge. What I do is very specialised, it's really technical. They'd be in a world of hurt if I decided to leave.'

'Well, whatever happens, you know Appa always has a job for you here with us.'

Shanti laughed, but it was more of a wince. 'I'm very grateful to your father, Amira. He helped me when my own father couldn't. That's something I will never forget,' Shanti checked they were alone and lowered her voice. 'But I don't think it's something he's ever going to let me fully repay. Sometimes it feels like he wants me to work for him forever.'

'Don't you want to stay with us?' Amira threw her a wounded look. 'You're not going back to India to live with your father, are you?'

'No, I don't want that either. I'm trying to bring my little sister out as well. It's not good for her to be living alone with my father,' Shanti took Amira's hands. 'Haven't you ever felt like you wanted to go out and do something for yourself? Make something on your own?'

'But I do. And I am,' said Amira, shaking both of Shanti's hands with excitement. 'I'm going to study optometry next year.'

'Is that what you really want to do? I've never heard you talk about it before.'

'Why not? Appa says you can make more money than a regular doctor. You can sell spectacles and lenses as well. Just four years of study if I do the accelerated program, then I'll have my own clinic. Appa is already looking to buy one for me.'

'Oh, Amira. Life is all mapped out for you, isn't it?' Shanti stroked her cousin's hand. 'Just make sure you're happy with the destination, okay?'

* * *

As much as Shanti was fond of her cousin, she knew where the loyalties in this family lay, hers included. Shanti's uncle had not only covered her London boarding school fees, he also gave her room and board when she earned a part scholarship to a German university. She studied computer programming during term, Indian restaurant management during holidays. By the time she graduated, her uncle was preparing to install her in one of his newer restaurants, but a tech recruiter offered her a position with the financial startup in London. She persuaded her uncle to let her go, partly by agreeing to send back a substantial cut of her meagre paycheck each month.

Once the startup imploded, he wasted no time in recalling her to Munich, offering a small studio apartment above one of his restaurants. She virtually begged a couple of ex-university colleagues to give her the role at Opod, but the arrangement drove her into a financial cul-de-sac of ongoing payments to her uncle.

'When are we going to get started on my catering website, eh Shanti?' asked her uncle as the extended family settled around the large table at the back of the restaurant. Shanti almost choked on her chapati. 'Amira tells me you could be leaving the travel company soon. Why you didn't share the good news earlier?'

'Papa, that's not what I said!' Amira wailed, but was shushed by her mother.

'I never said I was leaving Opod, Uncle. They're making some management changes before they list on the stock exchange, that's all.' Shanti shot a quick glare at Amira, who mouthed a 'sorry' and returned her gaze to her plate.

'Well, maybe you'll get a promotion.' Her uncle brushed his luxurious moustache as he smiled at her. 'More money and less work. Isn't that how it goes in these big companies?'

'You know I'm working almost as hard as you, Uncle,' Shanti smiled, trying to move the conversation along.

'And that is why you find it so difficult to meet a husband, isn't it?' her uncle winked.

The table broke into laughter, some genuine, some polite. She fumed quietly as the food made its way around the table. Experience had taught her that each time she earned a little more freedom, her uncle managed to add something to the tab. She was only paying interest, the principal was never reduced. What she needed was a wholesale buy-out.

* * *

'The coding is not the tricky part, it's basically a trading platform. But how would the actual swaps work? Something like a barista would be fine. Most retail would work. Even some low level entertainment gigs. But as soon as you're talking about skilled jobs, where you need to know what you're doing, then I think you're asking for trouble.' Shanti stretched and produced an XL-sized yawn.

'I know it's late there in *Cher*-many,' said Trent, 'but can you please turn away from the screen when you do that?'

'Why don't you just turn off the video? If you want table manners, you're going to have to start paying me,' Shanti countered.

'Ah, yes, I wanted to talk to you about that,' said Trent, moving in closer to his screen. 'I've decided to leave Mediclinical and concentrate on building this idea into a company.'

'For real?'

'For real. I just can't see myself working for my parents for ever.'

'Wow. I'm impressed, Trent. How'd they take it?'

'Fine, but I didn't call you to talk about my parents. I want to talk about us.'

'Us. What do you mean us?'

'I mean us as co-founders of this company,' Trent put his hands together under his chin. 'Shanti, if we're going to change people's lives, let's start with our own. Let's build this company together. You and me.'

'Whoah. I mean, it's a really cool idea and all, but to get it to where it's got enough scale to make money? You realise how much work that would take?'

'You've never been afraid of work, Shanti. In fact, that's why you're one of the few people I would even consider doing this with.'

'Flattery might work with all those Upper East Side girls you chase around the Village, but I need to eat. I got rent to pay. I've got my job, my family…'

'So do I, Shanti,' said Trent.

'Your family is a little different to mine, Trent. They're not keeping a ledger of everything you owe them.'

'Don't be so sure,' said Trent. 'Look, I've already got some seed funding lined up to cover hard costs for the development phase.'

'Did your parents decide to invest?'

'In a manner of speaking. But I'm only asking you to contribute sweat equity.'

'Sounds icky.'

'What I mean is you don't have to pay for your share of the company. I'm offering you equity.'

'What's the catch?'

'The sweat. We can't pay ourselves a salary for the first month, but we'll each have a stake in what is virtually guaranteed to become an extremely valuable part of the sharing economy,' said Trent with a flourish.

'Virtually guaranteed?'

'C'mon, Shanti, paychecks are for suckers.'

'Careful, you sound like you're begging. Not a good look for you.'

'I *am* begging, Shanti. You're the smartest developer I know. Hell, you're the smartest anything I know,' said Trent. 'You're way too smart to work for those pinhead Swedes you've been complaining about. You're too smart to work for anybody.'

'Except for you, it would seem,' she said with a smile.

'Not for me, *with* me. I'm talking equity. I'm securing a house somewhere cool and we're bunkering down as a team. It'll be like a working holiday but with a big fat payday at the end. Besides, you've pretty much sketched out all the tech we'll need already.'

'I was just spit-balling what you'd need for the trading platform. That's not a proper scope,' said Shanti, shaking her head. 'Besides, I'm not going to quit my job for you, Trent. It's the only thing keeping me out of a vat of ghee.'

'Didn't you say those Swedes boxed most of your team this week? Then they put your projects on hold? That doesn't sound promising.'

'A lot of stuff has gone on hold while the buyout's finalised.'

'Sounds like London all over again, Shanti. Aren't you worried?'

'It's the opposite of London, Trent. That was a shitty business, run by arseholes, which ran out of money because no-one wanted to invest,' Shanti pushed her hair back from her eyes. 'Opod is a solid business – '

'Also run by assholes.'

'Okay, agreed. Run by "assholes", who just got a massive injection of funds because someone wants to buy them. Totally different.'

'Except for the part where you did all the work but still ended up with no equity in either company,' said Trent crossing his arms. 'I've got some friends who would be interested in trialling the service. Some bike couriers, some people in PR, a camera assistant. I bet you have too, over there in Munich.'

'Maybe a couple of people, yeah.'

'We just need to knuckle down and build the prototype platform, put our friends on it, send it live and see if it takes off. Then you can decide if you want to be a co-founder of an incredibly cool and successful startup, or do database integration for some ungrateful Swedes who will probably outsource your job to Bangalore within a year.'

'Racist much?'

'Oh come on Shanti,' Trent waved her question away. 'You know what I mean.'

Shanti studied the slightly pixelated Trent on her laptop. Clearly, Southby had lit a fire under him. Every night for the past week he had peppered her with lengthy emails asking about platforms and technology, servers and cloud storage, transaction gateways and security. In the past, his ideas had been evaporated by the friction of having to figure out how to make them work. This time he was on a mission.

'Are those packing cartons behind you? Are you moving house?'

'I'm going all in, Shanti. I'm going to set up a scrum base in a low-cost city somewhere so we can do zero to launch in thirty days,' Trent held up a slim paperback with exactly those words on the cover. 'Co-location is the key to innovation. I'm thinking somewhere in South East Asia.'

Shanti found the idea of a few weeks away incredibly appealing, but she'd have to figure out what to tell her uncle. Overseas holidays weren't part of his repayment schedule.

'I won't quit Opod, but I might be able to help get you to launch. I've got a lot of leave owing which I have to use up before the merger goes through or I could lose it completely.'

'Perfect. We build the prototype on an existing e-commerce template and re-jig it to fit our idea. The book says we shouldn't be doing work someone else has already done. Shortcuts are the new black, Shanti.'

'Tell your book it's wrong. Building on someone else's tech is a house of cards. It'll either be buggy as hell or they'll just keep jacking the licensing fees,' Shanti pushed the hair back from her eyes. 'If you want me in, we do the build my way, with my code.'

'How long will that take?'

'Maybe six weeks to do it right.'

'Can't give you that long. Thirty days is the plan. All we need is a rough looking prototype and a good-looking team of founders. I need you to help me find a hipster.'

'Why on earth would we need a hipster?'

'It's all about the three H's,' Trent tapped the book's cover. 'I'm the hustler, leading the team, finding the deals. You're the hacker, making the tech decisions, doing the build. Then we just need a hipster to make everything look cool.'

'You mean a web designer or a UX lead?'

'I'm not sure what I mean, exactly. But you do, so I'm going to let you make this hire.'

'Except there's no money to hire them with, right?'

'Oh, Shanti, stop worrying about the lack of cash for today. Dream about the equity of tomorrow,' Trent threw his hands up, halfway between a beg and a prayer. 'We're going to have an awesome adventure, in a magical foreign land, building the best thing since sliced Facebook. Then we sell it to some fat VC guy and live very happily ever after. You'll have to beat the candidates off with a stick.'

'Do they have to come to Asia with us? And please don't choose India, ok Trent?'

'Now look who's racist.'

Shanti folded her arms, pursed her lips and stared into the webcam.

'You know I'm joking. Yes, they will come with us. Co-location is key. My seed funding will cover costs for the build period. Including travel and accommodation,' said Trent, rubbing his hands together. 'Mad design skills are table stakes. They also need to be pretty dialled in to what the cool kids are doing.'

'Anything else?'

'Don't hire someone who's a complete dick. We'll be living and breathing this thing together in the one house for thirty days. So pick someone you wouldn't mind spending serious time with, at close quarters. Do you have someone in mind?'

Shanti leaned back from the computer and gave her upper arms a gentle squeeze. 'I think I can get my hands on a pretty decent candidate.'

* * *

'Social media. Virtual reality. Augmented retail. Mega data. Drone-powered commerce. What do these things have in common?'

The entire agency had filed into the presentation area, squeezing onto the oversized timber staircase and spilling onto the polished concrete floor. A girthy man wearing a black and red striped shirt, like some sort of Freddy Kruger homage, paced the stage. His full head of tight ringlets was held back on one side by a headset microphone.

'Opportunity,' he paused and surveyed the room. 'In every one of these new technologies is an opportunity just waiting to be cracked. But you have to move fast. You have to be first. Because once it's been done, it's been done. And you don't get a gold pencil for making the first copy of someone else's fresh idea. Today's Friday. You know the drill. You have the entire weekend to generate a fresh load of award-winning ideas to pitch to me at our weekly Idea Slam on Monday morning. Let's go to work, people.'

Gavin waited for the stairs to clear before making his way back to his desk. He watched as several of his colleagues milled around the speaker, all trying to talk at once.

'Inspired by our fearless new creative leader?' a thin blonde girl paused as she negotiated the stairs.

'You mean feckless.'

'Careful Gav, that's treason,' the blonde girl shook her head and smiled.

'You going to turn me in?' Gavin stood up.

'More fun to watch you perjure yourself. I give it a week before you tell this dickhead to shove it,' she said, nodding towards Girthy Ringlets.

'Now who's talking treason?'

'We're all thinking it. You're the only one reckless enough to say it,' she shook her hair out and clambered down the last steps. 'Me? I like my paycheck too much.'

Seven days back from Southby and Gavin was still struggling with re-entry to real life. He sought comfort with his housemates and friends but their familiarity rubbed like a stone in his shoe. Although it took him a while to notice, his constant refrain of 'when I was at Southby' was proving to be a similar irritation to them. He milled about at staff drinks on Friday night just long enough for people to remember seeing him there, then made for the station.

'You should have called. I would have saved some supper for you.' Gavin's mother opened the door just past nine o'clock. She kept her long grey hair in a thick braid and her glasses on a chain around her neck. 'Are you staying the weekend? Where's your bike? Is Troy with you? I like Troy.'

'No, just me Mum,' said Gavin, kissing her cheek as he shuffled through the hallway. 'I meant to call you from the train but I zoned out.'

He fell into the worn sofa beside the small combustion stove. It had been mild enough in the city but here, where the suburban sprawl started to splinter into hobby farms and weekend retreats that dotted the ridges and gullies out to the National Park, nightfall brought a definite chill.

'Do you want some wine? It's a decent Shiraz.' His mother moved a pile of books from an armchair and settled herself in.

'Might have some later. I feel like I've been drinking constantly,' he said.

'Are you running away from a bad week at work?'

'I'm not running away from anything, Mum. I just wanted to come out and see you.'

'You didn't bring your bike, or your friends. Or any washing for me to do,' she nodded at the messenger bag slumped at Gavin's feet. 'You never were a good bluffer, son. You haven't improved much.'

'Shiraz, was it?' Gavin pushed himself off the sofa and sauntered into the kitchen. 'And yes, work is completely sucking, thanks for asking.'

'That's my job, remember,' she called from the living room. 'You sounded so excited last weekend when you got back from your trip to Hollywood. What changed?'

'The trip was to Texas, mum. And I think that's part of the problem.' He poured a glass and returned to the lounge room to top up his mother's. 'I saw so many cool ideas, people starting things, building things. So much energy in that week. Then I come back here and it's all just...'

'The same?'

Gavin nodded as he took his seat. 'Everything feels petty and small-minded, even my friends. It's probably just me. Thought it would be best to stay away from people for a couple of days before I say something regrettable.'

'So I'm not considered people?'

'See, I did it again. Sorry, Mum. It'll pass, I guess.'

'Except it won't,' she said. 'You can't put the genie back in the bottle. You're too much like your father.'

'You mean I'm an arsehole?'

'I didn't mean that,' she said, laughing a little. 'Do I wish your father was still here for you? Of course. But then I'd be wishing for him to be a different man. If you've seen something you think you really want, you won't be happy until you go and get it.'

'I don't know, Mum. It's a long shot,' Gavin pulled his beanie off and rubbed his scalp. 'Today I got an offer from some people who want me to help them start a new company. It's a killer idea and they seem smart, but I only met them the once, at that tech conference. I've been back and forth with their Chief Technical Officer this week. She's super smart and seems really, really nice. Indian girl, but she lives in Germany for some reason.'

'Are you more interested in the company?' his mother sat forward in her armchair. 'Or in the girl?'

'There's not really a company yet. It's just an idea for a service but if we can get it to work, it would be so incredibly cool.' Gavin smiled and took a slug of wine. 'Why do you always think everything is about the girl?'

'Like I said. You remind me of your father.'

Get into the chopper if you want to retain equity

'Whose crazy fucking idea was this, eh?' said Gavin as he climbed the stairs, drawn to the caramel-skinned girl in the yellow sundress.

'You can't change your life sitting on a sofa, now can you?' Shanti furled her parasol as she stood in front of the palace entrance.

Their emails since Austin had flip-flopped between serious technical discussion and flirtatious banter. Their Skype calls were usually followed by Gavin enlarging and enhancing her LinkedIn profile picture, studying her wide, dark eyes and trying to remember the exact contours of her body. He reached the top of the steps and leaned in for the reunion kiss – the catalyst for a sensational night of reunion sex.

'And you're just as crazy for agreeing to go along with it.' Shanti went to kiss him on the cheek, ducking a little as he made for her lips.

Gavin caught himself trying to re-manoeuvre and pretended to stumble on the top step.

'You okay?' she asked, placing a hand on his shoulder.

'I'm fine. Just the heat,' he covered, wiping his forehead with the back of his arm. 'Did Trent say where to meet him, exactly?'

'Ho Chi Minh City. Reunification Palace. Thursday. Around noon. That's all I got,' said Shanti, heading in through the main doors. 'He has a penchant for the dramatic.'

After Shanti had talked him into joining their 'little startup experiment' Gavin realised he knew almost nothing about Vietnam beyond what Trent had told them: high-octane coffee, cheap beer, dazzling local food, decent internet speeds, low rents and manageable visa requirements. At first Gavin had regarded his own dramatic resignation from the agency as a demonstration of both his integrity and his low tolerance for dickheads. But when Shanti explained that she had arranged a 'personal development' sabbatical from her job, it struck Gavin as a far more mature approach than his own 'scorched earth' strategy. So he borrowed Shanti's sabbatical story and claimed he was on a similar arrangement. Trent was fond of reminding them there was no real future in being an employee. The way he had been talking, they were about to write themselves an entirely new future, in both code and cash. All they had to do now was write the code.

* * *

Shanti drifted around the entrance hall of the palace, towing Gavin behind her. She stopped to admire a circular rug emblazoned with a pair of red dragons chasing each other through golden clouds, talons outstretched. A small tent-card sat on the edge of the rug, announcing: DON'T STEP ON THE CARPET.

'Tempting though, isn't it?' came a voice from behind them. They turned to see Trent grinning, arms folded. 'Can you believe this place?' he asked, extending his arms to welcome his partners. Gavin slapped a palm onto Trent's, while Shanti accepted a kiss on the cheek. They swapped the obligatory airline mini-reviews.

'You know why you're here, don't you?' asked Trent after a pause in the small talk.

'Of course,' answered Gavin. 'We're here to get this thing done in thirty days, just like the book. Got my copy. Read it on the plane.'

'Yes, thirty days is correct, but I meant right here, in the Reunification Palace?' Trent gestured past the rug, towards the corridor.

'Because you think it's cool, in an ironic way, and it makes a grand statement. And you like grand statements,' offered Shanti.

'As much as I appreciate the psych evaluation, the real reason we're in this palace is because it has a story to tell us. You guys ready for your company induction?'

They took a series of stairs to the basement, a drab and claustrophobic collection of small rooms filled with imposing desks and banks of rotary-dial telephones, connected by corridors that would not have felt out of place in a warship. Trent led them into a small two-room apartment, furnished with a desk, three telephones, a tactical map of the 'American War', a bed, a lamp and absolutely nothing else.

'This,' he gestured around the room, 'is how we've been working for the last couple of weeks. Each in our own little bunkers, relying on technology to communicate, following a map we've drawn that may or may not be connected to reality. And it's worked okay so far. We have the basic technology scope, a start on the visual identity and some ideas for the product roll-out. But now it's time to come out of our bunkers, form a team and start the real campaign on the battlefield. Let's take a look at what we're up against.'

He pointed up at the ceiling, smiled and walked out of the room. Gavin and Shanti followed him through the narrow corridors, emerging in a cramped hall filled with plaques and exhibits. It was crowded with tourists, mainly because it was the only room in the vicinity with functioning AC.

'Is this where you tell us we're going to war?' asked Gavin, raising an eyebrow.

'We need to be prepared to go into battle,' said Trent. 'Not only will we be fighting to build the product and to secure the next round of investment, but we'll also be fighting to control how our company is perceived. Because the market will want to dictate the story of what it is that we do. Take a look at these walls.'

They spent a few minutes jostling with the tourists, following the chronology of the palace as told by photographs, newspaper clippings, the odd medal and a handgun. A couple of images were instantly familiar – a burning monk, a tank smashing through tall iron gates, a line of desperate people trying to board a helicopter on the roof of a building – but the story this collection told differed slightly from the popular understanding the West had fashioned from the conflict.

The room told of a proud, hard-working people, whose rule had been interrupted both by meddling foreigners and traitorous, treacherous brothers. More than half of the display featured colour photographs of the palace serving as a gala reception hall for visiting diplomats, trade delegations and the odd, un-named western tourist. Essentially the story was: we had a few problems with the neighbours, who were acting like dicks, but they surrendered in shame so it's all good now and lately everyone wants to be our friend.

'Do you know who put this display together?' asked Trent, motioning around the room.

'Some officials from the Vietnamese Tourism Authority?' ventured Gavin.

'The winners.' Trent deepened his voice and adopted a chiding British accent. 'History is written by the victors.'

'Churchill never actually said that,' countered Shanti.

'He didn't?'

'Everyone attributes the quote to him, but there is no actual recording of it. Can't be found.'

Gavin regarded Shanti with admiration as Trent was momentarily taken aback.

'But I think I get your point,' Shanti reassured him. 'It's not just about building product. It's about delivering an experience and managing our reputation.'

'Exactly. And that's a big part of why you're here,' Trent turned to Gavin. 'Shanti told me she was impressed by your approach to user experience. How it's not just about efficiency on the screen, but making people feel part of the experience of being someone else, right from the start.'

Gavin shot a quick look toward Shanti, who gave a nod.

'The thirty days book talks about it a lot and I want us to keep it as a core focus: winning the market over, one user at a time. That's how we control the story of our company, how we appear like winners,' Trent paused, as if he were already at the microphone of his own presser. 'We can't leave it to the venture capitalists, or the incubators, the angels, the trade press or the bloggers. Those guys are just money in search of a story and if they aren't chasing ours, they'll use us to chase someone else's. So that's lesson one: we write the story of our company. Okay, time to level up.'

They climbed an uneven stairwell into a courtyard on the ground floor, open to the low-slung tropical sky. A severe garden of succulents sat at the centre of a ring of private apartments, their outer walls replaced by floor to ceiling glass panels, creating a small museum of executive living for five-star generals. Some of the apartments were connected to shared private dining rooms, the cherry wood tables standing to attention under cut glassware and jade-handled serving utensils. The bedrooms were upholstered in various shades of opulence but one design point united them: each contained one bed, a single. It seemed there was no time for getting to know your comrades when you were busy defending your nation from invaders, foreign and domestic.

'We are here, just like the generals before us, to get the job done.' Trent looked from Gavin to Shanti and back again, but neither reacted. He inhaled mightily and ploughed ahead. 'So this part of the story is about how we're going to be living and working together in a relatively confined area. We'll be eating from the same table, so to speak, but leading separate lives, right?'

Gavin had hoped to reach the palace early and talk to Shanti about their night together, but flight delays thwarted that plan. And he'd never quite found a segue to the topic during their emails. He'd waited for her to bring it up and, when she didn't, he was terrified that if he did, she would laugh it off as inconsequential, or claim it was a drunken mistake. His particular brand of male logic led him to believe that if he didn't ask her the question, he couldn't hear her say no. Now he decided it would be best not to talk about it, at all. Except, Trent *was* talking about it. And now, so was Shanti.

'London was different, Trent. I told you before that I have a policy on mixing business with pleasure: I don't.' Shanti said flatly, crossing her arms. Gavin was so entranced by the way her arms pushed her cleavage up and slightly forward he almost didn't hear her forceful dismissal of their budding romance.

'Look, we're all adults here and everyone is free to behave as they see fit,' continued Trent, looking slightly uncomfortable. 'I'm not here to tell you what to do, except that I kind of am. Same table, separate rooms. That's all.' His tone left no room for further discussion.

Shanti shot Gavin a look of disapproval. He countered with a wide-eyed, open-palmed show of innocence and then let her walk on ahead. Gavin wasn't sure which made him more uncomfortable: having their entanglement brought up by Trent as a potential operational issue or having it shot down so quickly by Shanti as a potential breach of her personal code of conduct. Maybe she was just putting on a show for Trent, to prove that she was genuinely committed. After all, Trent was the one pouring his own money into the project. It made sense she would want to impress him. Gavin decided it was a lead he should follow. He stared wistfully at the carved rosewood bedheads in the display apartments for a moment, then resolved to put on an even more forceful show of disinterest in romantic entanglements. At least for a while.

They strolled past open doors, roped off to protect the cavernous rooms decorated in variations of late-60s Asian Totalitarian Military Ruler. One room featured high-backed lacquer chairs with emerald cushions, arranged in a perfect circle. Another huge, rectangular room was dominated by a long conference table in high-gloss ebony flanked by two opposing rows of boxy leather chairs, the sort you might expect to find in mission control during the Apollo program. A pair of long, thin microphones sprouted from the centre of the table. It looked like the perfect room to sit face to face with your enemies while your minions served them glasses of tepid water and you threatened them with swift and decisive military retribution.

A tour group of French retirees shuffled past the open double doors on the opposite side of the space, pausing to take in the grand negotiating room and nod as if to say, 'Ah oui, that's exactly how I would have arranged my negotiating table if I was running a politically-troubled nation in Indochina during the Sixties.'

Gavin marvelled at how it had been virtually weaponised by its scale and structure. It was the sort of room that offered the opposing team of negotiators no better possible outcome than a quick yet honourable death.

'Is this the part where you tell us how we're going to handle decision-making?' asked Gavin, embracing the change of topic.

'I could see you securing us a good deal in a setting like this,' Shanti weighed in.

'Not here, exactly. But you've both got the right idea. We'll be doing a lot of presenting, a lot of negotiating, a lot of deal-making. And when we do, I want us to appear formidable,' said Trent. 'If we look ramen profitable, we're going to be funded like we're ramen profitable. So when we meet with investors and partners, I want us to look powerful and expensive to run. Which will make us look expensive to buy. Which is what we want.'

'Do we actually have to be ramen profitable?' asked Shanti.

Gavin didn't want to reveal his ignorance but it seemed like decisions were being made about food and money, both of which were too important to remain un-investigated. 'What's ramen profitable?'

'Valley-speak for a startup that is turning a profit on paper, but only because the founders are being paid survival wages,' Shanti offered. 'Just enough to buy instant ramen.'

'Sometimes they get paid in actual ramen. But seeing as we're in Vietnam, let's aim to be pho profitable. Or at the very least, bahn mi profitable,' laughed Trent. 'As discussed separately with both of you, my investment fund will cover flights and accommodation, a small per diem, plus any costs associated with the business. But otherwise, your only payment this month will be in the form of equity. So yes, "ramen profitable" is absolutely the model.'

'But your point,' Gavin gestured at the negotiating table, 'is that we want people to think we eat lobster for breakfast, right?'

'Seafood is pretty cheap here, apparently,' Shanti chimed in.

'Guys, please,' Trent said clapping his hands together loudly and bringing them up below his chin. 'A little focus. The plan is to *appear* well-funded.'

'Even though we're eating noodles,' Gavin added.

'Yes. Tasty, nutritious, authentic, bought on the corner, eaten in the street, Saigon noodles,' said Trent, chopping the air impatiently with his hands to underline each word. 'Got it? Good. Let's continue.'

Shanti suppressed a giggle like a naughty schoolgirl and Gavin's heart soared. They exchanged glances and scurried after Trent up another set of stairs.

They emerged into a vast room on the second floor that contained a bar, billiard table and grand piano. The entire space appeared to be tailor-made for a cadre of relaxing generals.

A circular orange sofa dominated the centre of the room and offered a perfect view of the fighter jets and tanks on the front lawn. The whole scene was a spit-polished highball ying to the battered water canteen yang of the lower levels.

'Can you imagine the parties that must have gone on in here?' said Gavin, wide-eyed.

'This Steinway must have seen a pretty varied repertoire,' said Shanti as she peered inside the open lid of the piano. 'I bet the nights started with patriotic workers' songs but finished with "I Am the Walrus".'

'Imagine if generals brought in a troupe of lounge singers, but they turned out to be sexy female assassins, sent to –'

'Okay, Gav, that's very good material,' said Trent placing a firm hand on Gavin's shoulder, 'but maybe you should save that storyline for your Tarantino homage. Now this was obviously the party floor, no matter which party was holding office.'

Trent paused as another herd of elderly French tourists flooded the room, fanning themselves with brochures while nodding appreciatively at the furnishings.

'It didn't matter how serious things got down in the bunker, or how badly the negotiations were going on the ground floor, you could always come up here to take a break with a game of billiards, a couple of fingers of fine scotch and, quite possibly, a little singalong with a pod of sexy yet deadly female assassins.'

Gavin gave a little fist-pump to celebrate the acknowledgement.

'We will operate in a similar fashion,' Trent continued. 'We will work these next thirty days like our lives depend on it but we will also pause and relax from time to time, provided we're meeting our development milestones. This should be fun, right? Otherwise, why bother?'

'I created a production timeline while I was on the plane,' offered Shanti. 'I'd like to make that a priority discussion this afternoon.'

'Excellent work, Shanti. Agreed,' Trent clapped lightly.

'And can we set up a time to talk about onboarding?' Gavin stepped forward. He wanted to demonstrate his commitment to the task. Especially considering Trent's earlier warning about mixing business with pleasure. 'If we don't have live support and conflict resolution systems fully functioning at launch, a couple of negative reviews can snowball pretty quickly. We'll never be able to turn it around.'

'And I want to talk to you about the affiliate marketing stream,' said Shanti, talking more quickly as she went. 'Airlines and insurance brokers pay referral fees that are more than decent. We could make almost as much revenue from that deal flow as on the life-swap commission itself.'

'Guys,' Trent broke into a warm smile, 'I'm really impressed by the thinking and yes we're going to tackle each one of these opportunities in the build. But first you're going to let me finish the company induction. Let's head upstairs.'

They made the final ascent to the roof where they found another small, upholstered bar, now serving as a drinks kiosk for tourists. Trent bought three beers and they wandered over to the edge of the terrace to look out across the city, wiping the chilled cans across their foreheads. The buzz of Saigon's thousands of motorbikes drifted up through the heat, accompanied by the slow shuffle of tourists' flip-flops on the roof. A slight breeze offered momentary relief.

Trent pointed to the terrace below where an ageing military helicopter sat beside some potted palms and a discarded market umbrella. 'There's our final chapter for today.'

'Don't get it,' said Shanti, shaking her head slowly.

'Is it something about hitting our targets?' ventured Gavin.

'Sort of. This is about what happens when it's time for us to get out. There are, theoretically, only two ways to leave a startup. One involves climbing back down all the stairs, winding up lost in the basement, alone, with nothing but rotary dial phones and single beds. The other way...' Trent trailed off, motioning with his eyebrows down towards the helicopter.

'Is by using our eyebrows?' suggested Shanti.

Trent smiled. 'Okay. It's hot and you guys are probably a bit jetlagged. I'll make this easy. The other way we get out is by chopper,' Trent gestured with his beer can. 'It's fast, it's furious and it can take you almost anywhere you want to go. But when it comes, we will have to get in quickly, because the load window is short. And the number of seats is strictly limited.'

'You're talking about having an exit strategy, aren't you?' said Shanti.

Trent nodded and took a pull of his beer.

'That's from the thirty days book, too, isn't it?' said Gavin, squinting against the flat midday sunlight. 'The wrong ownership structure, a product that doesn't scale or a lack of customer care systems can all scare off potential buyers. But if we set these things up correctly we become a much more attractive acquisition target.'

'Ten out of ten, Gav. Very strong summary,' said Trent with a wink. 'It may seem incongruous to be talking about the end when we're at the beginning, but it's one of the most common mistakes founders make. You don't wait to see what the exit looks like, you design it in advance.'

'It looks like cash, doesn't it?' asked Gavin.

'It might. Or it might be a stake in something bigger. Board seats. Speaking gigs. Our own VC fund. It's up to us,' Trent stretched out his arms. 'But before we leave here, we need a live prototype, a company structure, an operations plan, and a detailed picture of what our chopper looks like.'

'Sounds good.' Gavin tilted his head and drained his beer. 'What are you going to call the company?'

'I've got a couple of ideas, but right now I'm liking The Changing Room of Life.' Trent beamed.

Below them traffic lights changed to green, releasing a fresh swarm of motorcycles' revving. Shanti nodded slowly and finished her beer. Gavin passed his empty can from hand to hand.

'Either of you got a better idea?' Trent folded his arms.

'Shelf Life,' Gavin said quietly without looking up.

'What?' asked Trent, unfolding his arms.

'Say that again,' commanded Shanti.

Gavin cleared his throat and stood a little taller. 'Shelf Life.'

'That's sooo good, Gav,' Shanti's eyes widened. 'That's perfect.'

Gavin felt a little tingle and tried not to smile. Just like Tony Montana had told him during countless stoned repeat viewings with his flatmates: *First you get the money, then you get the girls.* Tony had also told him something about power, but Gavin couldn't quite remember.

'I love it, Gav,' said Trent, slapping him on the back. 'Shelf Life. That's fucking genius.'

Gavin stared out at the chopper and allowed himself a little smile. Through the shimmering haze of the tropical air he imagined the rotors slowly turning to life and the pilot leaning out the window giving him the thumbs up.

To compile is to be glorious

'Sales assistant in ladies' footwear.'

'So. Very. Creepy,' Shanti shook her head slowly.

'Only if you don't like ladies' feet,' Gavin said with a grin.

'I like it. Write it up,' said Trent, pointing at the whiteboard. The lounge room of the third floor apartment had been converted into a basic office. The fan blades did lazy circuits overhead while a motorbike droned past in the street downstairs. 'Okay, what's on the shortlist so far?'

'We've got barista, DJ, personal trainer, yacht broker, zookeeper, sports reporter, photographer's assistant, surf guide, nightclub door bitch, food reviewer, videogame designer, lifeguard and, thanks to Creepy McCreepface over here, ladies footwear sales assistant,' said Shanti, giving the whiteboard marker a little sniff.

'That stuff'll kill you,' said Gavin, stretching back in his office chair.

'We've been in this office since the middle of the afternoon. It's now almost three. I need something to keep me going,' said Shanti.

'Okay, are we happy with that inventory for launch?' Trent walked a small circle in front of the whiteboard. 'This is all white-bread middle-class M-rated fantasy stuff. Do we need more cool? More edgy? More dangerous?'

'We do, but it will come from the users. They'll see our list and say "my life is more interesting than that stuff", which will encourage them to register, which will boost our inventory,' said Gavin. 'Classic user-generated acquisition strategy.'

'Nice. Are we just listing them by job title? I thought the point of ShelfLife was that people get to rent the whole life, not just the job?' Shanti replaced the marker cap. 'So they get to experience the whole box and dice. The home life, the friends, the neighbours, the kids –'

'The wives and girlfriends,' said Gavin with a little too much excitement.

'The husbands and boyfriends?' Shanti countered with a raised eyebrow.

'That was my original idea, yes. There should be scope for full immersion, but I don't want to make it mandatory, otherwise it'll just scare too many people off.'

'But the titillation is important. The sense of possibility. It's how we sell SUVs in the suburbs. You buy one knowing that you'll probably never take it off road, but you love the fact that if you wanted to, you totally could. So let's set up the database tables to accommodate the social aspects and the home life as well.'

'Easy for you to say,' Shanti tapped her chin with the marker. 'We're trying to get the prototype live in thirty days, remember?'

'I'm not saying it's easy, but from a user's perspective we need to be more granular in the way we present it,' said Gavin. 'Split it out by pre-requisites. That'll reduce your incomplete rate.'

'How so?' asked Trent.

'The Host Lives where the professional component has no pre-qualifications go in their own category. This is stuff you can do with almost no training or knowledge. Like a valet.'

'Last I heard, you need a driver's licence to drive a car,' Shanti folded her arms.

'Yeah, well, fair enough, maybe that's a bad example,' Gavin rubbed his chin. 'Look at Door Bitch, Barista, Photographer's Assistant, and maybe the Food Reviewer. A bit of pre-reading and a cheat sheet written by the original life owner and I reckon most people could muddle through for a week without causing any major problems. Right?'

Trent nodded and Shanti blinked slowly.

'So put them in the walk-ins category, no prior experience needed. Then you've got things like Lifeguard, Fitness Instructor, Valet, thank you Shanti, and the Yacht Broker who all probably need some basic certification. Or Marty on the surfboat, there's a decent level of surfing ability needed there. Put those lives in a separate category and flag the professional pre-requisites up front so customers know what to expect before they browse. Much higher conversion rate.'

'Not the Yacht Broker,' said Trent, perched on the edge of a desk. 'My buddy from college moved to Florida and started dealing in yachts with nothing more than his high-school diploma. He actually suffers from sea-sickness. Now he's clearing a couple hundred grand in commissions per season.'

'Would he be interested in ShelfLife?' asked Shanti.

'He can't wait for us to go live. He's so bored of showing old rich dudes around Beneteaus but the money's too good so he can't quit,' said Trent, pushing himself off the desk and heading down the corridor towards the bedrooms. 'This is good stuff. You guys keep going, I need to pack.'

Shanti wandered over to the whiteboard to examine the list.

'Pack? Where's he going now?' asked Gavin in a low voice. 'We're starting to slip behind schedule, aren't we?'

'I think he's meeting some investors in Hong Kong at some big pitch fest,' said Shanti without turning from the board. 'Do we really need these sub-categories? Feels too complex to me.'

'Complex for us, but simple for the user. You want to make sure that every life the site serves them is one they can rent. That's the secret to reducing abandonment rates. You don't do this stuff at Opod?'

'Not really. That platform is very data-driven. Has to be because there's so much of it. But you're looking at the user first and then making the data fit.' She turned to face him. 'It's clever.'

Gavin put his hands in his pockets and shrugged. 'You just have to remember that these users are just humans. We all are.'

'I find humans frustrating. They don't follow patterns. They're unreliable.' She gave him a smile. 'You can't know for sure exactly what they're thinking.'

Gavin returned the smile. He wondered if this was an invitation to let her know exactly what he was thinking.

'Okay gang, I'm on the 5am to HK so I'm heading to the airport. Can I also task you to work up some options for handling the workplace associates, the people who have to carry the renter on the job for the week? Maybe revenue sharing, or credits towards a rental of their own?' Trent barely slowed as he trundled his cabin bag through the office. 'Our landlord promised to come by today to fix the shower head. His name is Mr Trung, lovely guy. See you in about twenty-four hours.'

Trent's luggage clacked down the three flights of stairs. Gavin sighed.

'I'm glad he finally left,' Shanti stretched her arms above her head. 'He gets so focused he assumes everybody else is just as happy to pull an all-nighter.'

'I'm kind of used to it. We do them all the time in advertising. But they're usually not productive like this,' Gavin motioned around the office. Every wall was covered in post-its and tearsheets, the by-product of a couple of weeks spent thinking and dreaming and arguing. Whenever Trent had described what he imagined ShelfLife could do, Gavin set about breaking it down into a series of human behaviours and reactions, while Shanti compiled the code to mechanise it. The beautiful yet fragile idea Trent had revealed to them in Texas just a few weeks earlier was finding form in lines of code. 'I think this is starting to look like it might work.'

'I think I need a break,' Shanti walked past Gavin, running a slender finger along his bicep as she went. 'Do you?'

She had told herself it was part pity-fuck, part stress release, but she harboured the suspicion she'd invited Gavin into her bed that morning because she liked him. She acknowledged she would be breaking her own code of conduct by sleeping with a colleague, then immediately found a loophole by telling herself this wasn't a real company. Ergo, Gavin was not a real colleague.

Still relishing the pleasure of her release and the deliciousness of their shared secret, Shanti suffered mental-replay interruptus later that afternoon when an email arrived from Opod. All development was being sent offshore. The belongings on her desk were currently being boxed. The 'Scandefuckers' had fired her while she was on leave. She retreated to her bedroom to make some phonecalls to Opod's

HR department, but they had all been let go as well. The receptionist was new and refused to put the call through to anyone in senior management. Shanti took a deep breath, went back to her desk and distracted herself from Gavin's puppy-dog eyes by working furiously through the afternoon.

* * *

'Does this qualify as a date?' Gavin grinned as they sat down at a plastic table in the middle of the street, surrounded by food carts. Strings of tiny lights swung gently in the warm breeze as waiters took orders with a nod and yelled them to the outdoor cooks. Shanti smiled but didn't answer. She waved a waiter over and ordered for both of them.

'That's amazing, how you're picking up the language so quickly,' said Gavin.

'What's amazing is how Westerners only ever speak English,' she shot back with a little more venom than intended. The barb struck.

'I was just trying to be nice,' said Gavin. 'After last night, I thought – '

'Whatever you're thinking, Gavin,' she held her palm upright, 'I need you to unthink it, okay?'

'Unthink it? I can still feel it, Shanti. Are you just wiping me away?'

'I'm not wiping anything Gavin. I like you and I really liked last night. But things have changed for me. I need to get serious about ShelfLife.'

'Me too, I really – '

'Gavin,' she held up an index finger. 'Just listen, OK? I'm not really on sabbatical from Opod. They forced me to take the leave I'd accumulated so they could get it off their books.

Turns out they wanted it off their books so they could fire me. While I was on leave.'

'Fucking bastards.'

'I appreciate the sympathy but still no talking for you, okay?' she paused, partly to dare him to fill the silence. 'Now that I don't have a job, I've got no way of keeping my uncle off my back. I need money for my rent, my board, my university tuition, my boarding school fees and for god knows what the fuck else he's quietly been adding to the bill all these years.'

Gavin's mouth opened a little, but he quickly closed it.

'Years ago, my dad lost all his money back in India and so his brother stepped in to pay for my education. My dad says it will be this big giant shame on our family if I don't pay my uncle back. And I kind of see his point,' Shanti slumped a little. 'So I *have* to get this site launched and cash in on all this VC money Trent keeps talking about, or...'

'Or what?' said Gavin, before covering his mouth with his hand.

Shanti waved his hand away with a faint smile. 'I go back to Munich and work for my uncle's restaurant full-time.'

'What, like a waitress?'

'And book-keeper, receptionist, coder of his shitty website, basically everything. So if this thing here doesn't work, I'm screwed.'

'I'm not on sabbatical either,' Gavin leaned across to place his hand on hers. 'I told my bosses to go fuck themselves and I quit.'

'When did you do that?' Shanti shook her head in disbelief.

'Pretty much straight after your first email asking me to come join you guys,' Gavin gave her hand a little squeeze. 'So this is all I've got, too. We're in this together, all the way.'

'Oh, Gavin,' Shanti withdrew her hand. 'Not all the way.'

'What do you mean?'

'If we're really going to build this site and get investors on board, I need to focus. You need to focus.'

'I'm focussing. I'm focused,' Gavin stared at her and pointed at his own eyes. 'Look: focus.'

'Not on me. On the work,' she brushed her hair back. 'So you and me, if we're working together, we can't be together, even for fun. I've been to this movie before. Not a great ending.'

'If that's the way you want it,' he withdrew his hands to his lap.

'I'm sorry, Gavin, really. It's just the timing. If it was any other –'

Their food landed inelegantly on the table, in a flurry of plates, cutlery and barked Vietnamese.

'Not that hungry, actually.' Gavin threw a crumpled wad of dong onto the plastic table, gathered himself up and ambled into the night. The flipside of his boyish charm was his occasional childishness. They did not appear to be sold separately.

* * *

For the first time in a long time, Shanti felt like crying. She sat alone in the office, staring at the whiteboards and post-its that lined the walls. All these fragments and acronyms, arrows and Venn diagrams that were waiting to be captured, wrestled into code and loaded onto a server, then pressed into service on a million laptops and smartphones in the hopes of turning dreams into cash. Right now, the whole thing looked so fragile that a stiff breeze could reduce it to confetti. Shanti felt the panic starting to rise and in response, she unleashed a torrent of tears, sweat and code that lasted through the night. Every time she paused, her mind wandered back to Gavin. To prevent the wandering, she leant more forcefully into the work. By the time she finished, fingers aching and shoulders perma-hunched, the ShelfLife site was a functioning prototype, ready for an upload of test data and its first round of de-bugging. She drew the blinds against the morning sun and fell into bed.

* * *

'Have you heard from him? Is he here?'

'Slow down, Trent. I just woke up, you just got in – very obviously – and I don't know what the hell you're saying.'

'What I'm saying is that I left you two alone for a little over twenty-four hours with instructions to write some code, design some pages and not spend any money. Instead, I come back to find he's missing, you've passed out and I have a voicemail from the Vietnamese Ministry of Home Affairs asking me to confirm Gavin's passport details. In person.'

'Oh shit.'

'Oh shit is right. Now, let's try this again: do you know where he is?'

'I have no idea, sorry.'

'When's the last time you saw him?'

'What time is it now?' she rubbed her eyes with the palms of her hands.

'Jesus, what have you two been doing?'

'I've been working, Trent. Okay?' Shanti snapped back. 'I was coding till about eight this morning, then I passed out. Do you think Gavin is in serious trouble?'

'It's entirely possible. Get dressed. We may have some bargaining to do.'

The office of the Vietnamese Ministry for Home Affairs was winding up for the afternoon and they wandered its halls for several minutes before being directed to the third level. At the end of a dim corridor they found a drab olive door marked with Vietnamese script in flaking black paint. A printout of the English translation was sticky-taped to the door: *Threats and Incidental Actions*.

The small man in a military uniform behind the large desk did not react when the door swung open. It was difficult to tell if he was awake behind his thick, tinted glasses. Three black plastic chairs ranged against the opposite wall just below a framed print of the president.

'Appointment?' asked the man behind the desk without warning.

'Yes I do,' said Trent.

'Your appointment letter?'

'I'm here about a passport verification. For Gavin Higgs,' Trent held his phone up while pointing at it. 'I have a message.'

'You have a problem.' The man spoke English as if he were reading from a textbook: precise, but without emotion. Trent couldn't tell if it was a question, so he hedged his answer.

'I'm hoping you can help me.'

'Yes. You will need help.'

'That's great.' Trent went for the presumptive close. 'I really appreciate it, Mr...?'

'General.'

'Mr General,' Trent said as he walked forward, extending his hand and unfurling a broad smile. This was a deal he wanted to close.

'Not Mister. General. General Trung. Take a seat, please.'

'General Trung? Then perhaps you know Mr Trung of Golden Star Electronics? In Quan Three? He's our landlord.'

'It is not important what your landlord is called. What is important is the damage caused by your associate Mr Higgs. Very big problem. Please, your seat.'

'I'm sure it was an accident,' Trent began, electing to play for the draw and lowering himself into the chair. 'And I am very sorry for whatever damages may have been caused.'

'Many motorcycles damaged. People threatened. Women insulted. Your associate did not control himself. Big problem.'

'Again, I must apologise.'

'Simply apologise is not enough, Mr Carlisle. You are the guarantor for Mr Higgs, is this correct?'

'He is my business associate. We work together. We all do,' Trent said, motioning towards Shanti.

'Yes. You are making something for the computer?'

Trent nodded towards Shanti. 'Here is our Chief Programmer.'

'Architect,' Shanti corrected.

'Chief Architect,' Trent continued.

'So pretty, and clever as well. Why you even need this one?' asked the General, pointing towards Trent. He smiled at Shanti like an oversized reptile surveying a much smaller mammal.

'Mr Carlisle has vision. He's a leader. Much like you, General Trung,' Shanti smiled back.

The General smiled a fraction. Trent realised Shanti held the stronger hand. He edged backwards in his seat.

'Why do you come to Vietnam to make this computer program, clever girl?' the General asked. 'You don't have enough computers in America?'

'Well yes, but we want to be part of a new industry in Vietnam. We see a bright future here. Many talented people,' said Shanti, eliciting another slight smile from the General.

'Yes, we have many internet business in Saigon. I also invest in these things.'

'Really? Perhaps you would consider looking at our business as well?' Trent leaned in again.

'I doubt that. Without your associate, maybe your business is not good investment,' the General smiled.

'May I ask where Mr Higgs is now?'

'That depends,' said the General, his smile vanishing. 'On his guarantor.'

Trent shifted in his seat. 'This sounds expensive,' he said to Shanti under his breath.

'Right now, Mr Higgs is in one of my department vehicles. I am yet to decide where that vehicle will take him,' said the General as crossed the room. 'I could choose to send him to the airport or… somewhere else.'

The General took a small notebook and a pencil from his top pocket, scribbled on the top page and tore the sheet out. He rose, crossed the room and handed it to Trent while smiling broadly again at Shanti.

'Can I ask you what this number represents, General Trung?' said Trent, holding the sheet of paper between his finger and thumb like a snake of unknown toxicity.

'That is the total of damages and fines owing.'

'I see. And would that be in Dong?' asked Trent.

General Trung laughed without humour as he strode back to his desk, taking out a Marlboro softpack and fishing for a lighter in the top drawer.

'You have the funds available?'

Trent looked back down at the scribbled figure. He most certainly did not have these funds available. At least not in this time zone. Even then, they wouldn't be his funds. They would be borrowed and then repaid, endlessly and incrementally, through a series of low-level administrative jobs in a far-flung corner of his parents' medical equipment empire, assuming they ever let him back in. He would commute from his one-bedroom apartment in a bland yet affordable part of New Jersey that was increasingly acknowledged to be almost safe, at least during daylight hours. He would live in this apartment for most of his adult life. He would never own anything of significant monetary value. His car would be second-hand and only intermittently reliable. He would never get laid again.

'General Trung, how long have you worked for the government?' Shanti asked, in a voice clear and bright, shattering Trent's Hallmark-esque nightmare.

'And you look after the finances as well as the computers?' asked the General, ashing his Marlboro on the floor. 'Impressive.'

'I'm in charge of Operations, General Trung,' replied Shanti with growing confidence. 'Do you know what type of software we're building here in your beautiful country?'

'I was not so interested to find out.'

'I don't blame you, General. Most software is very dull, but we're not building most software,' Shanti crossed the room to the General's desk and pointed at the Marlboros with her thumb. 'May I?'

The General took the pack, belted the base of it and thrust it forward to offer a stick, which she allowed him to light.

'What would you rather be doing, right now, if you didn't have to be here, dealing with troublesome foreigners?' she waved back across the room towards Trent.

'There are a few things I can imagine,' smiled the General, warming to the flattery.

'I'm sure there are, but I wasn't thinking of just going to a bar or a hotel across the street. A General can do that any day he wants, can't he? I was thinking of something far more exciting.'

'How exciting?' the General looked over Shanti as if he were assessing a brood mare.

'What's the most exciting thing you can think of, General?' Shanti took a long drag and let the smoke fall upwards into her nostrils. 'Where is the one place in the world you've always wanted to go? What would you do when you got there?'

The General tapped his cigarette pack on the desk and stared at Shanti. She held his gaze. Trent thought he might take up smoking himself if the tension got any higher.

'Maybe I would go to America, ride across the desert like a real cowboy. Share a smoke with the Marlboro man,' the General laughed savagely, waving his cigarette to underline the point. 'But why would you want to know such a thing, clever girl?'

'I want to know because our software can make that possible,' Shanti looked for somewhere to ash. 'We can let you be that cowboy, General, riding across those plains. Sitting around the campfire at night, telling stories and smoking your Marlboros.'

The General took an ashtray from his drawer and placed it on the desk. 'Would I have a gun?'

'Two guns.' Shanti took a long drag on her cigarette, eyes narrowing against the smoke. 'A shotgun and a six shooter, if that's what you wanted.'

The General tapped the softpack against the desktop and glanced at Trent. He leaned back in his chair and examined his cigarette closely.

'Tell me how does this software of yours work?' he asked.

Trent took the small sheet of paper holding the scribbled number, crumpled it into a ball and slipped it into his pocket.

* * *

Trung pulled the door of the van open and motioned for Gavin to climb inside.

'See, your friends are here,' the landlord clapped Gavin on the shoulder then gave a gentle push. 'We go now.'

Gavin stumbled into the seat as the door slammed behind him. He looked around to see Trent in the seat behind him and Shanti in the back row of the passenger van.

'Yay. You're alive,' said Trent from the back seat. 'Now I can fucking kill you.'

'Oh, man. Thanks for picking me up, although I probably could have got a cyclo or something. It's not that far,' he started to scoot across the seat to get comfortable. 'Wait. What's with the luggage? Are we going to a pitch fest or something?'

'Didn't they tell you?' Shanti asked from the back as the van pulled out into the clogged arteries of Saigon's roadways.

'Oh man, if one more person tells me about some scratched paint on a stupid Harley Davidson I'm gonna explode.'

'Do you realise how much shit we are in because of that bike?' said Trent.

'Do you realise that I just spent almost twenty-four hours in a filthy jail cell where no one spoke English?' said Gavin, rising out of his seat.

Trent stopped typing on his phone to look at Gavin properly. Gavin looked like shit. He also looked scared and confused. As angry and frustrated as Trent felt, he realised it couldn't have been a pleasant experience for Gavin either.

'Look, man, I'm sorry. You OK?'

'Yeah. I think so. I just need some sleep,' said Gavin, sniffing his armpit. 'And a shower.'

'I don't think we have time for either of those. Thanks to your little adventure last night, we now owe the son of the Minister for Forestry and Agriculture a mint Harley Davidson Fatboy.'

'That was absolutely not my fault,' Gavin started to protest.

Trent cut him off with a raised palm. 'Unfortunately, the son of the Minister for Forestry and Agriculture doesn't see it that way. And now we also owe a senior official from the Ministry for Home Affairs a week in Nebraska, living the life of the Marlboro Man.'

'What? You're not blaming me for that, too, are you?'

'No, Shanti's responsible for that one,' said Trent, returning to his phone.

'You're welcome,' Shanti folded her arms and sank into her seat.

The van lurched to the right. The chaos of overhead power cables, signboards, street vendors, motorbikes and two-stroke fumes fell away as they ascended a ramp and joined a parade of overloaded lorries and unregistered Mercedes barrelling along the highway to the airport.

'Where are we going?' Gavin craned to get a look at the scenery as it rushed past.

'Not sure yet. Still working on the leaving part,' said Trent without looking up from his phone.

'Leaving where?'

'The country. Mr Trung has a family friend who works at immigration. If we can get there before her shift finishes, she'll stamp our passports and we can leave tonight, but she won't enter the details in their system until she clocks on again tomorrow. Say goodnight Saigon.'

'Are you fucking serious?' Gavin threw his hands in the air. 'What if we get caught?'

'Caught is where you were about half an hour ago, remember? Or did you get so drunk that it's all just a blur?'

'Is that what you think happened? Is that what Shanti told you?'

'Nope, all she said was that you went to the seven eleven to buy a razor,' Trent turned to study Shanti for a reaction. Shanti pretended to study the traffic outside.

'I actually went out for a walk, to clear my head. It had been kind of a long day,' Gavin shot Shanti a glance. 'I walked past this dude who asks me if I like motorcycles. He's showing me his bike, then I get shoved from behind and I fall into the gutter. When I get up, all these bikes are lying on each other, the dude is yelling, girls are screaming and a couple of cops appear from nowhere. Next thing, I'm in jail. I think I got set up.'

Trent studied Gavin for a long while before placing a hand on his shoulder.

'Well, I'm glad you're okay. Really.'

Half an hour later the van turned off the main road, swept past the terminal, sped along a narrow laneway and came to a stop beside a series of hangars. Trung opened the driver's door and slid out. The noise from the hangar flooded the van's interior: shrieking whistles, shouting men, the insistent whine of reversing indicators, the dull throb of grinding machinery.

Trung slammed the door and shuffled out into the commotion. The whistling and shouting became handshakes and greetings.

'I swear Trung knows every single person in this town,' said Trent, shaking his head with admiration. 'Okay, get your stuff and be ready. This is almost certainly going to be surreal.'

The three of them watched through the aubergine window tint as Trung arranged himself in an old plastic chair beside one of the dock supervisors and handed around a pack of cigarettes. He was telling the story of his tenants, the ShelfLife founders, annotated with hand gestures, to the small crowd of airport workers.

Trung's hands made a typing motion and Shanti began a running commentary.

'He's explaining what we do,' she began, sounding more like David Attenborough than she had intended.

Trung's finger walked up and down an imaginary set of stairs several times, followed by a shrug of the shoulders. The whistleblower nodded for Trung to continue.

'He's saying we never complained about all the stairs we had to climb to get to the third floor.'

Trung cupped his hands together, grabbing something and brought them up to his mouth. He flapped his jaw a few times.

'Ha! That's Trent eating Bahn Mi. Every. Freaking. Day.' Gavin joined in.

Trung held one finger up on his left hand. He held up two fingers with the other. Then the single finger moved up and flew away, the whistle-blower following its imaginary trajectory.

'That's you, flying to Hong Kong a couple of days ago,' said Gavin, 'and us two staying behind to...' His enthusiasm evaporated as Shanti shot him one of her looks.

Trung made one hand into a loose fist and bumped it into the open palm of the other hand several times.

Trent turned to look at Gavin, then at Shanti. Neither returned eye contact.

Trung's hands flew up, fingers outstretched like a small explosion, and then drifted apart. He mimed wearing handcuffs, grasping iron bars, offering a salute and someone asking for money. The finale was a series of fingers tip-toeing gingerly along his own thigh, then flying away. He brought the curtain down by slapping his thigh. The laughter of the crowd could be heard inside the van.

'I think I get the picture now,' said Trent.

'Trent, look, it wasn't meant to – ' Shanti started, but was interrupted as the van door opened with a grinding moan. The supervisor gave the three a loose salute and a wink. He spoke into a walkie-talkie as Trung led them towards a large opening in the wall of the hangar, obscured by a hanging set of industrial plastic strips.

Shanti jogged a little to catch up to Trent. 'Are we getting smuggled out as freight?'

'I. Don't. Actually. Know,' Trent replied without moving his lips, eyes scanning left and right, trying at least to act calm, as it was no longer possible to remain inconspicuous.

Through the plastic strips and into a high-roofed warehouse, they snaked around a collection of refuelling trucks and baggage carts in various states of repair. Men in overalls stopped to stare as the founders rolled their luggage through the workshop. The wall on the other side of the cavernous space was punctuated by three regular-sized doors. Trung paused to read the Vietnamese script on each one, talking quietly to himself as if pondering a riddle. He settled on the left door, pushed it open and waved them through.

Trent glanced back at Shanti then Gavin, took a deep breath and strode into a small white office containing one large desk and one Vietnamese woman in a military uniform. Trung greeted the woman with a warm embrace and much nodding. They spoke for a short while, holding each other's hands and ending the conversation with a gentle laugh.

'I leave you now, Mr Trent Carlisle,' said Trung, stepping over their luggage.

'Thank you so much, Mr Trung. See you again,' said Trent, shaking his hand.

'I think perhaps not,' said Trung, closing the door behind him.

'Passports please,' said the woman.

The three founders scrambled for their documents and rushed to place them on the desk, like a border-crossing version of snap.

'One thousand for exit fee, please,' she said with a pleasant smile, like a shopkeeper toting up the milk, bread and papers.

Trent retrieved several notes from his satchel, placing them next to the passports.

'Each, please.'

Trent started to protest, then stopped. He peeled off more notes. The official placed both her hands on the stamper and pushed it onto each passport, making a sound like an oil drum being dropped from a balcony. She made some notations in a small notebook and handed each passport back with two hands, arms outstretched, bowing slightly each time.

'This way, please,' she said, gesturing to a door behind her desk. The three founders stepped through to find themselves airside of the immigration counters.

'I'm so sorry. Your flight today is cancel,' she said brightly. 'Please check with service desk to arrange another flight. That way.' She pointed along the corridor and was gone.

'I guess that's it,' Shanti turned her passport over in her hands, perhaps hoping it would reveal an answer, the way a magician's deck conjures up the exact card you were thinking of. 'Time to say goodbye and go home, right?'

'If that's where you want to go. Back to your comfortable job debugging confirmation pages in Munich,' Trent folded his arms and lifted his chin. 'Or resizing banner ads for some grocery chain in Melbourne.'

Gavin looked up, realising he'd just been dragged into a conversation that was fast heading towards an argument.

'Look, I'm sorry about what happened. I really am. But I quit,' he said.

'You can't quit,' Trent started to puff up. 'Because I'm going to fire you first.'

'No, man. I mean I already quit – past tense. Before I even came here,' Gavin put his hands up. 'There are no banner resizes waiting for me in Melbourne.'

'I thought you were on sabbatical like Shanti?' asked Trent.

'I got so excited about your idea, about working with you guys, I walked out of a review meeting with my douchebag Creative Director and never went back.' Gavin stared at the passport in his hand. 'Boxed up my things. Sublet my room. I think my housemates prefer the new guy; he's even freelancing at my old agency.'

'Wait, some guy is living in your house with your friends and working at your old job?' Trent started to laugh. 'You realise you've basically created a ShelfLife booking already?'

'When you put it that way.' Gavin thrust his hands in his pockets and stared at the floor. Shanti kept turning her passport over. Travellers wafted past, staring at schedule boards, mouths agape.

Trent broke the silence. 'I had some very promising meetings in Hong Kong. I was close to getting us to the next stage.'

'I completely forgot that's where you were,' Shanti looked up at Trent. 'Did you meet up with your mentor as well?'

'He wanted to introduce me to a couple of investors, but he needed to see something working first. We couldn't show him a bunch of code in different pieces. The timing of all this,' he threw his hands up and looked around the airport, 'couldn't have been worse.'

'It's not in pieces,' said Shanti. 'The site, I mean. It's actually close to being functional. I went on a code binge while you were in Hong Kong. The matching algorithm is working, so the site now pre-qualifies the applicants, gives the life-rentals a higher probability of success in the real world. That's why I was up all night.'

'Are you talking wireframes?' Trent stared at her.

'For now. But if Gavin's last round of page designs are all correct, which they have been so far, I just need to front-end it. We could probably put it on a staging site and upload the test data.'

'Jesus, Shanti, are you serious?'

'I think so, yeah.'

'You get this close and you still want to pack it in? Go back to Opod and wait to get boxed?' Trent put his hands on his hips.

'Already happened.' Shanti lowered her chin. 'Those Swedes fired me. By email.'

'Fuckers,' said Trent, smiling.

'That's what I said, too,' Gavin put his hands on hips.

'Huh,' said Trent, scratching his chin. 'Seems like we've got more in common than I thought.'

'You mean we're all broke?' asked Gavin.

'No. Well, yes we are broke, but I think I can fix that,' Trent put his hands together in front of him. 'Look, can I just ask you two, please, to promise me that you'll be strictly professional from now on?'

Gavin pursed his lips and nodded. Shanti rolled her eyes.

'I'll take that as a yes. Now, shall we get back to work and launch this company?'

Gavin watched Shanti, turning her passport over. A contract cleaner pushed an industrial vacuum past them slowly.

'Where?' she asked.

'Yes!' Trent clapped his hands together and brought them up under his chin. 'Thank you, Shanti. I promise it will be somewhere nice. Now what about you, Gav?'

'You still want me around?' Gavin looked from one to the other. 'I mean, after what happened?'

'Well I can't design and I think Shanti already has enough to do. So, yes, we still need you around.'

A security official paused to look Gavin up and down, frowning before he moved on. The three waited for the moment to pass.

'Jesus, Trent, can we just get out of this airport before Mr Trung's mojo wears off?' Gavin hissed. 'Buy some tickets to somewhere and let's go.'

'Awesome,' Trent said quietly. 'I need to make some calls. Why don't you two find wi-fi and do some work while we're waiting? I'll come find you.'

Shanti tapped her passport on her chin, but eventually handed it over. Gavin placed his on the stack. Trent smiled. 'I love it when a plan comes together.'

Shanti stopped Trent as he headed for the service desk. 'What did you mean just then, when you said we've got more in common that you thought? Apart from being broke?'

'It seems like none of us is needed in our old lives anymore. ShelfLife is all we've got.'

'What happened to your cushy sales job, working for your parents?'

Trent smiled and walked backwards, arms outstretched. 'That was a lifetime ago.'

I'm on a boat,
you're on a boat

Andy stared at the carving knife-shaped space one last time before realising there were exactly ten good hiding places for the knife to be at this moment. Five were under the pillows of the five surfers lying in the bunks on the port side of the *CrossShore*; and the balance of those hiding spots were likewise under the pillows of the five surfers lying in the bunks on the starboard side. It now occurred to him that the real Marty would have seen this coming and hidden the knife under his own pillow.

'You complete fucking idiot,' Andy thought to himself. 'You could have just stayed at home with a nice glass of pinot watching the rugby. But you had to decide you were bored with your life and try to change everything, didn't you? And look where it got you: in the middle of the Indian Ocean on a boat full of sociopaths who want to stab each other in the face. Happy now?'

Truthfully, he hadn't been happy before. The pressures of the mortgage, the prying of the neighbours, the hectoring of the current affairs shows, the suffocation of the emails, the trimming of the hedges and the enforced joviality of the school fund-raisers had all conspired to drive him as close to mad as he had ever been courageous enough to admit.

Seeking a new or, perhaps, forgotten definition of himself, he fossicked through the mementoes his life had produced. The bands that his own band had once covered in his parents' garage were still at the top of his CD pile, underlining the fact he still had actual CDs. The football stars he had once taped to his bedroom wall as a schoolboy were now on the board of trustees of his son's private school. He realised all his early memories were just signposts to exactly where he was now, which was the only place his life was ever going to take him. The only Kodachrome moment that hinted at a different possibility was a silhouette of himself standing on a dune, board under his arm, shielding his eyes from the dawn as he surveyed the waves. Staring at that snapshot, he wondered if that might have been the last time he truly felt like himself.

Andy had taken his return to surfing slowly at first: a weekend session here, an after-work paddle-out there. Nothing too serious. Until the moment he caught the last wave of a mid-week dawn patrol and rode it into an altered state of self-belief. This wave ambled in from the horizon, stood up, broad shouldered and polished. It paused for a moment to collect Andy before falling elegantly over itself again and again, taking a diagonal path towards the shore. It was serene and thrilling all at once. Crucially, Andy did what he always hoped but never truly expected he would do on a wave this good: not fuck it up. The better the wave, the less the surfer has to do to ride it well, and this wave was perfect. Andy gave a slight stall on the back foot, a bit of a forward crouch to release the rocker, a shift of weight to the heel, a smooth, steady opening of the shoulders and that was it – a weightless, noiseless tube ride, followed by a clean exit and a climb to the lip before a wide, powerful cutback, spray lighting up in the warm rays of the early sun.

Boom.

Like an addict desperate to salvage the remains of a fading high, Andy immediately began searching for a bigger hit. In between meetings, in the lunch queue, watching junior netball, in every spare moment, he Googled opportunities to recapture that moment. The global surf travel industrial complex was mining the planet for new waves on a daily basis, and, on the internet at least, all the waves looked perfect, empty and fairly approachable. Similarly, all the fishing boats converted into mobile surf caravans looked sturdy, spacious and more or less luxurious. Andy knew this couldn't universally be true, a fact quickly confirmed by the flaming, ranting, chest-beating, xenophobic cauldron of surf discussion forums. By the collective reckoning of the rabble the waves were hoaxes, the camps were flea-pits, the boats were death traps and, no matter where you went, there were far too many cashed-up young Brazilians with multiple ju-jitsu trophies and absolutely no surf etiquette.

This surf trip will change your life.

Those seven words followed Andy around the web for days, like a teenager who doesn't want to be seen at the shopping centre with her parents but has no other way of getting home. He started seeing those seven words flashing beneath his inbox, next to his search results and alongside the tedious stream of backlit photos of his dull colleagues' even duller offspring. It followed him into his secret browser tabs of dominant milfs, amateur creampies and interracial threeways.

This surf trip *will* change your life.

So simple, so perfect. A life-changing journey to a place where the primary activity was surfing. Andy desperately wanted to step out of the brogues and the cufflinks and the regular dental check-ups and car servicing and school reports and calendarised matrimonial sex to leap into the ocean and become, if only for a short while, the stall-to-tube-to-cutback guy. Could it be possible that these seven words held the key?

Click.

A small gallery of faces filled the screen. Some were standing in sleek corporate offices, dark nightclub interiors, tropical landscapes, famous cities, a stable full of horses – even what looked to be a fully-fledged BDSM dungeon. But only one tableau interested Andy, a shining square of turquoise framing a wiry, tanned twenty-something man. Tongue poking out, wearing white-framed wayfarers and a green trucker's cap, the man stared at Andy from the screen, sending all the other profile pictures to the periphery. The figure leant over the railing of a sizeable boat, his left hand making a peace symbol, the splayed fingers perfectly framing the open mouth of a wave as it barrelled past the tropical background.

I'm Marty. How'd ya like to be me next week? read the caption.

From a quick skim, it appeared that Marty was, in fact, offering a week-sized slice of Marty's life, for the reasonable sum of USD2450, travel and booking fee not included.

Click to meet Marty.

The video loaded and a smaller, more pixelated version of Marty started to sway from the rigging of the timber boat. After a nervous sideways glance he addressed Andy directly.

'Hi, I'm Marty Durant! Thanks for checking out my ShelfLife profile. I live and work on the mighty *CrossShore*, a deluxe sixty-three foot timber surf charter boat in the magical

Mentawi Islands of Sumatra, Indonesia. My life is pretty rad, but it's also pretty sweet. I get to pick the best spots, surf all day and hang with the guests. The local crew are great workmates and my boss is the best bloke, even if he is a little crazy sometimes. Seriously, you'd have a hard time picking a better ShelfLife to live for a week. So leave yourself behind, book a week and come and be me, Marty the Deckhand.'

Andy sat back. This was *exactly* what he had wanted: a chance to *be* the stall-to-tube-to-cutback guy. The week's life rental included full board and meals, professional indemnity insurance, and a list of tasks that seemed no more difficult than cleaning up after a family barbeque. On the downside, there were about eight to ten 'on-duty' hours a day, the 'possibility of sea-sickness', the need to 'mediate minor guest disputes' should they arise and some 'occasional light manual labour'.

Marty had not yet been reviewed or rated, but he was a 'verified ShelfLife host' (whatever that meant) and, most interestingly, his booking calendar showed he had slots available. Andy clicked through to a few of the other profiles, read the FAQs, scrolled through some of the testimonials and scanned the founders' bios. The site was billing itself as 'the Airbnb of lifestyles' and, at the bottom of every page, kept asking 'Who would you rather be?'

Andy decided he rather wanted to be Marty the Deckhand, thank you very much. He completed the application form and was overjoyed to find a pre-approval email in his inbox the following morning. All that ShelfLife required now was confirmation of his surfing ability, via a short video clip of him at his local break, a recent medical certificate and half of the booking fee. A few days after that, he received a confirmation phone call from ShelfLife's customer support team. The young man reminded Andy to sign the waiver and indemnity forms, and to familiarise himself with the ShelfLife instruction manual, *How to Be Marty the Deckhand*. Andy printed out a copy, tucked it in his briefcase and re-read it every spare moment he got.

* * *

The crossing from the Sumatran port town of Padang to the Mentawi Islands was uneventful, at least from Andy's perspective. The 4am wake-up call, the motion-sickness tablets, the rolling ocean and the tropical sun all conspired to put him asleep within minutes of stepping aboard. He woke in a fog to learn from Chook, the captain of the *CrossShore* and his boss for the week, that a favourable current and slight tailwind had delivered them to the closest of the decent surf breaks in the island chain with about an hour of daylight to spare. The guests would be in the water on Day One, which always made for a smoother start to the trip.

Marty's instruction manual had explained that some international guests had been on planes and in check-in queues and transit hotels and gate lounges and taxis for thirty-odd hours before they even set foot on the *CrossShore*, and often became disgruntled to learn there were still hours more sailing to be done before they arrived at the mythical waves of the Mentawis. And even when they did, it would probably be too dark to see, let alone surf. Some guests, unable to contain their pent-up excitement, would paddle out in the gloom, get washed in over the reef and spend their first night of the trip scrubbing tiny pieces of fire coral out of their shallow wounds with a toothbrush. According to the manual, this was # 3 on the 'Top 5 worst possible ways to start a surf trip'.

The *CrossShore* slid into anchor beside a left-hand break known as Scarecrows just as the rays of the setting sun basted the tops of the palm trees deep orange and the opposite end of the sky started to blush with the purple of early nightfall. Only one other boat was anchored nearby, although most of its human cargo appeared to be pouncing on anything that looked like a wave.

'It's bad form to just rock up and let our guys paddle straight out,' said Chook, grimacing as he peered through the forward window. 'Like farting in an elevator. Makes it unpleasant for everyone.'

'Maybe if we just let half of them go?' suggested Andy. 'Five guys isn't so bad, right?'

'Fuck it,' said Chook with an air of fatalism. 'It's the last half-hour of light. We'll deal with the fallout after dinner. Might make a nice first job for you, eh Marty?'

Chook slapped Andy on the shoulder and made his way to the back deck, where the ten guests were pulling boards out of covers, threading leashes and screwing fins into plugs. He tried to set some ground rules – don't descend as a pack; wait for a few waves to go through before paddling on to the peak; let the guests from the other boat take the bigger waves; don't act like dickheads – but most of the guests had waxed up and thrown themselves over the side before Chook made it halfway through his list.

Within minutes, the lineup descended into chaos.

Words were spoken, leashes pulled and drop-ins became standard operating procedure. The surfers from the other boat gave up in disgust, cursing and complaining as they paddled home in the fading light. Chook sent Andy over to the other boat with a slab of beer and an apology. They would all be sharing these waters for the next week, it made no sense to start out as enemies.

'Thanks for the beers, mate, but honestly, you guys are going to be needing them more than us,' said the tanned, balding captain of the other boat as Andy stepped aboard.

'Yeah, it was a bit of a tense crossing and Chook just had to let these guys get wet, y'know?'

'Oh yeah, we all get that on Day One. Sometimes it's easier just to do the crossing at half-throttle and arrive after dark,' said the captain, taking a long pull of his beer, 'But you guys have a special case on your hands this time.'

'What do you mean?'

'Jesus, mate, haven't you seen who's on your boat this week?' The captain's voice rose in disbelief. 'Chook must have been fucking desperate for revenue is all I can say.'

'Yeah, Marty told me there was a last-minute cancellation or something. Had to put two smaller groups together to fill the booking.'

'Where is Marty, anyway?'

'He's taking a break this week,' said Andy, using the cover story he'd agreed with Marty. 'So I'm sort of filling in for him.'

'Wow! So you're the guy who rented Marty's life for the week?'

'He told you, huh?'

'And he gave you *this* week? With *this* group of guests?' the captain asked, his register continuing to climb.

'It appears so.'

'That Marty's a fuckin' clever cat, mate. Half of your guests are Brazil nuts,' the Captain handed another beer to Andy. 'And the other half are Seth Effricens, mate.'

'Is that bad?' asked Andy, eyebrows raised in hope.

The captain let the equation hang in the air for a moment before solving it with the crack-hiss of a ring pull.

'Bad enough when they're in the same ocean.' The captain looked back across the bay to the *CrossShore*. 'But in the same boat? Madness.'

Andy took the tender back to the Crosshore. He clambered up over the duckboard and into the main dining area to find the two groups of surfers crowded around opposite ends of the dining table, heads bowed, shovelling forks full of pasta. A gap in the middle of the table marked the no-man's land where neither Zilla nor Saffer would enter, lest it be taken as a sign they were comfortable in each other's company. Chook sat on the railing, just on the edge of the light, surveying the truce and chewing slowly.

After dinner the two groups broke out the cards. The South Africans played kaluki and the Brazilians truco. The tension slowly faded as the soporific effects of jetlag and carb loading won out. The guests drifted away from the table like autumn leaves, disappearing in ones and twos, until Andy and Chook were alone on the back deck sharing a bottle of rum. The Indonesian deckhands quietly went about cleaning and stacking and folding and storing, trading jokes and good-natured insults in low, happy voices.

'Aren't you worried about how these guys are going to get on?' asked Andy.

'Could go either way, I reckon,' said Chook, sipping slowly. Marty's manual described Chook as a former oil-rig worker who took up surf boat charters to get a change of scenery. It also listed him as possibly bipolar but generally 'a top bloke'.

'I need you to identify the two ringleaders. Get them on side and they should keep the rest of their guys in line.'

'What else do you need me to do?' Andy rolled the tumbler between his palms. 'I mean, what else would Marty normally handle, besides peacekeeping?'

'Get up early and paddle over to check the break,' Chook nodded towards the waves crashing in the darkness. 'And then get back here and make sure everyone's boardies are pressed.'

'What? Like ironing?'

'The iron is in the cupboard next to the galley.'

'Seriously?'

'I will not tolerate creased boardshorts on my boat,' Chook put his rum down and stared at Andy.

'Umm, okay. Do you have an ironing board, or do I just use the dining table?'

Chook stared at him a fraction longer before breaking into laughter and clapping him on the back. 'Ah, you seem like a good bloke, Andy, but you've got to stop trusting people so much.'

* * *

Andy was woken by Chook tugging on his ankle, letting him know that he was late for work. A greasy fog lingered above the sheet-glass ocean. Andy threw himself into the water and the awakening was immediate. Clambering on to his board he started paddling when he heard laughter.

'Andy!' called Wayan, the ship's cook, from the boat. 'Other way!'

Navigating by the muscular sound of waves crashing onto reef, Andy found his way through the mist to the break. The stillness of the air and the water had conspired to magnify the sound, and Andy was relieved to find the swell had dropped overnight. A set of very approachable three footers emerged from the dark, stood up on the reef and then rolled through the lineup forming playful walls that tapered away to gentle shoulders. He resisted the temptation to snag a couple of rides before going back to report the conditions – Marty's cheat sheet had been specific on that point. The two tribes were getting ready to surf the way marines prepare for combat – with sullen intensity and one eye on the enemy.

Wayan motioned for Andy to take some toast, drawing him close enough to whisper, 'That one, blue shorts. And that one, yellow shorts,' indicating the leaders of the respective packs.

'Thanks, Wayan.' Andy raised his slice of toast in salute.

'Good luck. Enjoy.'

Blue Shorts, a heavy-set, tattooed Brazilian, stood on the duckboard waiting without grace as Chook bled the fuel line of the tender. Yellow Shorts, a wiry, weather-beaten South African, leapt over the side, breaking the water with the tip of his board and disappearing below the surface. He emerged several metres later in full competitive paddle, head bowed and arms stroking. The remainder of the guests lemminged after him, churning the water to foam with a series of entries of varying cleanliness.

'Get out there, try and keep the peace willya, Marty?' Andy nearly jumped at the sound of Chook's low, gravelly voice in his ear. 'Take the boat.'

He understood now that the messing about with the fuel line had been a ploy to convince the impatient surfers to paddle the several hundred metres to the break. This gave Andy plenty of time to speed over in the boat, position himself in the lineup and let a few waves roll through, demonstrating for the guests the kind of patience and magnanimity he was expecting. He felt like a deputy headmaster placing his foot on the ball while talking to the over-eager junior soccer team. But as the pack emerged from the fog, thrashing through the water at pace, the feeling changed to that of a frail village elder waiting for the Mongols to thunder down from the steppes.

The pack steamed in as a lull in the swell enveloped the line-up in stillness. The ten surfers settled in a circle around Andy, assuming he was an experienced surf guide and talented surfer.

'Morning fellas. Haven't had a chance to meet all of you. Well, any of you. My name's Andy,' he started with as much confidence as he could. 'Or you could call me Marty, I guess. If you want.'

A bird on the shoreline gave a loud cry and took flight. It was the only sound in the bay. The surfers stared past Andy towards the source of the swell.

'Where are you guys from?' asked Andy.

A small wave collapsed onto the inside reef.

'Well, I'm from Sydney. You guys ever surfed there?' Andy ploughed on, comforting himself with the thought that this is what he was paid to do. Except that he was the one who had paid.

'Yeah. I surf there. Is okay.' It was a young broad-shouldered Brazilian with close-cropped hair. He spoke with no real enthusiasm and his eyes never left the horizon. 'Some waves, very crowded.'

'That's 'cos there's too many fucking Zillas in Sydney,' said the South African in the yellow shorts, a smile playing across his lips. 'Too fucking many in the Mentawis, too.'

Blue Shorts lowered himself onto his board, took two deep, powerful strokes and glided past Yellow Shorts, missing his board by inches. He came to a stop directly between the South African and the likely direction of the next set of waves. He sat back up on his board and placed his hands on his hips, muscles tensing.

'Looks like game on, eh boys?' said Yellow Shorts, addressing his countrymen, with a smile that bore more resemblance to a threat.

Andy weighed his options. He was close to making a general appeal for calm when a set materialised, prompting all ten surfers to paddle towards the same small patch of ocean as fast as physically possible.

The paddling turned to shoving as several surfers wheeled around under the lip in unison. Arms flailed, legs kicked, warnings were yelled and ignored. The circus was repeated on each wave of the set, leaving the pack to untangle leashes and inspect boards for damage. The whitewater bubbled as the current dragged them further over the reef.

'You go this one?'

It was the short-cropped Brazilian kid who had surfed in Sydney but found it crowded. He'd waited patiently while his countrymen sacrificed themselves at the altar of aggressive drop-ins, and that patience was now being rewarded.

'I think this one is yours – ?' Andy offered, bringing his inflection up to ask the kid's name.

'Renato,' he said, stroking into the pocket of the incoming wave and timing it perfectly.

By lunchtime the tally was three damaged boards (two crushed rails and one fin chop) and ten frayed tempers. Almost zero waves had been ridden without some sort of drop-in, fade, snake or other infraction. To add sand to the gears, the swell was clearly dying, delivering sets less consistently as the day wore on.

Andy managed to get a little more conversation out of Renato before Blue Shorts barked at his tribe in Portuguese, presumably ordering them to stay focused on ensuring that no South African got a wave without having to fight for it. The

South Africans appeared happy to oblige, until Yellow Shorts declared himself 'really fucken hungry, ay' and signalled for the tender to pick them up. Deprived of opponents, the Brazilians followed suit.

Chook arranged for Wayan to serve lunch at opposite ends of the boat.

'Mind if I join you fellas?' Andy tried to sound confident, but suspected he had not been entirely successful.

'Long as you don't try and snake me while I'm eating, ay fellas?' said Yellow Shorts, trying to make it sound like a joke and also failing.

'Don't worry, I promise I'll wait my turn for the sauce bottle,' said Andy, which drew a couple of small chuckles. 'Which part of South Africa you guys from?'

One of the younger guys, lanky and blond, said they were from Durban. Andy had seen this kid catch a couple of waves that morning and, despite the jostling and blocking, he had surfed with the relaxed, fluid style of someone born to the water. The kid turned out to be Yellow Shorts' nephew and this was his first big overseas surf trip. The other three worked for Yellow Shorts, or were related, or both. Chook had been hovering, nodding appreciatively as Andy made small conversational inroads with the group, until he overheard Yellow Shorts explaining the family business: a small back-to-base home security and response company. In South Africa, it meant the phone was always ringing.

* * *

'Fucking hell. Private security contractors. All we need now is for the Zillas to be some kind of Ju-jitsu masters,' said Chook, staring at the ocean.

'Why? Have you talked to them already?' asked Andy.

'Don't tell me, please, Jesus fucking Christ. Are you kidding?' pleaded Chook.

Andy shook his head and reached into the cooler for a beer. 'They've just won their regional championships. But a couple of their team-mates are back in jail for assault, so that's why there's only five of 'em.'

'Marty, you clever prick.' Chook drained the last of his Bintang and tossed it over his shoulder. It made a small splash before sinking.

Chook put the hammer down and made the crossing to Playgrounds in record time. He was working on the theory that if they could tire the guests out with uncrowded waves, then load them up with carbohydrates and alcohol, the crew stood a better chance of keeping a lid on the situation each evening. Andy's job was to convince each tribe to go to a different break for the afternoon session while Wayan assembled an avalanche of food.

'Hey Renato, I got a secret spot for you guys,' said Andy, making his way forward to where the Brazilians had been pointing frantically at every break as it swept past.

'Yah, I think Chico, he going to say where we surf now,' Rento answered, jerking his head slightly to indicate Blue Shorts.

'Okay, but tell Chico I've reserved the tender for you guys and I can take you to your own spot. No hassling for waves.' Andy turned and went back down to the main deck where Chook was trying to sell Yellow Shorts and his merry band of security goons on the bowling little left-hander breaking just next to the anchor point. Eventually the offer of exclusivity won them over and the waxing and fin-installing and sunscreening began in earnest. Chook and Andy watched in mild despair as everyone tried to get their boards out of the rack at the same time.

The South Africans grumbled to Chook that the Zillas were going in the tender. The Brazilians, via Renato, who had become the unofficial translator, made it clear they felt it was unfair the Saffers could simply paddle to the closest break. Both groups were promised compensation in having the roles reversed tomorrow. It was like dealing with a scrum of resentful, entitled toddlers, except they each stood around six foot tall and were trained to break into either your house or your ribcage.

Andy's session with the Brazilians started calmly enough. A small group of bodyboarders who had been surfing the peak by themselves took one look at the tattooed tribe piling out of the tender and made for the shore. A few smackable three footers rolled through to start them off but it wasn't long before the drop-ins and snaking and naked aggression surfaced yet again.

'What is going on?' Andy gestured in frustration towards the inside of the break, where two of the Zillas were cursing each other in Portuguese and untangling their boards as whitewater rolled through the impact zone.

'Is just how we do,' Renato said with a shrug. 'Whole life we fight. Just to survive. Out here, same.'

Andy played a cat-and-mouse game with the fractious knot of Brazilians who seemed to want a wave only if someone else wanted it first. Once the floating melee washed through the lineup, he had a few minutes to pick a wave of his own before the civil war resumed. He was enjoying the wide open faces of these Indonesian waves which, although small (and getting smaller), had the energy of thousands of miles of uninterrupted Indian Ocean behind them. They propelled his board with an urgency and grace he seldom found in the confused soup of Sydney's beachbreaks.

Every time he spotted a promising-looking lump on the horizon and spun his board into position, he found Renato had done the same, and several metres closer to the critical take-off spot. No matter. Andy smiled broadly, gave an encouraging yelp and watched as Renato not so much jumped to his feet as let the wave fall away beneath him and casually placed his board where the ocean had been. The young Brazilian disappeared behind the peak for a moment before unleashing a series of frothy explosions off the top of the peeling wave as he travelled down the reef. Inspired, Andy could feel his own confidence growing, his turns getting sharper and his stalls getting a little more definite with each wave.

'Turn your foot more straight,' said Renato as they sat at the take-off spot, willing a set to arrive before Blue Shorts and co paddled back out.

'My foot?' asked Andy.

'Yah. Front foot. Dis one,' Renato slapped his left thigh and then pointed at the nose of Andy's board. 'Make your toes go to the front more. Is better for speed. Try, this wave! Paddle deeper! Go now! Go!'

Even though he was sitting deeper and, by the unwritten rule of Surfer Law, had priority, Renato was coaching Andy into the approaching set, encouraging him to paddle deep into the peak. The water drew off the reef as the line of swell gathered itself up into a wave. Andy saw the coral heads as they appeared to rise massively, inevitably towards his fragile board and exposed flesh.

'Go!' Renato's voice was now more command than encouragement. Andy's arms responded, digging deep into the blue one last time before grasping the rails of his board and pushing it down into the void. For a second, Andy was weightless, his head leading his body in a trackless arc toward the shallow reef. Gravity asserted itself and the board started to descend. Andy's feet made contact with the deck just as the rail sliced into the steep, smooth face of the wave. The acceleration was fierce.

The wave opened up for a moment then enveloped him in a cocoon of diamond blue light and white noise. It spat him out through a vortex of foam onto a wide, open face of momentum and possibility. He carved his way, top to bottom, as the wave kept pushing all the way to the inside of the reef.

It was a different wave, geographically and temporally. But as he kicked out into the calm of the channel, Andy realised it was the same wave, at heart and in spirit, as the one that had led him here, to this very spot. He had become that stall-to-tube-to-cutback guy. He had changed, officially and spiritually, into Marty the Deckhand.

'Why? Tell me why?'

Andy's reverie was shattered by a face, angry and in need of answers, filling his field of view. It was Chico, with more questions than vocabulary.

'What?' Andy struggled to make sense of his new predicament.

'Why take Renato wave?' said Chico, pointing the take-off spot. 'Not you wave. Renato wave.' He jabbed his meaty forefinger into Andy's chest.

Andy was now the target of waterborne aggression, as the rest of the Brazilians drew in around him, partly following Chico's lead but mainly thankful for the opportunity to direct their frustrations at an outsider.

'Okay,' Andy raised his hands, 'Renato wave. Got it. No problem. Every wave can be Renato wave. You're the guest.'

'No! Every wave my wave!' yelled Chico, his breath landing on the bridge of Andy's nose.

Renato had kicked out from his last ride and paddled over, yelling in Portuguese. Chico yelled back, without moving his face from Andy's. Clearly, he wasn't buying Renato's version of events.

Another set rolled through, unridden. Chico leaned forward and glared one last time at Andy, spat violently from the side of his mouth and paddled back to the take off spot, laughing and talking to himself. The others followed behind at a distance, like a pack of dogs trying to avoid the random beating they knew their master would inevitably dispense.

'What the fuck, Renato?' asked Andy when the pack was out of earshot.

'Yah, sorry man. Chico, he very crazy,' said Renato, watching his friends gather in a tight knot to jostle for the next set. 'He just want to fight. Always.'

'What did you say to him?'

'I told him: if he hurt you, or people from the boat, he maybe go to jail. He say he don't care. But I tell him, no Brazil jail – Indonesia jail,' said Renato, watching the horizon. 'I tell him to stop fighting, just enjoy surfing. Maybe he listen. Maybe.'

'Thanks Renato. You're a good kid.'

The two of them waited for a set to appear and the pack to ride to the inside, but the ocean had gone flat, as oceans are sometimes wont to do. Chico paddled around in small circles, muttering and slapping the water. He waved for the tender. 'Here no more waves!' he yelled. 'We go.'

'Chook, we might have a real problem here,' Andy whispered to the skipper once they were all back on board. 'Chico, in the Blue Shorts, he's a fucking nutcase. Just lives to fight.'

'That's only half the problem,' Chook drained another beer and watched the South Africans, who were treating the other peak the way a pride of lions treat a zebra. 'The Saffer in the Yellow Shorts – his mates call him TP.'

'TP? Like toilet paper?'

'Stands for Tupac, his hero and role model. Showed me pictures of his gun collection last night. Sounds like the kind of guy who goes around begging for someone to give him a reason to pull the trigger.'

'Oh, fuck.'

'Fuck indeed.'

A series of splashes from the rear of the boat caught their attention and they leaned over the railing to see the Brazilians paddling for the break in the bay. Andy called out to Renato. 'What are they doing? They're not supposed to go to that wave!'

'Chico don't care,' said Renato as he stood on the transom, board under his arm. 'He want to surf there.'

'Get out there, Renato,' Andy pleaded. 'Tell him to come back before he starts some serious shit.'

Chook called out to his crew in heavily-accented Indonesian. They started scurrying about, hauling in the anchor and tying down the topside equipment. Wayan sauntered below and started prepping.

'What's the plan now, Chook?' asked Andy, 'We just sail off and have a nice, quiet dinner somewhere while they kill each other?'

'Good idea. Then we motor back and pick up the survivors? Whaddaya reckon?' Chook was grinning like a maniac.

'Umm, is that legal?' asked Andy.

'For fuck's sake Andy, I'm kidding mate. I just want to scare 'em back into the boat and then feed 'em up as quick as we can. Go tell 'em I'm taking 'em to a secret spot.'

When the two packs returned to the boat, they found Chook standing on the transom, arms folded, flanked by his Indonesian crew. The duckboard had been drawn up, making it almost impossible to climb aboard. As the surfers milled around like sullen schoolboys, Chook announced the new rules for the duration of the trip. The front half of the boat would be the favela, the back half would be the shantytown and the middle half would be for the crew.

Andy figured it wasn't the time to point out that one boat couldn't have three halves. His job now was to ensure the warring nations had as little contact with each other as possible. Chook drove the *CrossShore* at full throttle, making it difficult to move about the deck, and Wayan started dishing up mountains of food. The crew took up positions through the middle of the boat, forming a human cordon to keep the nations apart. It felt like a hostage situation, although it was difficult to tell who the hostages were. For his part, Chook had started taking cans of Bintang prisoner, interrogating them for alcoholic content and then tossing their lifeless bodies overboard.

The drone of the diesel engines wore away at the tension, replacing it with tedium. Chook put the boat slightly abeam of the swell to introduce a yawning sideways motion. The pacing and fidgeting and glaring and scheming began to subside as general unease crept first into the stomachs, then into the hearts and minds of the ill-prepared. Andy was glad Chook had told him to take some motion sickness pills.

'Fuck me, that was close,' said Chook, perched on the back of the captain's chair, steering with his feet.

'Impressive trick,' said Andy said.

'Won't last. Most guys get their sea legs by about day three,' Chook said. 'We're gonna have to come up with a more permanent solution. I'm thinking I might put one lot ashore for a couple of days.'

'You're going to strand them on an island or something?'

'Sort of, but we'll make it feel more like an adventure. I reckon the Saffers might go for it, actually. Make it like a hard-man contest.'

They talked as the boat ate up the nautical miles in the darkness. Chook gently cursed the real Marty once more for his cunning. Andy marvelled at the absurdity of people who fly thousands of miles and spend thousands of dollars to escape their everyday lives, only to bring their complications with them. They finished the beers in the small bar fridge in the cockpit and Chook convinced Andy to go below decks to mix up a couple of dark and stormies.

'A real sailor's drink,' Chook explained with a smile. 'Because I reckon you might have earned it, Marty.'

Relaxing for the first time since stepping aboard, Andy eased himself down the ladder and crept into main cabin, where the sleeping crew occupied every cushioned surface. This was more like it, Andy thought to himself as he stepped between the bodies on his way to the galley. This was life on the ocean. Making your bed wherever you can find space, too exhausted to care. Charting a course through the dark, in search of your very own secret spot. Keeping a level head and besting your enemies using only your rat cunning and the angle of the swell. Drinking rum and talking long into the night with your captain. Drifting off to sleep, dreaming of the waves that will greet you with the dawn.

'Thanks, Marty,' he said to himself with a smile.

He switched on the small lamp above the bench and gathered the required ingredients: glasses, ice, rum, ginger beer, limes, chopping board. He stared for a moment. There, in the dim light of the galley, it became terrifyingly apparent the large, dull carving knife was missing.

'Here. I have it.'

Andy could just make out a figure emerging from the cramped circular stairway that led up from the forward cabins. As the figure came closer, the light from the galley fell first on to the dull metal of the large blade.

Andy raised his palms and started backing away. The cramped galley offered him nowhere to go.

'Look, I...' but Andy couldn't think of how to convince a man pointing a knife at him to stop pointing a knife at him. He slowly edged his right hand down to the bench, feeling for the heavy wooden chopping board.

'Chico took it. But I take it back,' Renato stepped fully into the light of the galley and offered the knife to Andy, handle first. 'Now, you take. Otherwise big problem.'

'Fucking hell, Renato,' said Andy, shaking his head and putting his hand to his chest, breathing deeply. 'Does Chico know you took the knife back?'

'I think no. He still sleeping,' said Renato.

'No sleeping!' said another voice, again from the top of the stairs. Andy reached for the galley light switch, revealing a furious Chico.

Renato rolled his eyes before turning to Chico and exploding into high-velocity, emotional Portuguese, using the knife as punctuation.

'Having trouble, boys?' came a snarl from the other side of the cabin.

Andy, Renato and Chico watched TP move into the light, backed by his tribe and cradling something heavy. Muffled voices from below deck became louder as the remaining Brazilians appeared at the top of the stairwell behind Chico.

Chico barked at Renato, who looked at him for a moment, shook his head and moved toward to Andy with the knife, offering it handle first.

Chico threw himself at Renato with a half roar, half grunt, sending them both to the galley floor. Andy stepped back, taking the knife with him. Both groups of surfers surged into the cabin, fists raised.

The overhead lights came on and half a dozen bright flashes of steel brought the activity in the main cabin to a halt. The crew were all now in a low crouch, armed with long curved Parangs, the traditional knife of the Indonesian archipelago. The Zillas and the Saffers were subdued by the sight of so much steel, so carefully sharpened and so deliberately pointed.

The scrape and click of a rifle bolt wrested everyone's attention from the field of Parangs. Chook sauntered into the cabin, holding a crusty yet serviceable weapon at his hip and flagrantly breaking one of his own on-board rules: no smoking in the main cabin.

'If you are not a crew member of the *CrossShore*,' commanded Chook through his cigar, 'your job now is to drop any object in your hands or in your pocket. Even if that object is your cock.' A series of dull thuds issued from both sides of the cabin. 'Keep going.' A second round of thuds followed. Chook kept the rifle at hip height, pointing it first towards the Brazilians and then at the South Africans. His crew gathered up the torches and screwdrivers and fins that the guests had abandoned to the floor. Judging by how calmly Chook read the riot act to the surfers, Andy suspected that this scenario was not without precedent.

The surf trip was now officially over. The guests had breached the terms of the charter they had all signed, specifically regarding the use of weapons. The *CrossShore* would make for Padang harbour where all guests were to be offloaded. All fees and charges paid by the guests were to be forfeited. No refunds would be granted. No correspondence would be entered into. Chook paused to draw on his cigar, the shotgun continuing its slow sweep of the cabin. Everyone was to be confined to bunks until the *CrossShore* made land. Except for Blue Shorts and Yellow Shorts, who were to be assigned the bow head and the stern locker, respectively. This last detail was not in the charter agreement but, as he was the one holding the shotgun and had had 'an absolute gutful of this bullshit', Chook decided it was his prerogative to amend the terms as he saw fit.

To close proceedings, Chook announced that the guests, and any known associates, were no longer welcome on the *CrossShore* for this or any future charters.

'Now, do any of you stupid fuckers have any stupid fucking questions?'

The guests stared at the floor, realising that their dreams of surfing the Mentawis were now officially over. Chook motioned with the shotgun. 'Off you go, then,' he said.

'I thought you said you didn't smoke?' asked Andy as the surfers melted back below decks without a sound.

'Only on special occasions,' grinned Chook, patting the shotgun and winking at his crew.

Dawn crept into the harbour as the *CrossShore* pulled up to the dock. Andy stared at the bags on the back deck, waiting to be offloaded. He might be able to change his flight, but more likely he'd have to kill a few days in Padang before heading home. Angie had been right. ShelfLife had been too good to be true. Although, for a moment, he had almost truly become Marty.

A hand landed heavily on his shoulder. 'Can I buy you a beer?'

Andy summoned a smile, but a grimace emerged. 'Maybe the real Marty would have said yes, but it's a bit early for me. Thanks, Chook.'

The Captain retained his grip and took a long look. 'You know, you did a bloody good job out there. Not sure Marty would have been as cool under pressure, to be honest. That's half the reason I wanted to get him off the boat this week.'

The remainder of Andy's smile began to spread.

'He was going a bit crazy, the last few trips, and I knew he needed a break, but I didn't want to go shorthanded.' Chook retrieved his hand and employed it to casually scratch his own crotch. 'When he told me about his mate's business, this life swap thing, and then you came into the mix, y'know, sensible business guy, I thought it was the perfect answer. Until these fuck-knuckles started World War Three.'

'Thanks Chook, but better to end it now, before someone gets hurt for real.'

Renato lifted himself off his luggage and walked along the jetty, to the side of the boat. He squinted up at Andy.

'Sorry boss. Chico no good. He too crazy,' Renato gestured towards the figure in the Blue Shorts, slumped on the parched timber of the jetty. 'My friends, they sorry too. Everybody sorry.'

'You're a good kid, Renato. But the captain says you guys are too dangerous. It's over,' Andy's shoulders fell. 'For all of us.'

Chook looked to Andy and then back to Renato. 'No. Just him,' he pointed to Chico. 'And him,' he pointed to TP, also on the jetty.

'I don't want to hang around this stinking harbour for the rest of the week. You've still got a few days of being Marty, and there's a decent swell filling in from the south tomorrow. Whaddaya say we get back out there?'

Chook waited for Andy to register, then allowed himself a small smile. He climbed up on to the transom, hands locked on hips, and addressed the surfers milling on the jetty.

'All right. Listen up, you fuckwits,' Chook's voice boomed across the quiet bay. 'This here is the *CrossShore*. It is a surf boat. It was built for surfing. Not for fighting. Or moaning. Or sneaking around with knives or any other cowardly bullshit like that.'

The surfers on the dock abandoned their fiddling with their gear and took a couple of shuffling steps towards the boat.

'Here are the new rules: only four guys in the water at any one time. No more separate meals. No more separate cabins. Zillas and Saffers, chose a new best friend. You bunk together. This is your last chance to tell me if you do not understand.' Chook cupped a hand behind his ear. 'Good. This is your last chance to tell me if you do not agree.'

Renato offered up a rapid-fire translation for his Brazilian brethren, who then nodded in agreement.

'Okay. No problem. We only want to surf,' said Renato, his eyes pleading to be allowed back on board.

'And how about you dickheads?' Chook asked the South Africans, who were quietly arguing amongst themselves.

A stocky, ginger-haired guy with a serious beard spoke up. 'Yeah, all right. We just want to surf. Us three.'

'What about you? Whatever the fuck your name is?' Chook pointed at the remaining South African, who oscillated between the boat and the ailing Yellow Shorts.

'Name's Craig. And I. I mean. Look, it's… Aw, fuck man, I'm married to his sister,' said Craig, pointing at Yellow Shorts. 'If I leave him here, she'll kill me when I get home.'

'Suit yourself. All right, everyone who wants to surf, grab your stuff and get back on the boat.'

The *CrossShore* reloaded with military precision. Whether they were more motivated to get back to the waves or to get away from their respective leaders wasn't entirely clear, but their new-found compliance wasn't lost on Chook. He hit them up for a few hundred US dollars, each, to cover the extra fuel before the boat cast off.

'Everyone better get on like the fuckin' Brady Bunch or I offload all of you on the nearest island. Which may or may not be inhabited,' Chook warned with a grin.

'I'm not sure *The Brady Bunch* was ever broadcast in Brazil,' said Andy.

'Missed out then, didn't they? That Marcia was a minx.' Chook swung up onto the ladder and disappeared into the wheelhouse. The twin diesel engines started their rumbling, industrious hymn. Andy was going to be allowed to be Marty for just a while longer.

* * *

Crash-landing back to his Sydney life like a returning astronaut, Andy found himself not so much changed as re-wired. Gone were the slightly hesitant answers, the dweeby fashion choices, the safe restaurant suggestions. It was as if someone had taken Andy, the generally likeable, generally competent corporate banker and shaved off the generalities. He was more expansive in meetings, more assertive in the line up, more aggressive in the shopping centre carpark. He reached for the TV remote without hesitation. None was more taken with the new, improved Andy than his wife, for whom he also began reaching without hesitation.

Word spread quickly through the investment banking community of the mild-mannered mid-level risk analyst who clicked a web link and became someone else for a week: a seafaring, knife-wielding, Bintang-chugging, tube-riding legend. Everyone wanted the password, the secret recipe, the keys to the kingdom.

'No, seriously Andy,' they'd ask, standing shoulder to shoulder at the office urinal. 'How did you do it?'

'Do what?' he'd reply, smiling to himself.

'How'd you change your life?'

Downward dog day afternoon

'A drug dealer in Los Angeles, a DJ in Sweden, a celebrity chef in Taipei and a dominatrix in London,' Shanti read from the print-out, her other hand shielding her Bellini from the jostling crowd.

'What? Another one?' grinned Gavin.

'You can never have too many dominatrix,' announced Trent, as much to the room as to his colleagues. 'Or is that dominatrii?'

'Dunno,' said Gavin, 'they didn't teach the collective noun for dominatrix at my school.'

'At this rate we're going to have to learn it,' said Shanti, scanning the list.

'Or invent it,' said Trent.

'A whip,' said Gavin, with a little too much enthusiasm. 'It should be a whip of dominatrixes.'

'Too obvious,' said Shanti. 'How about a clamp?'

'Perfect,' Trent said with a smile. 'A clamp of dominatrii.'

'I don't get it,' said Gavin.

'Oh Gav,' Shanti placed a hand on his cheek. 'You want everyone to think you're mister urbane, but you're just an innocent country boy at heart, aren't you?'

Gavin blushed and reached for Shanti's hand, but she withdrew it as quickly as it had landed. Trent called for another round. It was their first night out together since escaping the wreckage of Vietnam. It also felt like the first time they could exhale. Trent's emergency phone calls from Saigon airport had secured a rambling villa in Bali, part-owned by his business mentor and currently between tenants. The near-deportation experience had given the team a renewed focus and they had fast-tracked the site for launch.

'Some of those are going to be impossible to get insurance for, don't you think?' asked Gavin.

'It's not about possibility, it's about affordability. Everything is insurable, for a price,' Trent took a sip. 'We just have to factor that into the listing price and then let the market decide.'

Securing the first 'Marty the Deckhand' rental had required a frantic round of smoke and mirrors by the founders, who created the façade of a much larger company. Once Customer #0001 had confirmed he wanted the rental, the logistics of delivery became the team's focus: turning Marty's ramblings into an instruction manual, arranging flights and transfers, negotiating an equitable split of the fee for Marty's boss and, crucially, verifying that Andy the Banker had the basic surfing skills to perform Marty the Deckhand's job for a week.

The effort had all been worth it. Marty got a break from the boat, Marty's boss got a break from Marty and Andy got a new lease on his own life. Andy was telling the world and the world was starting to listen. Web traffic, sign-ups, enquiries, referrals, backlinks; by every metric, ShelfLife was starting to go 'next level'. So Shanti fretted about infrastructure capacity and security threats while Gavin spent his time pacing and muttering, 'But how do we scale?' in a self-defeatist mantra. Trent, however, believed wholeheartedly in one of the last maxims of his startup launch bible: the need to celebrate all wins.

Ordering tools down, Trent led the team to a sprawling beachside bar with a superb view of the sunset over the Indian Ocean. Both the music and the crowd were growing in intensity but the three founders barely noticed, transfixed by the ream of site analytics Shanti had printed out and the story it hinted at. For ShelfLife, the genie appeared to be out of the bottle. And so, therefore, were the rums, vodkas, gins and anything else Trent could put on his last functional credit card. The list of individuals who had offered their lives up for rent was long and varied enough to silence the nagging question hanging over the founders since Saigon: should they just shut the whole thing down and head home to their former lives?

'I see potential in the drummer in Belgium, the gardener on Maui, the tea taster in Sri Lanka, maybe the stockbroker in Chicago as he's just a pit runner and also the woman in fashion publishing in New York,' said Gavin, running his finger down the list.

'What does she do in fashion publishing?' asked Trent.

'Wait a minute,' Gavin stalled as he retraced his way back to the listing. 'Ah, here it is: junior ad sales co-ordinator.'

'Forget it. That's the worst job ever. Not worth the negative ratings from all the wide-eyed kids from Idaho who pay three thousand dollars for a week of taking dictation, doing coffee runs and getting yelled at.'

'Ohhh, we've got a Private Investigator here,' said Shanti. 'In Scotland. Just like in all those carbon-copy crime novels.'

'Would that even be legal?' asked Trent.

'I don't see why not,' she replied without looking up, 'he's a private citizen, self-employed – oh wait, it's a she – so she'd be within her rights.'

'Should be fine. We can restrict it to people with basic security or military training to make it safer,' said Gavin. 'It's not like she's an actual cop or anything,'

'Wait. We've got one of those too,' said Shanti, leafing through pages. 'From a village on Malaysia's east coast.'

'Awesome. That's like number three on our list of requests. The market's clamouring for cop lives,' said Trent, swirling the last of his drink and chugging it.

'I reckon we should leave law enforcement alone. It's just asking for trouble,' said Gavin. 'The easiest to manage are lives in some kind of buddy arrangement. Like Marty and Chook. They can take it in turns. One gets a break while the other carries the renter for a week. Then they swap. No need to do a revenue split if they each take an even number of rentals.'

'That's good, Gav, really good,' Shanti's eyes widened. 'I can set those parameters in the listing so they have to comply or it will be an invalid record.'

'Guys, I love the enthusiasm, I really do, but we're supposed to be having fun,' Trent smiled. 'All this brainstorming and coding will still be waiting for you in the morning. This dance floor will not, so get on it. Oh, hey, back in a sec.'

Trent shimmied past the bar where a knot of barefoot partygoers, illuminated by a bank of powerful rooftop spotlights, stomped a thin strip of sand into submission. Among the flirting and dancing and high-fiving that was ramping up on almost every square foot of the club, Gavin and Shanti continued to pore over their list, pausing either to laugh out loud or shake their heads in disbelief at some of the lives that were now available to rent: an elephant guide in Phuket, ski instructor in Chamonix, a bartender in Maui, a tattooist in Shinjuku.

'Oh, remind me to rent that one myself,' said Gavin.

'Which one?' said Shanti, trying not to spill her drink on the print-outs.

'The Shinjuku tattooist. That's what I'm going to do with my earn-out.'

'You're going to be a tattooist?' Shanti raised an eyebrow. 'Won't you need to get a bunch more tattoos yourself?'

'Nah. Well, maybe a couple more. I don't want to draw the tattoos on people, I just want to own the shop. I'll have a motorcycle café in the front and do the ink in the back room. On the beach somewhere. Oh, and a boat.'

Shanti shook her head.

'What? It'll be my money. I can spend it how I wanna,' Gav shot back. 'What are you going to do with yours? Give it to charity, I suppose.'

'Some of it, yeah.'

'And the rest?'

'No, you'll laugh.'

'No I won't,' Gavin took another swallow. 'Promise.'

'All right, I want a place on top of a mountain where I can sit by myself and nobody is invited.'

'Lame,' said Gavin.

'Shut up,' Shanti scowled. 'Anyway, you should park those dreams until we get out of revenue neutral. If we don't get some serious revenue in soon, we might get swamped by our own traffic. Our hosting provider issued a capacity warning earlier today. We need an upgrade.'

'Make sure you talk to Trent before you go upgrading anything. I don't think there's a lot of gas left in the tank, credit-wise.'

'What do you mean?'

'Trent told me earlier that the closest thing we've got to liquidity is the next round of drinks.'

'Seriously?'

'Maybe. And it looks like he's about to spend it on those Eurotrash girls in the bubble skirts,' Gav nodded to where Trent was dancing and talking with a pod of girls in all the shades of fluoro.

'But we've got the traffic. We've got all these people signing up. We can't let him screw this up because of a simple cashflow issue. C'mon, let's talk to him now.' Shanti started across the bar.

'Shanti, wait. Let Trent enjoy himself. We've all got a night off. I thought we could, y'know, talk about things, now that the site is up and working,' Gavin placed a hand on her arm.

'Gavin, we're not just colleagues, we're business partners.' She shook her head as she brushed Gavin's hand away. 'And if you think the hard work is behind us, you're facing the wrong way.'

Shanti crossed the floor. After a moment, Gavin followed.

'Please don't tell me we're about to run out of money, Trent. Not when we've worked this hard,' Shanti put her hands on her hips.

'Okay, easy, it's supposed to be a celebration tonight,' Trent turned to the group of girls. 'Excuse me, ladies. One moment, please.'

He guided Shanti to the edge of the dance floor, where the waves came ashore.

'Trent, if I need to upgrade our infrastructure tomorrow, can I do it?'

'Tomorrow? No, I wouldn't do it tomorrow,' he held a hand up to pause her. 'But very soon we'll be in a much better position financially. We can take advantage of this amazing traffic you've generated and grow ShelfLife like it's hydro skunk. But please do not use my credit card tomorrow.'

'Jesus, Trent, why didn't you tell us?' asked Gavin.

'Worrying about the site is your problem, worrying about the money is my problem, OK?' said Trent.

'How bad is it?' Shanti asked.

'Bad? No, not bad,' said Trent between sips of his mojito. 'This is good. Very good. We wanted to take on investors, remember? Now we can prove there's demand for our service, we're in a much stronger negotiating position.'

'So running out of money is a good thing?' Gavin shrugged.

'No! Well, yes. Kinda. Look, we're exactly where we want to be right now,' Trent opened his arms wide. 'We've done the hard yards, now we just take our amazing site and our awesome list of signups to my guy and say "show me the money."'

'What guy? The guy who owns the villa?' asked Shanti.

'My mentor, yes. Part of the agreement I struck with Charles gives him first refusal. He's flying in tomorrow and he's very excited. He's the tap and all we need to do is turn him on.'

'I think we should meet him, too.'

'What kind of money are we looking for?'

Gavin and Shanti spoke simultaneously and Trent placed a finger in the air while taking a long pull on his straw, taking him almost to the bottom of his glass.

'That is a helluva good mojito. Yes, Shanti, you will meet him. I think you'll like him,' Trent turned from one partner to the other. 'And the kind of money that we're looking for, Gav, is technically known as "all of it". Now, who feels like dancing?'

* * *

Two o'clock was the default business lunch slot in Seminyak. Any earlier signalled you were new in town and yet to tune in to the local pace of deal making among the 'barefoot and boardshorts' business mafia. Any later, you struggled to get service. Island wisdom held that if you could afford to live in Bali permanently, among the small-block property developers, graphic designers and furniture exporters, you probably had something working for you, financially, back in the real world. The living here was reasonably cheap but it certainly wasn't free. On the other hand, choosing Bali hinted that whatever money you had on tap was a casual flow at best. If you had a genuine fire hose you'd be taking breakfast in your spa in Aspen or tying up at your berth in Split.

Trent had spent his first week in Bali chasing rumours of serious wealth, but found mainly trust-fund kids and early retirees. Charles had provided a few introductions, mainly people in the restaurant business, but they were only interested in expanding their restaurant businesses.

'That's why I'm not based here full-time,' Charles explained as he settled into an oversized wicker chair. 'It's all playboys and play money. The real money is in the north. This is Asia's leisure suit.'

The front of the restaurant opened up onto the street, but a dense row of lipstick palms kept the humming and beeping of motorbikes and vans at bay. White tablecloths and carved artworks completed the separation from the tropical chaos outside. Industrial airconditioning units pushed a chilled breeze through the open dining area and out into the street, where it was obliterated like a vampire in the morning sun.

Charles scanned the menu. 'How has your team found the villa?'

'It's been great, but it's probably the only part of Bali they've seen. I've been working them pretty hard.'

'Same partners as before? The hipster and the hacker?'

'Yes, Gavin is doing UX and design. Shanti did the build and is handling the back end. They've been fantastic. And they're totally committed.'

'So what does that leave for you to do?' Charles glanced up and gave a sly smile.

'Like you said, Charles. Someone has to provide leadership.'

The waiter took their orders. Most of a bottle of rosé disappeared while Trent got a recap of Charles' professional trajectory: seventeen years with mid-level consulting firms; offered a golden parachute during a takeover; stole some clients and built them a procurement portal; kept the IP and on-sold it. Between fees from the IP and a growing portfolio (some real estate investments, a couple of tech ventures and a stake in a junior miner) Charles' tap flowed freely enough for him to search for something new to water every six months or so.

Their meals arrived and they were spectacular. It was hard to say who had got to Bali first: winners of the private-wealth lottery (like Charles), or the two-and-a-half-star chefs wanting to escape the 'reviews & revenues' treadmills in the brutal, fashion-driven dining capitals of the west.

'Why did you do it?' asked Trent.

'Do what?'

'Walk away from your consulting job at the big end of town?'

'Money, I guess. Now where's that wine list gone?' Charles twisted around in his seat, searching for a waiter.

'You would have been making plenty as a consultant. There must have been something else?'

'Oh, I guess I was feeling stale, wanted to feel a little bit more in control of my life.'

'Why didn't you do something more dramatic? Shave your head and move to Tibet?'

'I almost did something very much like that, but the red tape made it too much of a ball-ache.'

'So you became an independent consultant,' said Trent, slicing into his crusted fillet of sea bass. 'You wanted to feel like you were changing your life, but you didn't want to lose the life you had, right?'

Charles leaned back from his steak and looked into the distance for a moment. 'Yes, I suppose, when you put it in those terms. But what's with the psychoanalysis, Trent?'

'Just testing. To see if you'd be attracted to the service we're building. I think you would be. I think a lot of people would be.'

'I thought you were developing some sort of marketplace for the sharing economy?' Charles sliced his steak carefully. 'Like a house rental or a job swap thing?'

'What we've got goes far deeper,' said Trent. 'We've built a service that lets you change your life. Maybe for a week, but in some cases it's a little more permanent.'

'How do you mean?'

'Well, take our very first paying client.'

'You're already in revenue?' Charles put his cutlery down and glanced around the restaurant. 'You didn't tell me you'd got that far.'

'And the best part is, he found us. It was a cold lead. Shanti used a profiling algorithm and poured our entire ad spend on re-targeting. Followed him for days until he made an enquiry. We got him signed up and on the plane within a week.'

'What? Like a holiday booking service?'

'Much deeper than that, Charles.' Trent explained what had happened to Andy, adding, 'All these augmented virtual theme-park nanny-state experiences aren't cutting it anymore. Too fabricated. People want something authentic, something genuine. That's the real product we're offering here.'

'Amazing,' said Charles. 'But it's going to create a lot of margin pressure if you've got to pay to attract both sides of the trade. That model only tends to work at scale. Where did you find the surf guide?'

'He's a friend of Gavin's. Was going a bit troppo, according to his boss.'

'Who's this Gavin again?'

'The hipster. Great design skills, really understands the user experience. Came from a big agency in Melbourne. Great guy.'

'You trust him?' Charles raised an eyebrow.

'Sure. Now,' said Trent, fishing in his satchel, 'I want to show you our web analytics, Charles. Our site is taking off, which is why I wanted to talk to you sooner rather than later. I haven't forgotten our agreement.'

'What am I looking at here?' said Charles, squinting and holding the printouts at arm's length.

'I don't think we're going to have too many cost pressures on the inventory side. These are the people who have registered on our site since customer number one started sharing his life rental experience on social media. We haven't even had a public launch for ShelfLife yet.'

'ShelfLife?'

'That's the name of our company, Charles. We designed our site like shelves in a store. Except our shelves offer a range of interesting and exciting lives from all over the world. If you see one you like, we can rent it to you. You live it for a week, then put back. What do you think?'

Charles continued scanning the list, flipping the pages until he had reached the end. A waiter refilled their glasses.

'This is remarkable, but there's an unmanageable level of risk in some of these propositions, Trent. I mean, you've got ambulance drivers, stuntmen, porn stars, ski instructors, combat soldiers. These are just lawsuits waiting to happen.' He folded the stack in half and placed it on the table.

'I'm in violent agreement with you, Charles. Some of these lives are clearly not suitable for our model,' said Trent, tapping the printout. 'Most of the careers you've pointed out are requests. These are the standard fantasies people have. But the bulk of the list is made up of orders we think we can fill: baristas, photographers, park rangers, tour guides, sportscar salesmen, stockbrokers.'

'Stockbrokers?'

'Just the low-level guys, the pit runners. Our initial range of lives for rent is drawn from people we know, like Marty the surf guide. For the next tranche we're focussing on lives that operate in a team-based environment so the renter has in-built support during the rental period,' Trent dabbed his mouth as the waiter cleared the plates. 'Now, to your point about risk mitigation: Shanti is building a pre-matching algorithm that scrapes a renter's social profile. This tells us if they have the basic skills for minimum job proficiency. Have they ever worked in hospitality? Did they complete college? Do they have a criminal record? We can pre-qualify for almost anything. It's the same tech the recruiting industry uses for candidate screening.'

'You have been busy,' said Charles, showing faint signs of a smile. 'But I strongly suggest you get some legal counsel on board, and a risk analyst.'

'I'm not sure we have the capacity to add serious headcount right now. We're only just coming out of beta.'

'Don't think of them as overheads, Trent, think of them as profit centres. A good RA can help broker a wholesale deal for insurance coverage, which we then break up into individual policies and on-sell to customers on both sides of the transaction, at retail rates. Fabulous margins.' Charles steepled his fingers beneath his chin. 'How's your cashflow?'

Trent winced inwardly. 'We're in reasonable shape.'

'Is that why you traded points in your hot startup for a few weeks' rental in a half-renovated villa?'

'Well, we're staying lean to show our management discipline. I'm following the book you recommended. All the founders are.'

'Look, it's okay,' Charles raised a hand. 'I'm here to help. Matter of fact, I want to join you. I love your idea and I'm impressed with what you've been able to build in such a short space of time. I'm also impressed with you as leader. I'd like to talk about a more formal investment.'

'That's great news, Charles. Thank you.' Trent twisted his napkin under the table in excitement.

'This is a critical time. Your team needs an established base, and you need to focus on growth. To the exclusion of everything else.'

'I totally agree, Charles. The team is loving the scene here. Lots of energy, lots of young entrepreneurs. I think we'd fit right in.'

'Oh god no, not here,' Charles snorted. 'This is all make-believe. The only money I've put into Bali is in property. Scratch the surface and you'll find all the startup kids here are spending their parents' money. A lot of the businesses are just laundromats for nose candy. The infrastructure is unreliable all the way down to the power grid, the corruption levels are well north of annoying and, besides, there are just too many temptations here.'

Trent rubbed his temple, as if he were trying to erase a problem. 'So where do you suggest?'

'My services are currently being retained by a very serious group of active investors. They offer tax incentives and government assistance. They are looking for the kind of opportunity your business represents and I'd love to introduce you to them. But first I need to know what shape you're in financially.'

Trent took a deep breath. He'd spent so many years constructing elaborate stories of success to mollify his parents that he'd almost forgotten what it was like to level. Or why you'd even need to. Trent pretended to study his wine glass. The book advocated that a founder should project confidence to the world while keeping 'the kimono open' with those you trust and rely upon. He knew he was about to rely on Charles. In that moment, he decided to trust him as well.

'Running on vapours. I'm down to my last credit card.'

'Don't sweat it, old chap. In fact, that's a good sign. Now, can you get your hands on a hundred grand?'

Trent stopped midway through taking a sip and the wine splashed up over his lips. He tried to pretend that was the way he normally drank wine.

'Because if you can,' Charles leaned in as far as his girth would allow, 'I'll match it.'

Trent tried not to let his disappointment show. A hundred k would vanish like smoke once they started to ramp up.

'That's not the actual investment, in case you were worried,' Charles grinned, showing he'd read Trent like a menu. 'It's just to prop up the balance sheet and pump the initial valuation. Then I'll recommend you to my investors. They'll snap us up. Nothing surer.'

'How quickly do we need to have this balance sheet funding in place?'

'That's up to you. But without it I can't move forward. If I take this deal to my institutional investors in your current state of liquidity, they'll use their incentives to flood the balance sheet, take you out of effective equity and put you on salary.'

'They can do that?'

'Can and will. It's not pretty, but that's how the game is played. I recently engineered exactly that play for another group of investors I consult to. Got them total control of a mid-tier e-commerce travel platform in Europe without breaking a sweat. You're lucky you've got me as a gamekeeper, Trent. I usually play the poacher.'

'And how much cash do you think they'll want to invest?' said Trent, trying not to sound like he was trying to sound disinterested.

'If you're looking for the payday, my boy, you won't find it in this round. These investors give you the tools you need to reach your payday: office space, staff, marketing budgets, legal counsel. This way gives you far more bang for your buck, trust me.'

'I learn something valuable from you every time we meet, Charles,' Trent raised his glass.

'Well I wouldn't be earning my share if I didn't bring something extra to the table now, would I?' said Charles as they clinked glasses. 'Now, how quickly can you get hold of your side of the cash?'

'It's kind of locked up at the moment. Technically I'm not supposed to touch it.'

'How so?'

'It's holding company stock.'

'But the stock is legally yours?'

Trent nodded.

'The way I see it –' Charles signalled to the waiter for another bottle, 'you can either be a minority shareholder in your parents' version of the future, or make a serious investment in your own.'

* * *

'Breathe in. Feel the energy come into your body,' said the slim, dark-haired woman as she padded through the room. The bodies on the mats around her inhaled, more or less in unison. Shanti let the earthy scent of the incense linger in the back of her throat, imagining that this was the energy the teacher spoke of. She wanted to believe she would be ready to tackle the change requests and updates and debugging and capacity upgrades and affiliate negotiations and tracking reports waiting for her back at the villa.

'Shanti,' a gentle voice pried her away from her task list, 'don't forget to breathe out again.'

Shanti opened her eyes to find the teacher's face hovering above her own, a ceiling fan circling without urgency in the background. A ripple of laughter rolled through the room and was subsumed by the waterfall of gamelan coming from the portable speaker on the window shelf.

'Yes. Sorry, I was…' Shanti offered.

'Somewhere else. Be here with your body, Shanti,' the teacher helicoptered out of view and resumed walking among the students. 'It's a beautiful temple.'

* * *

'You want to do something tonight?' asked the instructor quietly as she watched the others file out of the studio and into the early morning sun.

Shanti had been lingering, pretending to look for something in her shoulder bag. 'I do,' she said with a smile, 'but can I meet you later? The boss is on a trip to meet some investors. He keeps sending me emails with a hundred different requests.'

'Sure. I'll be at that new bar those guys from Zimbabwe opened just down from the temple. Called The Inverted Octopus, or something equally pretentious.' The instructor settled on the bench next to Shanti, their shoulders almost touching.

'What if I'm late?'

'Then I might be a little bit tipsy.' The instructor's eyes widened as she moved closer. 'And who knows what I might agree to at that point.'

'Then I'll make sure I'm not too early,' Shanti purred, deliberately rubbing her shoulder against the instructor's as she rose to leave.

Shanti made a mental note to slap herself the next chance she got. The schoolgirl act was completely off brand and she needed to put a lid on it before anyone noticed. It wasn't that Shanti was immune to the charms of her own sex, but this whole lingering glances, holding hands, getting-to-know-you business was new for her. Low-calorie stress relief was really all Shanti required right now, yet Amber's relentless honesty and cosmic intensity was drawing her into a more emotionally-charged entanglement. It was thrilling, but it did not sit well with the task list. She wrestled the small motorbike off its stand, donned the open-face helmet and gave it a couple of sharp raps with her knuckles. It was time to get back to work.

* * *

'You look happy this morning,' said Gavin, almost as a question. 'I'd say yoga agrees with you.'

Shanti fumbled with her bag and blushed, but made no effort to hide it – her caramel skin did that already. Her ancestry had not always provided upsides. The racism she had encountered in Europe was relatively easy to avoid when breezing through a city for a weekender, harder when you take up residency. By contrast, her skin offered almost complete invisibility in England. For a girl who didn't really belong anywhere, the nowhere she had felt most comfortable was in London. As a gentle breeze brought jasmine, incense and benzine fumes through the open windows of the villa, the cobblestone streets of Shoreditch seemed very distant indeed.

'You see the note from Trent overnight?' asked Gav. 'He sounded pretty pumped.'

'He sounded pretty drunk, actually,' said Shanti, unlocking the small safe in the bottom of the kitchen cupboard to retrieve her laptop. 'How come he suddenly had to rush to Singapore? Wasn't he going to set up a meeting for us with guru Charles? We haven't even met the guy.'

Flipping open the laptop and waiting for the apps to load, Shanti distracted herself with a few mild leg stretches while conceding that Gavin's choice of old-school Jamaican dancehall dub was probably the right choice for the morning ahead.

'Site's kinda slow this morning,' Gavin called from the kitchen. 'Anything crazy happen while we were asleep here in paradise?'

'Yes and no. Traffic is up in Hong Kong. Looks like the expat bankers there have discovered Andy's surfboat story,' said Shanti, scrolling through her inbox. 'We're also getting a decent kick out of our appearance on BetaList yesterday. And apparently, a crew of low-level LA gangsters are planning on renting out their lives to middle class white kids. They've done the math and reckon renting will be more profitable than "dealing in crack and bitches", which surprises me.'

'Not really. That Freakonomics guy found the same thing. Unless you're the king, you're a slave.'

'Is that a rap lyric, Gav?'

'It's possible,' said Gavin.

'Oh, hey, the Honduran government is considering banning us and we have an interview request from a PhD student at the University of Arizona.'

'Interviews are Trent's wheelhouse,' said Gavin, returning with a plate of cut papaya and lime.

Shanti stopped scrolling at an email with the subject line: *Pre-emptive bandwidth throttle – urgent response required.* It was from their hosting company.

The pieces started snapping into place for Shanti. She scanned the email for key phrases: valued customer…high levels of traffic activity…payment history…ensure continued service… mutually agreeable solution…blah, blah and furthermore blah.

Diving back into the safe, she retrieved a small ring binder, located the banking details, logged on and surveyed the fiscal landscape of the official ShelfLife operating account.

'Do you have any money?' asked Shanti without looking up from the screen.

'I got maybe a coupla hundred US on me. How much do you need?'

'No, I mean like real money, that the company can borrow.'

Gavin walked behind Shanti, leaning in to peer at her screen. 'What's going on?'

'Our hosting provider has got us on throttleback because our traffic is spiking,' she looked up at Gavin with a frown. 'And we haven't been the most timely in settling our account.'

'Hey, making things look good is my department,' said Gavin, raising his hands. 'I thought keeping dollars in the bank was Trent's job.'

'Me too,' she muttered, attacking the keyboard.

'Did he say when he was coming back?'

'Tomorrow if things go well.'

'And if they go badly?'

'Maybe never.'

After several failed attempts to reach Trent, Shanti knew she would have to contact the hosting company. She made a cup of green tea and walked into the small courtyard to make the call.

'I need to speak to someone about our hosting account. We're on throttleback at the moment,' she said as calmly as she could.

'Yes, I'm sorry about that. Standard policy, you understand.'

'It's really affecting our business, so I wanted to see how we could go about getting un-throttled.'

'You mean, besides paying your hosting bill?'

She gave a small, nervous laugh. 'Well, yes. We're kind of pre-revenue right now, but we're accelerating pretty hard and –'

'We've been monitoring your company since you got out of beta. At your current trajectory, your next bill from us would be somewhere between twenty and twenty-five thousand dollars, US.' He paused to let the figure sink in. 'We're very impressed.'

'You are?' Shanti's tone conveyed more surprise than she wanted it to.

'We have a special program designed for what we call our "high potential" customers. That's people like you. I'd love to talk to you about the benefits of the program.'

* * *

'We have an image problem,' said the immaculately dressed woman on the other side of the large desk. The small meeting room was bleached by overhead fluorescents, which made two dancing rectangles of the woman's fashion-forward glasses. It was impossible to read her eyes. Trent suspected the entire situation – the room, the lights, the eyewear – had been calibrated for precisely this effect.

'I'm not sure exactly what you mean, Ms Lim,' Trent said, not wanting to offend his hosts. Charles had prepped him the night before: keep it calm, keep it professional, and don't start flirting unless she does first.

'There's no need to be polite, Mr Carlisle,' said the younger, but equally well-tailored man sitting next to her. 'The Google auto-complete results are quite specific: rich, clean, healthy – '

'And boring,' Ms Lim cut in. 'That's the part we need to fix. It's a directive.'

'You're saying the government wants Singapore to appear more exciting?' Trent probed.

'Just to be clear, my colleague Mr Shaw and I are not officially representatives of the Singapore Government. Our organisation is a private think tank and incubator. We are closely aligned with many government policies and priorities, but I think you'll find that goes without saying for most organisations on the island.'

'Of course. My apologies, Ms Lim. I'm just trying to understand your objectives so I can see where ShelfLife may or may not have a role to play. You were saying something about being boring?'

'The issue we have is that the average Singaporean is convinced their life is boring, even though the life of the average Singaporean is relatively stimulating, when measured against the global index,' said Ms Lim, adjusting her eyewear. 'That has translated into a global perception. It's affecting tourism, trade and, to a lesser extent, direct investment.'

'Our three-year target is to have our name disassociated with boring,' added the younger Mr Shaw.

'We'll evaluate our progress and recalibrate our goals at that point, depending on directives,' said Ms Lim.

'That's when we'll be aiming for exciting,' Shaw jumped in, earning himself a withering look from his colleague.

'It's always good to have a plan.' This was Trent's third meeting of the day. He'd met with a government-backed incubator and a private VC firm, which sourced all of its funding from the government. The meetings had all been attended by similar pairs of Singaporeans: a young, enthusiastic chatterbox accompanied by an older, more circumspect leash-holder. This particular meeting also contained an older white man in a boxy tweed jacket and thick glasses.

'A key plank of our strategy, Mr Carlisle, is to attract early-stage technology businesses to develop services that ameliorate the perception of a lack of vivacity among the population and the urban environment.'

'I see,' offered Trent, trying to disguise the fact that he didn't.

'Our innovation consultant, Mr Archer-Ellis, believes your company has developed a product that may offer this type of service. Which is why he sent you to us.'

'We think your company is cool,' Shaw enthused. He was stared down again by Ms Lim.

'I'd like to introduce you to our macroeconomics consultant, Professor Jensen,' Ms Lim motioned towards the greying white man in tweed. 'He is helping us evaluate your offering against our selection criteria.'

'Well, yes, can I just say that my official remit is actually to recommend fiscal policy to stimulate innovation, growth and – ' the Professor was shut down by a raised finger.

'And today, Professor,' said Ms Lim, lowering her finger and taking up a sheet of paper from the desk, 'we would very much like your opinion of Mr Carlisle's offering.'

'Let me bring up my report,' said the Professor, tapping the screen of his tablet.

'Executive summary, if you please,' commanded Ms Lim.

'ShelfLife appears to offer a low-risk, high-impact methodology that enables people to briefly experience the sensation of genuinely changing their lives, facilitated by an online platform, optimised for desktop and mobile,' the Professor removed his glasses.

'Would you say that's an accurate description of ShelfLife, Mr Carlisle?' asked Ms Lim.

Trent sat back for a moment and smiled. 'Broadly, yes. Although we prefer to say that ShelfLife lets our customers be who they really want to be.'

The three interviewers on the other side of the table stared at Trent.

'It's just a tagline. We're market testing it at the moment,' said Trent. 'We're also testing "Rent the life you never dreamed you could own". That one's mine.'

'Well, whatever the final slogan, our citizens want a service like that,' said Mr Shaw.

'Our citizens *need* a service like that,' said Ms Lim, wresting the conversation back from her junior. 'We've spent the last fifty years improving every possible standard of living metric. We've raised health standards, literacy rates, life expectancy, home ownership, private vehicle ownership, mobile phone usage and access to Starbucks.'

'We've also reduced crime, disease, unemployment, working hours, commute times, traffic jams, distance to shopping malls and queue-times at amusement parks.' Mr Shaw stabbed the table repeatedly, as if he were playing a tiny game of statistical whack-a-mole.

'What my colleague is trying to say,' again she admonished him with her manicured eyebrows, 'is that we are running out of aspects of our citizens' lives that we can visibly improve. Well, not us specifically, the government is. You see in Singapore everything is amazing but no-one appears to be happy.' She sat back in her chair and removed her glasses.

Mr Shaw started to speak, then caught himself. He looked to his colleague for permission. Ms Lim rubbed her eyes and waved for him to continue.

'Pending Professor Jensen's assessment, of course, we'd like to suggest you base your company here in Singapore as part of our innovation program.'

The Professor then launched himself into the conversation like a child chasing a ball onto the road. 'And I welcome the opportunity to make that assessment, but before I do I need to make one thing clear.'

'I think we'll park your discussion of fiscal modelling and import duties for the moment, Professor,' Ms Lim slammed on the brakes.

The Professor sank back into his chair and removed his glasses.

'We want ShelfLife to help our citizens experience…shall we say, change and excitement,' Mr Shaw smiled. 'Do you think you can help them scratch that itch?'

'Yes, I think we probably could,' answered Trent with a broad smile. 'Provided the terms are equitable.'

Mr Shaw moved to slide a crisp manila folder across the table. Ms Lim brought an index finger down to halt the document's journey.

'Before we open the kimono, so to speak, we need to know a little more about the inventory of your site.'

'Of course.' Trent could barely take his eyes off the folder.

'Do you currently have any listings for, say, a physical therapist for a professional rugby union team?'

The land of
First World problems

Shanti paced as the aircrew joked and fussed over their computers in preparation for the onslaught of human freight leaving Denpasar airport. She licked her dry lips and cursed the security guards who had insisted she dump her water bottle at the gate lounge x-ray check. With one eye on her carry-on bag, she performed a quick circuit of the lounge but found no taps. Her head started to hum. It had been an exhausting few days.

All seats were occupied so she hovered by a large concrete planter box where her phone and laptop were charging, nestled within a forest of others. An insistent buzz emerged from the stack, prompting several lurking passengers to take half-steps towards the digital crèche to see if it was their device braying for attention. When no-one rushed to claim the vibrating phone Shanti figured it must be hers.

Shanti had been dealing with so many people over the past week – Germans wanting to know why she wasn't coming home, Singaporeans wanting to know why she was coming, Trent wanting to know why the code was doing this, Gavin wanting to know why the user interface was doing that, nervous ShelfLife hosts wanting to know what they should do while someone else was being them, nervous ShelfLife guests wanting to know exactly how much of someone else's life they would be getting, hosting companies wanting to know where all the traffic was coming from and how it would be paid for – she could no longer be selective about the calls she answered. Any of them could be important. Most of them were.

'Shanti speaking,' she tugged the power cable free of the nest.

'It's not too late, you know.'

This exit was not as hasty as their ejection from Saigon, but not all the boxes in Bali had their bows tied as neatly as they should have. Now one of those boxes was calling.

Shanti faced the full-length window, watching the tropical downpour sweep across the tarmac, sluicing off aircraft as they nosed towards their assigned gates.

'Babe, why are you leaving?' Amber's voice floated down the line like jasmine on a breeze.

Shanti closed her eyes to the thrumming in her temple. She had a perfectly valid reason for leaving Bali, but Amber's voice was making it hard to locate.

'I don't think you should get on that plane. We were heading somewhere important, remember?'

Shanti did remember. In the beginning, there had been flirting. Then drinking. Even dancing. As ShelfLife found its feet, then took off at a sprint, Shanti had converged with Amber at similar velocity, but it didn't take Shanti long to realise they had been imagining past each other into entirely different futures. 'Holiday romance' was how Shanti tried to frame their entanglement; 'soul mates' was Amber's leash-tugging counter. Like children with unfettered access to the ice cream tub, they continued to devour each other's attention even as they knew it would ache.

'Don't go back to those people, Shanti. They're not good for you.'

Amber used 'those people' to refer to Trent, his mentor and the faceless money men of Singapore. In Amber's eyes, they had rolled in like a tropical squall and removed her sunshine. Trent had phoned from a bar forty-seven storeys above the streets of Singapore, babbling about valuations and exit strategies. Gavin and Shanti had danced around the villa until the details emerged: in return for a significant investment, the incubator would require an equity stake and for the company to relocate to the city state immediately. Shanti railed at the lack of consultation. Gavin moaned at moving countries again. Trent was incensed by their ingratitude. The conflict raged until Trent's phone battery died. When he had set foot in the villa the following morning, he delivered an ultimatum: any founder of ShelfLife who was not in Singapore within one week would no longer be considered a founder of ShelfLife.

'You know the money won't make you happy,' said Amber.

The absence of it wasn't making Shanti particularly joyous either. As much as she wanted to pull the technical rug out from under Trent in that moment, Shanti conceded it would be professional suicide. The last thing she wanted to do was go home to her uncle and spend the rest of her days serving Kashmiri naan to the good burghers of Munich.

'This will change you, Shanti. I'm worried for you.'

As the point of departure approached, Amber mounted a series of ninja attacks on Shanti's self-belief. Except these ninjas threw spiritual affirmations and wore tie-dyed fisherman's pants. Shanti had always found it easy to leave her casual boyfriends. Leaving her first casual girlfriend was proving a more difficult dismount to stick.

'I don't need you to worry for me, Amber. I need you to dream for me,' Shanti cupped a hand over the mouthpiece to block the noise of the departure lounge. 'I've got to go, babe, okay?'

'You'll be bored. You'll feel trapped,' Amber began to sniffle. 'I know you.'

'How can you know me? You only just met me. Last month, you and I didn't even exist.'

'But we do now, don't we?'

Shanti sighed and ran her fingers through her hair, but couldn't reach the ends cleanly. She hadn't even had time to brush this morning. And her mouth was furry.

'The trade winds are shifting, the moon's energy is building,' Amber began with renewed enthusiasm, 'How much longer can you fight this, my honey bee?'

Shanti was no stranger to spirituality, but she detected something closer to manipulation in Amber's celestial arguments.

'I think my ship is sailing in another direction right now,' said Shanti, trying to close the door as gently as she could.

The sobbing began in earnest. Shanti rolled her eyes, but also bit her lip.

'Amber, look, I don't want to wind up in a dead-end life with my uncle on the other side of the world. I need to focus, OK?'

A crackling, blowing sound crashed over the departure lounge as the gate attendant fumbled with the microphone.

'Shanti?'

The phone vibrated in her hand. She held it out and squinted. A US number she didn't recognise.

'I'm boarding now. I have to go,' Shanti turned to see the flock of passengers rush the gates like seagulls at hot chips.

'If this thing does change your life, who will you be then?'

'I'm always going be me, Amber. I'm pretty sure of that,' said Shanti, just as the call dropped.

Who will you be then? The question careened about in Shanti's head. Maybe that was a reason she'd only dated boys up to this point: sure, they wanted to get in most places but at least they didn't seem to get lodged inside her brain.

She shuffled down into the jetway where every passenger was impatient to buckle in so they could get a head start on sitting down for the next couple of hours.

Staring through the small convex window as the airport terminal slowly backed away from the plane, Shanti felt a tap on her shoulder.

'Miss, can you please stow your laptop for takeoff?'

Dragging her focus back into the present, she asked the attendant for some water.

'After take-off, Miss, but I will need you to stow that.'

Shanti looked down to find the laptop sitting, appropriately enough, in her lap. She opened the seat pocket but as she lifted the machine, she noticed something stuck to the underside. In contrast to Gavin's heavily-stickered laptop, Shanti maintained the outside of her computer exactly as she maintained the innards: clean, neat, ordered, unblemished. Turning it over, she discovered a small adhesive sticker on the battery cover, one she was certain she had removed long ago. Flipping her machine open, she discovered it wasn't her laptop.

* * *

A tsunami of sweat broke out in the time it took Gavin to wrangle his luggage from the boot of the taxi and into the air-conditioned foyer of the office tower. He took the lift to the twenty-third floor and found himself in a small lobby. The signboard on the wall indicated only one tenant: Vertica. Gavin opened his backpack to retrieve a small black notebook. He rifled through the pages to confirm he had the right building and the correct floor, but the name on the signboard meant nothing to him.

The frosted glass door at the end of the corridor swung open and a blast of airconditioning rushed into the lobby. A couple of Chinese youths emerged, talking simultaneously in a mishmash of English, Mandarin and html5. They wore colourful hi-top sneakers, brand new denim, knitted long-sleeve tops, dramatically undercut hairstyles and horn-rims. They pointed at each other's handsets, occasionally swiping or tapping on the screens and jabbing repeatedly at the elevator call button.

'Excuse me, guys,' said Gavin.

The Chinese youths were visibly startled, but made no sound.

'Umm, yeah, I'm looking for my office,' Gavin continued. One of the youths blinked. The other reached slowly for the elevator button without breaking eye contact and gave it another careful jab.

'Do you know where I can find ShelfLife?' asked Gavin, making an effort to sound friendly.

'No,' the youth replied with a note of disappointment. The elevator bell struck true and clear. The other youth jabbed the call button again, just to be certain, said, 'Sorry' and disappeared. The doors hushed themselves to a close and the elevator excused itself.

'I see you've met the neighbours.'

Gavin wheeled around to see Trent standing in the doorway, wearing a pale linen suit and a grin the size of a Bentley.

'Mate, it is good to see you,' said Gavin. 'I thought I was lost or something.'

'You are very much found, my friend,' said Trent, striding out to the lobby where the two men exchanged bro hugs, keeping their hips spaced apart and pummelling each others back's gently with closed fists. 'You just land?'

'I did,' said Gavin. 'They don't serve food on these short flights so I'm pretty hungry.'

'We can fix that. Great food around this area. I might have found you some decent coffee, too,' Trent said as he marshalled the luggage stack. 'Although, as an American, I completely accept I'm not qualified to make that call.' Trent paused in front of the glass door, pulled a keycard from his pocket and waved it near a small square mounted on the wall. 'Let's go inside, take a look at our set-up. It's a bit different to Seminyak, but I think you'll like it.' Trent pushed through into the brightly lit space beyond.

The floor was roughly circular and arranged in a hub-and-spoke layout, with long rows of desks radiating outward from the central core of lift shafts and bathrooms. Laptops and monitors sat cheek by jowl along the desk surface, in an alternate facing pattern to maximise occupancy. Circular conference tables, mobile whiteboards and small clusters of bright red sofas interrupted the long rows of desks. Everything looked like it had been delivered yesterday and the air smelled faintly of cleaning fluid and carpet glue. As he walked along the rows, Gavin could see the harbour through full-length windows that wrapped the entire floor. Hundreds of cargo ships and oil tankers dotted the sapphire waters of Singapore's harbour, waiting to unload and reload.

A small army of mostly young, mostly Asian programmers stared either at their monitors, their phones, or both. Even in these numbers they produced almost no noise. A few glanced up to assess Gavin and his luggage as he passed by.

'Did you hire all these people in the last week?' Gavin whispered.

'We don't actually have any staff just yet. These are all the other startups the incubator is backing,' said Trent as they passed rows of workers. 'These guys here are doing a thing called Maidly. Fractional ownership of domestic help. And those guys along there are looking at real-time market-based pricing for higher education. Think NASDAQ for degrees.'

Every wall and partition was a whiteboard, and every whiteboard was covered in task lists, infrastructure diagrams and business plan outlines.

'This whole floor is for startups like us?' asked Gavin.

'This floor plus another two above us. Literally every day another bunch of dudes walks in, sits down, plugs in their laptops and starts building a new company. If they make their milestones within three months they get to stay another three, with another set of milestones. Beat your targets and you get to move upstairs.'

'What's upstairs?'

'Kinda the same as this, but the fit-out is much nicer. Lower density, bigger kitchen, more meeting rooms and fridges have beer.'

'What do our fridges have?'

'Energy drinks and hydrolytes. This place is even sweatier than Bali.'

'And where's our meeting room?'

'See that big cube of frosted glass near the middle? Just one, for everyone to share.' Trent guided Gavin by the shoulder. 'Come on, we're over here.'

Trent walked around the perimeter of the floor, nodding occasionally to individuals as they glanced up from their screens. He reached some vacant chairs at the end of one of the rows and parked Gavin's luggage beside the window, which overlooked an office tower under construction and a massive hole in the ground next to it, where another building would soon begin to rise.

'Some view.' Gavin placed his hands on his hips.

'Yeah, well, the ocean views were all taken. But a window seat is better than aisle, which is definitely better than middle. This is us.' Trent gestured to four chairs, two facing two, each with a computer-printed sheet of A4 taped to their backs that read 'shelf life'.

'Comic Sans? Are you fucking serious?' Gavin yanked off the sign and let it fall to the floor.

'I knew that would get you,' Trent laughed. 'C'mon, let's get you some breakfast.'

A whirring noise – part vacuum cleaner, part chainsaw – sliced through the hushed atmosphere of the office. Everyone seated went full meerkat, straining to locate the source. Trent jogged towards the centre of the floor, waving for Gavin to follow. 'Oh man, she's got the prototype working again. You have to see this.'

A knot of people had formed around a group of sofas, but they reared back in unison as the whirring sound increased in pitch. A tiny helicopter swung above the group, halting and swaying as it moved, causing some to duck and others to gasp. A ripple of applause broke out and spread through the floor, followed by a couple of hesitant whoops.

'Haven't these guys seen a drone before?' Gavin scoffed.

'A drone, yes. But the mind-control part is pretty new.' Trent pointed to a young man, sitting on one of the red sofas, arms folded as he smiled at the tablet cradled in his lap. He wore an elaborate skullcap knitted from sensors and wires.

'OK Tran, do a sweep and look for the red X on the ground near me.'

Gavin turned to the voice and saw a tall, slender woman in black leggings and tank top standing by the far window. Trent was standing next to her, grinning. Skullcap guy swept his eyes left then right, and the small lens on the front of the drone followed suit, hovering above an X of red duct tape on the carpet in front of the black-clad woman.

She offered a double thumbs-up to the camera and the drone released a small package, which landed near the X, before whirring back towards its take-off position. The woman leant down to retrieve the package when a loud snap stole the attention of the room.

The crowd let out a collective shriek. People scrambled for cover as tiny pieces of helicopter showered nearby desks. Gavin dived behind a large concrete column.

'What the fuck, Tran?' the black-clad woman's shout erased the momentary silence in the room.

Tran winced as he peeled the sensor cap from his scalp. 'Sorry, boss. I think I sneezed.'

Gavin felt a hand on his shoulder.

'It's a cool idea, but they've still got some kinks to work out. Now, how about that breakfast?'

* * *

Trent led him across the street and down a shaded, narrow laneway between two tall buildings. Within minutes Gavin was sweating again. Brightly coloured market umbrellas stood like garish toadstools at the base of a sombre forest. The footpath was awash with plastic stools and foldable tables. A flock of ancient bicycles and heavily stickered small-capacity motorcycles surrounded the makeshift restaurant like animals gathering at an oasis.

'There aren't too many places like this left. Any building older than a quarter-century is slated to be torn down and redeveloped,' Trent pulled a couple of stools out from under a table, looked up to check they had the protection of the umbrellas and began ordering, using mainly hand signals.

'Sorry I had to leave Bali on such short notice, but it was important to show the investors we're committed. You understand, don't you?'

'Yeah, I get it. I'm just not used to how fast these startups move. I went and stayed with Marty for the last couple of nights. Shanti went to some sort of retreat with her yoga instructor. She's coming in on a flight later tonight,' said Gavin. 'It'll be good to get the band back together.'

An old Chinese woman in t-shirt and shorts shuffled up to their table, her flip-flops scraping in protest as she deposited two glass mugs of milky tea. Trent waved away Gavin's feeble attempt at a wallet fakey and handed over a bright green note. The woman counted out the change methodically, releasing each coin as if it were a child she may never see again.

'There's no tipping here. It's totally amazing,' said Trent. 'Some stuff is crazy cheap. Like this breakfast.'

'I guess you're paying for the ambience,' Gavin joked as one of the motorbike couriers fired up his modified two stroke: the sound bounced off the concrete walls of the narrow laneway like bullets, the smell of oxidized oil wafted through the stall.

'And some stuff is stupid expensive. Cars are the worst. And booze. And office space.'

'But I thought our investors are covering the rent?' asked Gavin, taking a chunk of the roti and popping it in his mouth. 'Oh wow, this is good.'

'I know, right? They'll be covering rent for a while, but nothing comes for free in this town,' Trent took a mouthful of his tea. 'The going commercial rate for this sort of space in the CBD is around fifteen per square.'

'Is that high?'

'Fuck yes, that is high. Have you never rented commercial space before?'

Gavin shook his head.

'That's almost up with Tokyo prices and not far behind Hong Kong. But it looks like I'll be travelling a fair bit, so you can give my seat to one of the new hires when they come on board.'

'And we're supposed to just keep on pounding the keyboard while you jet-set around the place?'

'Don't be too jealous, man. It's hard work getting up on stage and pitching at hackathons.'

Gavin raised an eyebrow.

'OK, some of it can be fun,' said Trent. 'If it makes you feel any better, I'm putting in a submission for us to feature on a panel at the next SXSW. If we get selected you can go and do that one.'

'For real?' Gavin's mood brightened.

'Scout's honour. But first, we've got to sweat this little puppy, show that we're serious about creating revenue. We've probably got three months to demonstrate genuine scale potential and maybe six to get cashflow positive before they turf us out and give our space to the next bunch of hopefuls.'

'What about the cash they're investing?'

'It's a mixed liquidity round of funding, so not all of their investment is in the form of cash.'

'Is any of it in cash?'

'Yeah, there's still a component but it's not the focus of the deal,' Trent adjusted his glasses. 'Charles is helping me with the equity structure so we're covered there. I decided against taking cash because then you have to spend it at full retail rates just to buy all the things we're currently getting at wholesale. We get more efficiencies this way.'

'Actually, that reminds me. I wanted to ask you if it would be possible to save a few shares for Marty?'

'Why would Marty get any shares?'

'I spoke to him before I left and he sounded a bit jaded. He's not sure who he's supposed to be when he's renting out his life to someone.'

'He doesn't need shares, he needs a shrink. Besides, we need to see where the dilution lands first. We don't want to be giving more shares away.'

'What dilution?'

'With the new investors and the injection of capital. You'll probably wind up with more shares, actually.'

'More?'

'Well, more in quantity, but they'll represent a smaller percentage.' Trent fished his chirping phone out of his pocket and stared at the number. 'Smaller slice, bigger pie is all.'

'You need to take that?' Gavin nodded at the phone.

'No. It's my mother. I should definitely not take that,' Trent pocketed his phone. 'But remind me to call my father when we get back to the office.'

'Have you seen some of the new listings?' said Gavin.

'I know, right? There's a makeup artist in Hollywood, a champagne maker in France, a trust fund kid in Mexico and a finance minister from somewhere in Eastern Europe.'

'You're kidding?'

'I'm a bit suspect on that one, but Charles reckons it's probably legit. We might put that one up in our specialist skills section.' Trent glanced around and lowered his voice. 'We've got plenty of people browsing, but most seem too nervous to commit. Bottom line is we haven't taken that many bookings.'

'But Marty told me his life is booked out for the next couple of months. That's why I want to do something to keep him sweet.'

'The deckhand is great. He's absolutely one of our star listings. But surfers are a naturally adventurous bunch so it's not hard to convince them to take a risk.' Trent paused to take a slug of his tea. 'Now we need to move beyond the early adopters, get some slightly more mainstream customers.'

'Like who?'

'You ready to do some work, partner?' Trent pulled a printed list out of his shirt pocket and unfolded it on the plastic table. 'On the host side, we need more rock singers, fitness instructors and, get this, mothers of young children.'

'Seriously?' Gavin put down his tea. 'You think we should get mums to sign up as hosts?'

'I don't. Shanti does.'

Gavin raised an eyebrow as he leaned over and took the sheet. 'She's talking to you?'

'Only about work stuff so far, but I think she's coming around,' Trent laughed, but it was of the nervous variety. 'She gets very passionate about certain things, but then she's also very focused on the work. We could all benefit from being a bit more like her sometimes. She doesn't let anything get in the way of her goals.'

'That part I *have* figured out,' said Gavin, resting his chin in his palm.

'So she ran an analysis of general search queries and the social listening bots she has running. Seems like single women want to take the "married with children" life for a test drive before they sign up for real. It's a genuinely underserved market.'

'So now we need a bunch of mums who want to rent their lives out for a week?'

'Correct. But we've got no idea where to start.'

'Zumba and book clubs.'

'What?'

'At my old ad agency, we did a massive research project on stay-at-home mums for some tired old biscuit brand we were trying to re-launch. Turns out these women are doing Zumba and forming book clubs.'

'Book clubs? That's still a thing?'

'Uh-huh, apparently it's a by-product of the *Fifty Shades* industrial complex juggernaut. They're still reading mummy porn like it's never going to go out of style. A whole industry sprung up around it: sewing patterns for lingerie, light bondage classes, sex toy demonstration morning teas. It's kind of disturbing.'

'It's kind of hot.' Trent glanced at his watch. 'So what did you agency geniuses do with the research?'

'We came up with an awesome new name for these biscuits,' Gavin splayed his hands like he was unveiling a rabbit. 'Big Os.'

'Huh?'

'Y'know, like orgasms. But the client didn't go for it.'

'I'm not surprised.'

'Hey, we've some dominatrix profiles on the site, so why don't we target suburban mums, offer them a dominatrix ShelfLife to rent as a kind of *Fifty Shades* theme-park ride. Then, while they're away, they can rent out their mummy life to young single women who want to try before they buy. It's like a twofer.'

'Twofer?'

'Ad-speak. Two for one.'

'Jesus, Gav,' Trent shook his head. 'Is everyone in ad agencies as smart as you?'

'It's not smart if you do what the data tells you to do, that's just common sense.'

'And if the data is telling us that women are dissatisfied with their current lives,' asked Trent as he rose from the table, brushing crumbs from his trousers, 'we should be offering them a new kind of satisfaction?'

'Yes. Exactly. And the crazy thing is that the dissatisfaction is generally caused by the men in their lives.'

'Wow. You really do learn something every day.'

* * *

'Finally. Here they are,' Charles stood and opened his arms wide as Trent and Shanti made their way to the booth. 'We were getting worried about you two. C'mon, take a seat, get comfortable.'

There was a little shuffling but the plush, curved banquette easily accommodated the newcomers to the group.

'I think Trent knows everyone here and vice versa but Shanti, let me introduce you around, starting with myself,' he made a small bow. 'Charles Archer-Ellis, entrepreneur and change agent. Originally from the UK but not for some time. And this is Douglas, who's the ringmaster here at Vertica.'

A young Chinese man stood up quickly. 'Great to have another girl coder on the floor. We need a lot more of you. Really we do.' He shook Shanti's hand so vigorously he had to readjust his glasses.

'A lot of passion for the tech industry, has our young Douglas. And here on my left is Ping.' A tall, thin young woman in a clingy black dress offered a smile.

'Ping is originally from Malaysia – not that we hold that against her – and is developing an autonomous delivery service to help NGOs, which is well and good, but I'm trying to get her to see the bigger opportunity. She could change the world if she put her mind to it.'

'I see what you did there, Charles. Very flattering,' Ping held a slender hand out for Shanti. 'Welcome to Vertica. And to Singapore.'

'Tran is the brains of Ping's team,' Charles swivelled to the other end of the group.

'Literally!' Trent broke in.

Charles laughed. 'Yes, sometimes literally. He joined us from Hanoi, via MIT, to lead the development of the neural control mesh that underpins Ping's network.'

'And I'm also looking into sneeze suppressant technology. How are you?' Tran shook Shanti's hand as the group laughed.

'What's with the sneeze joke?' asked Shanti as she slid onto the banquette.

'Tran flew another drone into a wall this morning,' Ping took a sip of her martini.

'You forgot the part where he was flying it with his mind. How was your flight?' Gavin leaned over and gave Shanti a peck on the cheek.

'A bit of turbulence on take-off. The flowers at the airport were a nice surprise, though,' Shanti smiled and glanced at Trent.

'Good to see you two made up,' said Gavin.

'Trouble in paradise?' Charles raised his eyebrows as he took a sip of his scotch.

'I'd call it a robust strategic discussion, right Shanti?' Trent winked.

'Yes, let's call it that,' said Shanti with a tight smile.

A sequinned waitress appeared and took their drinks order. The bar began filling up with partygoers who all seemed to have been dressed by 'vulgar & expensive'. From their vantage point by the window, Shanti could see almost the entire city centre, more than fifty storeys below. Traffic snaked its way across the edge of the man-made bay, curling around the floodlit craters of building sites that dotted the city grid like teenage acne. A forest of cranes dominated the skyline while plane after plane swooped gracefully into the nearby airport.

'Incredible view, isn't it?' Charles landed himself next to Shanti.

'There's a lot going on out there.'

'You get a chance to see the offices on the way in?'

Shanti smiled politely. 'No, Trent took me to the apartments. Shower and change, then straight here. I've never been to Singapore before, it looks like an amazing city.'

'It'll be great when it's finished. A bit like this little business you're building.'

'How so?'

'Well, it's a bit of a construction site right now, but we'll get some operations people on board to put some process in place, ramp up the marketing and then scale out to other territories.'

Shanti stiffened a little, her eyes narrowing. 'You don't think we've got the right infrastructure in place?'

'Oh, I'm sorry, I didn't mean the site,' Charles chuckled and patted her arm. 'The code is beautiful, so I'm told. Not that we had a burning need to build custom code, but now that you've written it and it all seems to be working, we might as well keep it. The important thing to remember is that the business of ShelfLife is not the website.'

Shanti paused, trying to neutralise her expression before Charles had the satisfaction of knowing he had offended her. 'And what do you think *is* the business of ShelfLife?'

'Don't worry, people generally get that part wrong about internet startups. I'm talking about the business behind the business. That's where Trent is going to need the most help.'

'You don't think he knows what he's doing?' Shanti frowned.

Charles tilted his head. 'He's got amazing ideas, I'll give him that, but he doesn't seem to know much about cashflow, for starters. Or have you seen differently?'

Shanti stole a glance at Trent, who was deep in conversation with Ping. She'd lost count of the number of calls she'd fielded from vendors and suppliers wanting to know when they were going to get paid. Trent had assured her it was how all startups were run. He even seemed dismissive when she tried to get him to focus on their debtor list, so she'd paid several of them in lieu, crediting them with free ShelfLife accounts. Most were yet to be redeemed. It would be a relief, she admitted to herself, to have a grown-up in charge of the financials.

'Of course, he's also got his mother to worry about now,' Charles downed the last of his scotch and straightened his cuffs. 'Excuse me, but I've just spotted an old chum from

Europe I've been meaning to catch up with. Pretty connected in Belarus. Something to do with the Finance Ministry. You wouldn't believe the sort of cash people like him have to invest. Lord knows where it all comes from.'

Charles shuffled off the end of the banquette and sauntered across the room. Shanti turned to see Gavin, Tran and Douglas comparing sneakers. Ping still held Trent in her thrall, speaking softly yet earnestly about something that appeared to be very far away.

Shanti excused herself and made her way to the bar, as much for something to do as for a drink, and felt her limbs go heavy. The effort of relocating her life, yet again, while appearing nonchalant had suddenly caught up with her.

'Whoah, you look smashed, Shants. You okay?' Gavin went to hold her by the forearm, but she brushed him away.

'Oh, god, I wish. Just feeling a bit overwhelmed, I guess. This isn't really my scene. Hey, what's with Trent's mother?'

Gavin made a 'huh?' with his face and resumed drinking, tapping his feet to the pulsating music.

'Charles reckons there's something going on there.' She raised her voice above the music. 'He also thinks maybe Trent is not the best person to be handling the money side of the business.'

Gavin shrugged. 'Maybe. It's not like we've had any money to handle, have we?' It was hard logic to fault, in its own way. 'Besides, we're going to need a lot of people to handle all sorts of things. Trent reckons we have to scale up pretty quickly to reach our targets, otherwise it will be harder to attract investment for the next round.'

'Trent reckons? Or Charles reckons?'

'What does it matter now, Shanti? We're buckled in and we've just got to do what we need to do in order to get paid,'

Gavin smiled and raised his glass. Shanti held her hand aloft to make an air cheers.

'Oh! You have got to check out what Tran and Ping are doing with drones. Their startup is called Rotronica and it is literally completely mental.'

'Gavin, you have got to stop using the word literally when you mean figuratively or I will literally kill you.'

'No, I'm serious. They're using mind control.'

'Literally?'

'That's what I said. So, you know how people are using drones to do parcel deliveries? Well, Ping is going to use them to deliver medical aid in Africa and places like that. It's totally doable, but the bottleneck is the lack of pilots.' Gavin paused to watch as two girls in microskirts sashayed past, smiling at him over their shoulder.

'Saving lives in Africa?' said Shanti, poking him in the ribs.

'Oh yeah, so she's developing a system that lets anyone fly these drones just by thinking about it. Almost no training required.'

'Sounds amazing.'

'I know. And she's also trying to build a self-replicating network, where the drones fly out to the edge of their range and deliver the parts for the next village to assemble a new set of drones. And then it just keeps repeating.'

Shanti shook her head in disbelief.

'Tran's pretty much a genius at this neural control stuff and Ping is all gung-ho about saving the world.' Gavin nodded back to where Trent was hanging on every word. 'I think Trent's pretty smitten, to be honest. You know he was training to become a doctor?'

'He was enrolled once, which is not quite the same thing. I think he only did it to avoid working for his parents at their med-tech firm. And look how that turned out.'

'Anyway, I think it's cool, saving lives and stuff,' Gavin shrugged and looked out over the dance floor, which had become more populated. 'Kinda makes our thing look a bit frivolous.'

'Hey, I need a favour.' Shanti tried to sound casual.

'What the hell is Charles doing with those crazy-rich Asian milfs?' Gavin turned back to Shanti, who slapped him on the arm. 'Sorry. Sure, whaddaya need?'

'Did our investors say anything about getting new equipment?'

'Dunno. Only got here this morning myself. Why?'

'I might need a new laptop.'

'And I need to find some married women who are also mums,' Gavin nodded to the beat as a clutch of wealthy older Chinese women danced past.

'Ew, that's gross.' Shanti slapped Gavin on the upper arm again.

'Hey, if you don't want to keep the dog, don't get upset when it strays,' he grinned and she slapped him again, but with more force. 'I'm kidding. Sort of. You know that search analysis you did for Trent? He said you found a segment of young women who want to test drive motherhood.'

'It's become quite a thing. One blogger even has a book deal.'

'OK, so, I was thinking we convince some mums to rent out their lives for a few days, to give these test-drivers a go,' Gavin scratched his head to simulate deep thinking. 'And then I remembered we've got a few dominatrix and madam listings now, right?'

'Supply and demand.'

'Exactly. We just need a steady supply of jaded, wealthy married women who need a break from their kids and husbands.'

Shanti looked out over the dance floor as Charles shuffled back into view, thronged by older women. A couple were locals and several were expatriates. They preened extravagantly, pearls shaking and curls bouncing as they laughed and air-kissed, handling Charles like a pony for sale.

'Maybe they're closer than we think.'

Milf duds

The door swung open and a shaft of light stole into the bedroom. Clare heard the thud of shoe connecting with floor, followed by another. A gentle wrestle, a muffled rustle and a pile of clothes, she presumed, followed them. The covers rose and a body, heavy and ungraceful, wedged its way across the bed, coming to a stop just behind her back.

'Hmmm.' A man's voice. 'I thought you were still at the resort with the yoga group.'

A hand snaked across her thigh, rode up her torso and enveloped her breast, giving it a firm squeeze. She stiffened, unsure what to say. The part of her that stiffened the most, however, were her nipples.

'Did you finally duck off to Bangkok to have that boob job you've been threatening?' He kneaded her breast with more conviction, then flattened his palm and pressed her erect nipple back into the soft mound of flesh. 'The surgeon did a great job, baby. They feel fantastic.'

He swung his hips forward and she felt his member tapping against the small of her back. Clare cleared her throat. 'Are you Matt?' she said in a small voice.

The man froze.

He leapt backwards out of the bed in one movement, catching his feet in the sheets and crashing to the ground. The bed was an enormous teak thing, painted to resemble an antique opium lounge. The distance to the floor was substantial. Clare switched on the bedside lamp and leaned out over the edge of the mattress. The man on the floor had curly brown hair and a solid build. He was probably in very good shape a few years ago, but was now carrying the extra padding that comes to so many men in middle age. He clutched the sheet to his chest to cover himself, unaware that it reached only down to his navel. His eyes darted, his brow furrowed and his penis throbbed involuntarily.

Clare recognised him from the footage Lisa had included in the pre-briefing video. 'Yeah, you're Matt,' she said, extending her hand. 'Hi, I'm Clare. Lisa probably told you about me.'

Matt took her hand cautiously and shook it. 'She said something about a friend. Might be staying. This week. While I was out of town.' Each phrase ended with an upward inflection as he searched for reassurance. 'Are you the friend?'

'Sort of.' Her gaze slid down to Matt's exposed crotch. 'She said you probably wouldn't be home for another week or two, at least.'

'Conference got cancelled,' Matt propped himself up on one elbow and tugged at the sheets for more coverage. 'Look, I thought you were my wife. I'm sorry, for grabbing you.'

'Don't be. That's what's supposed to happen.'

'What?'

'Really? Didn't Lisa tell you why I'm staying in your house this week?'

'Oh god, she did tell me something actually, about a house swap or job swap or something,' Matt rubbed his face, as if the effort in remembering his wife's words had caused immediate exhaustion. 'Wait, she said someone wanted to test-drive her lifestyle? I thought she was talking about real estate. I honestly have no idea, sorry. We haven't been speaking much lately.' He looked up at Clare, waiting for an explanation.

'I'm staying in your house because, for this week, I *am* Lisa.'

'That doesn't make any sense.'

'It is unusual, yes, but it's also the truth. Lisa rented her life to me for the week. Are you sure she didn't tell you?'

'What are you talking about? How can you rent someone's life?'

'Oh, I know. It sounds wild, but it's just supposed to be a little bit of fun for us girls. There's this new website that makes it so easy, just like renting a holiday villa. A friend of a friend put me onto it.'

'No, I mean, why would Lisa want to rent out her life?'

'Maybe you'd have to ask her. But she told me that you'd be away on business and you probably wouldn't mind anyway, that you two have friends from out of town who stay all the time. Besides, your maid is here to make sure I don't get anything spectacularly wrong with the kids. They're adorable, by the way.'

'My wife let a complete stranger move into our house? And look after our kids?'

'Oh god no! Not a *complete* stranger. We have some mutual friends. It's a funny story, actually.'

Matt cut her off with a raised finger. 'Where is she?'

'You don't know where your wife is?'

'I know where she's supposed to be. Chiang Mai or Chiang Rai or Chang whatever. Some sort of yoga detox spa. She loves all that shit.'

'Maybe you should give her a call.'

'Stay here.' He rifled through his clothes and found his phone.

As soon as Matt left the room, Clare grabbed her own phone and started texting Lisa, hoping to give her some warning. It would be a shame if her week had to end now, and even more of a shame if she didn't get to sample the F part of being a MILF.

* * *

'Who was that?' asked the dark-haired woman in tall leather boots and nothing else.

Lisa slung her phone into her handbag. 'Oh, nothing. Just a little commotion on the home front.'

'In my experience, commotions on the home front are rarely little.'

'I just had to get my husband up to speed with our arrangement this week.'

'You didn't tell him? That's cheeky of you.' The blonde opened a large timber wardrobe and flicked her way through an ordered selection of bras, bustiers, corsets, masks and capes.

'I suppose so, Gretchen. But I honestly didn't expect him to be home until late next week. We've had a don't-ask-don't-tell thing going on for a while now.' Lisa ran a wooden brush through her long straight hair.

The room was long, narrow and well organised. One wall was dominated by a timber shelf, heaving beneath a pharmacy's worth of beauty and hair products. A large mirror, framed by small naked lightbulbs, gave the impression of a back-stage dressing room – which in effect, it was.

'Is that something you two agreed to explicitly? Or just a polite way of saying that you don't talk about your sex life anymore?' Gretchen asked, rubbing a clear lotion onto her breasts and under her armpits.

Lisa lowered herself onto a wooden stool. 'I guess it just happened that way, didn't it?' She pulled the brush through in strong, deliberate strokes. 'I assume he goes to places when he's travelling.'

'Places like this?' She stretched a shiny black bodice into a loop large enough for her head to pass through unmolested.

'Oh, he doesn't much like the rough stuff, more's the pity.'

'Or maybe he doesn't like it rough with you,' Gretchen smirked and ducked into the bodice, snapping it onto her chest like an elastic band.

'You know, normally, I would be furious at hearing that. But I think I'm starting to get it now. These men,' Lisa gestured past the heavy wooden door at the end of the room, 'they can't ask their wives for what they want. They're afraid it will change the way she sees him.'

'They should be afraid. You can't respect a man who asks you to stomp on his balls and then pays you for it.' Gretchen threw her head back and laughed like she was on a college drinking team. 'Oh, Lisa, I like you, darling, but you are so innocent sometimes.'

'I'm not innocent.' Lisa rose and shook her hair out, tossing the wooden brush onto the bench.

'Yet you are a long way from guilty, my dear.' Gretchen nodded at the brush. 'Bring that, I think it may be of use today.'

* * *

Matt placed his phone on the kitchen bench, not quite believing what his wife had just told him. Clare's life-rental story checked out. Lisa even scolded Matt for not paying attention when she had explained it last week while at some over-priced faux-French restaurant in a newly-renovated hotel near the river. But then again, every restaurant in Singapore was faux-something and charged the equivalent of Togo's GDP for two mains and a bottle of red, so remembering the venue was going to be no help. He had to admit he'd forgotten all about the conversation. He'd probably been checking football scores on his phone under the table.

Never mind. Now he had a deal: a 'hall pass' for the week, which she encouraged him to use, provided no questions were asked, in either direction. As much as he wanted to know where his wife was and what (or whom) she was doing, the deal was too sweet to refuse. Even better: Lisa seemed to be under the impression it was all her idea.

He slapped his abdomen a couple of times, puffed out his chest, walked back to the bedroom and threw the door open. 'Hi Honey, I'm home.'

'Come here,' Clare grinned and patted the space on the bed beside her, 'tell me all about your day.'

* * *

The sex was awkward and fumbling, and not just at first. Matt was careful not to appear too familiar with the mechanics of fucking unfamiliar women and Lisa had been mindful of appearing too hungry. As they lay in the oversized bed, their heart rates returning to resting, he admitted a large part of the thrill of sleeping with women who were not his wife came from the knowledge that he shouldn't be sleeping with women who weren't his wife. Lisa's blessing had made it feel that much tamer. The conversation stalled for a while as Clare searched for something comforting to say, until she realised Matt had fallen asleep. Assuming this was all part of their routine, Clare picked up a novel from the small stack on Lisa's night stand.

'Urgh, clit lit,' she said to herself as she scanned a few pages. 'If this is the quality of sex you get when you marry and have children no wonder you end up reading this tosh.'

* * *

'Window cleaner?'

'The smell reminds them of hospitals,' said Gretchen as she finished wiping the gurney down and removed a handful of instruments from the autoclave. 'The bright lights are another trigger. We're just taking shortcuts to their memories. You did very well today. You seem to have a knack for this.'

Lisa blushed and looked down, her hair partially covering her face. 'Oh, I don't know. I'm just doing what they ask me to do.'

'Of course you are, darling, but the trick is to get them to ask. They can never do that with their wives.' Gretchen rearranged the instruments in a neat row on the table. 'Finish the chair and then we're done. I've asked some of the girls to meet us for a drink.'

Lisa sanitised the various crops, paddles and flails, returning them to their allotted places in the open cabinet in the room they called "Emergency". Nachtmusik was one of the more established dungeons in Berlin, well known but not strictly famous. Gretchen had been running the place for the last decade and preferred to keep it discreet, cultivating a clientele that was mostly local and overwhelmingly regular. Half of the girls who worked there were experienced domination professionals, the other half were a rotating cast of travellers, part-timers, students and artists. Gretchen's talent lay in knowing what a particular client might want for any given session: steady hands or fresh faces.

A few of those hands and a couple of those faces were now gathered around a bar table in Kreuzberg, Berlin's most recent answer to Williamsburg. Once a migrant ghetto, the suburb had been terra-formed first by gays then by hipsters. The speakeasy-styled bar was accommodating both tribes this evening, many of whom kept throwing glances at the striking group of women in an attempt to divine their sexual allegiance.

'It's only a matter of months before the breeders start buying up warehouses, demanding organic sourdough and segregated footpaths for baby strollers,' Gretchen spat. The girls cackled and called for another round. The drinks had been coming at velocity and Lisa was struggling to stay abreast.

'You rented Dominique's life for one week, just like that?' asked a slim Hungarian girl with fierce blue eyes and cheekbones like balconies. 'Why?'

The table fell silent and looked to Lisa.

Lisa took a large mouthful of red and smiled. 'You know those men who pay to see you – us – every day?'

A table full of nodding.

'Do you ever think about their wives and their girlfriends?'

A pause, followed by a table full of shrugs.

'That's me. I was at home every day, with the kids, reading interior design blogs, wondering where my husband was but not really caring, and I thought to myself: *How did I get so old?* I was becoming depressed, I think.'

The girls nodded – less in agreement, more as a sign to continue.

'I got a phone call from a man my husband knows through work.'

'Did he ask you to stomp on his balls?' asked Hungarian cheekbones.

Gretchen slapped the young girl lightly on the arm and motioned for Lisa to continue.

'No, he's sort of an investor. Startups and websites and things. One of his companies has a new service he wanted me to test-drive. All I had to do was let another woman pretend to be me for a week.'

The Hungarian clapped a hand to her mouth. 'Oh my gott! So you're here, pretending to be Dominique, while another woman is in your house pretending to be you?'

Lisa nodded.

'This is amazing. What does your husband think?'

'I think he's getting more comfortable with the idea,' she smiled and reached for her glass. 'I know I am.'

'And how about your life here with us? Are you getting more comfortable with that?' Gretchen swirled her drink.

'Well, I've certainly learned a few things,' said Lisa glancing around at her audience. 'But I wouldn't mind lying back and letting someone else do the work for a change.'

The girls roared with laughter. Hungarian Cheekbones produced a twenty euro note and passed it to Gretchen, who slipped the cash into her bra.

'What's funny? What's the money for?' Lisa's head swivelled, seeking reassurance.

'Oh darling, don't worry. We can definitely put you on the receiving end. Everybody wants to give up being in control now and then,' Gretchen winked at the girls as they giggled into their drinks. 'I'm only surprised it took you this long to ask.'

* * *

Although it was 33 degrees Celsius and what felt like 110 per cent humidity, Clare shivered as she inched forward in the taxi queue. She'd spent most of the morning lying on a marble slab, covered in chilled volcanic mud, bathed in the frigid zephyrs of industrial-strength air-conditioning and left to contemplate her steadily declining core temperature while her therapist disappeared into a bubble-popping game on her phone. It was only when Kate – the cheat sheet from Lisa described her as *your bestie from the school mums group* – returned from the pedicure room and raised the alarm that Lisa was rescued. An aggressive shiatsu massage and a botanic facial brought her back to life. Clare left the spa feeling she'd been beauty-parlour water-boarded, almost four hundred dollars poorer and unable to fully rotate her left shoulder.

She air-kissed her temporary bestie, who promised to call about the school fund-raiser, and walked out of the cavernous mall to the taxi rank. The heat marched in through the pores, hitched a ride on the bloodstream and kicked over the starter motors on her sweat glands. Her taxi arrived a few minutes after the perspiration. On the short ride home she fished the crumpled post-it from her handbag and reread the note Matt had left on the bedpost: *That was fun. But I'm sure I can do better. C U after lunch?*

She was sincerely hoping so. After last night's fumble she was looking forward to a do-me-over. Clare trotted up the driveway, half-expecting to find him waiting, perhaps with his tie loosened and shirt unbuttoned, prowling the kitchen and barking orders at subordinates on his mobile phone. Instead, Clare was greeted by Lisa and Matt's live-in maid.

The help is called Julia, the cheat sheet offered. *Reasonably trustworthy, great with the kids, less so with the dog (not many dachshunds in her village back in the Philippines). You can play with the kids any time you like, but leave all the real work to her – that's what she's (mainly) paid to do.*

'I go and get the children now, Mrs Lisa,' said Julia nodding and offering a little bow. 'I think Mr Matt already come.'

'Already come?' Clare stopped.

'Yes, already. About maybe one hour,' said Julia with a shy smile. 'I take the children to music lesson, then gymnastics class. Then I come home to make pasta for dinner, OK?' She hefted a violin case under her arm and trudged off through the thick afternoon air.

Clare smiled at herself for misunderstanding Julia. That post-it note must have given her a one-track mind. She climbed the stairs and found Matt's clothes strewn across the floor of the bedroom. If someone else always picked them up, she thought, I'd probably leave them there, too. She pushed open the door to the ensuite and watched Matt's silhouette through the frosted glass of the shower, thinking he looked much better in rough outline than fine detail. Never mind. She cleared her throat loudly to announce herself.

Matt spun the taps shut and opened the door, smiling. 'Hand me the towel if you don't mind. No, not the green ones, they're Lisa's. I mean, they're yours. I'm brown.'

'How was your day?' she handed him the towel and let her glance linger on his wet body. 'Julia's accent is too funny. I got a shock for a second when she said you already came.'

'She did? God, I'm so sorry,' Matt stopped towelling. 'She has to learn to be more discreet. Just give me a little while and I'll be ready to go again. Promise.'

Clare gave a laugh, not knowing what else to give. 'What are you saying?'

Matt also gave a laugh. 'Nothing. Umm, did you enjoy tennis?'

'Spa, actually.' Clare crossed her arms. 'Did you just sleep with the maid?'

Matt wrapped the towel around his waist and shuffled past her into the bedroom, his eyes avoiding Clare's.

'Oh my god, you just slept with the maid.' She followed and found him sitting on the edge of the bed, running his hands through his wet hair, which was showing early signs of retreat.

'I was kinda horny all day, wondering if you got my note. Then I came home to find Julia cleaning the bathroom in one of my old t-shirts, sopping wet. She was bent over, scrubbing the wall and everything was jiggling about.'

'Are you serious?' Clare put her hands on her hips.

'Don't get mad at me, it was Lisa's idea,' he began, then his eyes widened. 'Actually, that makes it your idea, doesn't it?'

'Wait. What?'

'When you interviewed her, remember? She had said her rate was four-fifty a month for standard, or six hundred including headache duty.'

'Headache duty?'

'Julia's last employer paid her to sleep with the husband any time she had a headache and didn't want to do it herself. You thought it was funny at first, but then decided it was pretty smart. If you're going to outsource the cooking, the cleaning, minding the kids all day, why not just add fucking your husband to the list?'

'Matt, look, I'm not really Lisa.'

'This week you are. You told me. And my wife told me to treat you just like I would treat her. You girls started this little game, I'm just playing along.' Matt rose from the bed and walked towards her. 'So that's our little secret, Lisa. Now you know that I know that you pay the help to suck my cock, because you don't want to do it anymore.'

'Urrgh. Why are you telling me this?'

'It's what we do, honey. We fight about something – usually nothing – then I apologise. Then you apologise. Then we fuck,' he shrugged.

'We do?'

'I'm surprised Lisa didn't put that in your little instruction book,' Matt opened his arms wide and let the towel drop. 'I'm sorry, baby. Let me pop a Viagra. I'll make it up to you, promise.'

Clare retreated downstairs to the kitchen to process the situation. Matt hung around for about half an hour, wavering between sulky and playful. When he became doubtful Clare would sleep with him again, Matt declared the situation to be 'too much like real life', packed a carry-on and headed for the airport. Apparently, there was another conference he might as well be at.

* * *

'Ow. That hurt,' said Lisa with an intake of breath that conveyed irritation more than actual discomfort.

'Oh god, I'm sorry,' said the tall, skeletal man standing behind her, wearing only boxers and long socks.

'That's kind of the point, isn't it?' she shot back.

'Well, yes, but I don't want to really hurt you. It's difficult for me to tell.'

Lisa wriggled out of the ropes that pretended to secure her to the bed. 'Give me that.'

The man handed her the leather tawse as if he had been caught with something embarrassing. He watched as she walked slowly behind him and brought it hard across the back of his thighs. The intake of breath was more heartfelt in his case.

'See. A little flick of the wrist, making sure to keep the implement completely flat. Or it will hurt.' She struck him again. 'And not in a good way.'

He let out a whimper and reached around to rub the backs of his legs, but she swatted his hands away.

'Nah-ah. Only Mistress gets to make it feel better.' She struck again, drawing a little yelp. 'Now do you want to try again?'

There was no answer.

'For god's sake, Hans, you're the one paying for this.' She brought the tawse down again. 'Now, are you going to give me a good thrashing? Or do you need more instruction?'

* * *

The two women sat facing each other across a small plastic table in a quiet corner of the airport.

'Did you sleep with my husband?'

'I wasn't sure what the rules were. Your cheat sheet hinted at it, but it was a bit vague.'

'I know, I'm sorry. I left it a bit open-ended in the rental details. I guess I wanted to see what would happen. And how I would feel about it. Did you?'

'Only the once.'

'That's all?' Lisa slid her sunglasses up on to her head. 'Was he that bad?'

'It wasn't bad. But not as good as I thought it was going to be. I probably wasn't much better myself,' Clare gripped her coffee with both hands. 'We were going to have another go at it, but after I found out about the maid, I couldn't quite bring myself to do it again. I'm sorry.'

'Oh, don't be,' Lisa waved the concern away. 'You managed to work through the arc of my entire marriage in about seventy-two hours.'

'Your kids are gorgeous, though. If I was guaranteed to get one like your little Lizzie I'd be tempted to start a family right now.'

'Oh, I know. You're not supposed to have favourites, but she makes it hard not to.' Lisa looked out through the window as another plane rolled backwards from the terminal. 'If only you could have the kids without having the husband. But I'd still keep Julia though.'

'You're not leaving him, are you? Not because of me?'

'No. He makes too much money, quite frankly. And I don't mind what he did with you. Or with Julia, for that matter. I thought it would bother me, but I guess I already knew,' Lisa toyed with her necklace. 'And I had *my* fun, don't you worry.'

'You weren't at a yoga retreat, were you?'

'No. I was not,' she smiled the way a recently-fed cat might. 'I was making 500 euros a night, hitting complete strangers in the testicles.'

Clare lurched forward to catch some of her coffee as it escaped from her mouth. 'You did what?'

Lisa slid a napkin across the table. 'I had so much fun. You just wouldn't believe it.'

'You're right. I don't believe it.' Clare dabbed at her chin. 'Who wants to be hit in the balls?'

'Lawyers. Bankers. School principals. Weedy, clever men who find themselves in positions of authority. Secretly, they don't believe they deserve it. Some of them just like the sensation of pain.'

'Did you have to sleep with them?'

'Not unless I felt like it. It was an old-school dungeon in Berlin.'

'You've been in Germany this whole time?'

'I know! It sounds so naughty when you say it like that. But Matt and all his work buddies fly halfway around the world to sit in one meeting. They think nothing of it. Why shouldn't we?'

'I suppose. It just seems like a long way to go.'

'Not when there's so much fun to be had out there in the real world. I miss it already,' Lisa checked her watch. 'But what about you? Did you enjoy being a wife and mother? Apart from the sex, I mean?'

'It wasn't what I was expecting, to be honest.'

'Let me tell you: it rarely is,' Lisa pushed her empty cup to one side. 'I wish I'd been able to dip my toe in the water before I took the plunge. I had no idea what I was getting into.'

'I mean, I wasn't prepared for the way you have it all set up. Matt isn't around much, we ate out all the time, Julia looks after the kids, there wasn't that much for me to do. I know I was only pretending for a week, but it didn't feel like a real life,' Clare stopped herself. 'I'm sorry, I didn't mean to criticise. That was rude of me.'

'I'm not upset.' Lisa placed a hand on Clare's. 'I'm glad I got to do this. And I'm grateful to you for saying that. I think I needed to hear it from someone else.'

'No, that's not right,' Clare shook her head. 'I feel terrible.'

'Who gets to say what's right, Clare? I think everybody should get the chance to rent their life out, turn around and take a long, hard look at themselves,' Lisa stood up to leave. She kissed Clare on the cheek. 'They might be surprised at what they see.'

Double bonus
happiness from the skies

'The dangers are quite significant, Ms Menon. Or may I call you Shanti?' said Professor Jensen as he slid his palms across the table. Shanti leaned back. She'd had quite enough of leering English professors during boarding school. 'You can't always predict how the human mind will react when presented with unfamiliar situations. Particularly when actions become disintermediated from consequences.'

'How so?'

'ShelfLife is how so. To the trained eye, it's obvious that it's your raison d'être.' The Professor adjusted his glasses. 'Granted, it's not your typical economic disintermediation, like all these so-called disruptor services. More in a behavioural sense. I'm not surprised your advisor is recommending someone like me.'

'Actually, our advisor is recommending we get a psychologist,' Shanti nodded thanks as the waitress delivered coffee.

'He's only half right.' The Professor stirred his cappuccino until the foam disappeared. 'If you bring a traditional cognitive psychologist on board, you only get behavioural risk mitigation in an entirely theoretical model. Psychologists have wonderful insights, but they don't know how to apply them to economic mechanisms. That's why you need me. A behavioural economist with a double doctorate in psychology and economics. I'm the complete package.'

'Impressive,' Shanti cupped her latte, as if warding off the cold. It was almost mandatory for retailers in Singapore to provide a microclimate that denied its proximity to the equator.

'Not so much impressive as valuable. Behavioural economics is becoming the driving force in business model design,' the Professor sipped his cappuccino. 'HBR ranked it fourth on its annual list of emerging skills that all high-performance teams need to master. It would be quite a coup for your little startup to have me on board.'

'So why are we lucky enough to have caught your attention, Professor?'

'Can I tell you a secret?' he gave a sideways glance.

'We're all friends here,' Shanti nodded for him to continue.

'See, that's what I like about Singapore. Everyone is very open in their communications, very transparent. Easy social terrain to navigate. I want to stay here.'

'Why can't you?'

'I've been advised by the Singapore government that my oversight role with the investment co-op is, sadly, not to be renewed.'

'What frightful news.'

'I'm glad you see it that way,' he went to pat her hand, but found only the tabletop. 'I have to find another source of employment within thirty days, or I will be forced to leave the country.'

'Why don't you find something temporary while you're looking for a better opportunity?'

'What do you mean temporary?'

'I don't know, anything really. Get out and about, soak up that social terrain. Find something in hospitality, perhaps?'

Jensen snorted. 'Heavens, no. Why would I do that?'

'Because you so badly want to stay,' she said. 'Besides, what's wrong with hospitality?'

'It's manual labour, for a start, but even if I were to sink to that level, the visa requirements state the role has to be commensurate with my skills and experience.'

'That must be a challenge,' said Shanti.

'You've no idea. My skillset is incredibly specific and experience levels are undeniably high – not boasting, just stating facts. But I am determined to find the right role. My only other option is to find a spouse who is an employment pass holder. I don't suppose you'd be free for a wedding this weekend?'

Shanti stared.

'I'm joking, obviously,' he rushed to reassure her.

'That much I assumed.'

'So a role with ShelfLife would be perfect for me right now. At least until I can secure a role with the Finance Ministry. I'm keen to move into national economic policy.'

'The only problem I can foresee is that we don't actually have a role open at the moment,' said Shanti.

'Of course you do. Archer-Ellis told me he was very concerned you kids are handing out life rentals like candy. You have no checks or balances. No psychological screening. It's only a matter of time before something blows up.' The Professor interlocked his fingers tightly. 'Psychological profiling is an incredibly complex process. Thanks to my dedicated training, I can vet potential matches with a high degree of accuracy, safeguarding your investors from any potential embarrassment or financial liabilities.'

'Wait, are you proposing we check every potential ShelfLife rental manually? Do you realise how long that would take?'

'Yes, but I'm sure I could develop a series of profile templates and checklists that would enhance the efficacy of the process over time.'

'Professor, we're a digital business. We're scaling incredibly quickly. There's no way we can introduce a manual process performed by one person,' Shanti shook her head as we spoke. 'If Chuck wants us to filter out the crazies, I have a fairly sophisticated matching algorithm that should do the job. I developed it to power a personalised travel recommendation engine.'

'I think you vastly overestimate our ability to codify the human condition.' Professor Jensen scribbled on a notepad, tore the page off and handed it to Shanti. 'Archer-Ellis wants some parental oversight on your little project and I'm the person he recommended to provide it. I expect to hear from you shortly.'

'What's this?' Shanti squinted at the page as the Professor rose and straightened his jacket.

'That's my monthly salary requirement,' said the Professor, stooping to collect his briefcase. 'Very similar to the package in my current contract.'

'Is that what the co-op was paying you to advise on their startup investments?'

'As the old saying goes, Ms Menon, if you think it's expensive to hire a professional to do the job, wait until you hire an amateur.'

* * *

'So I'll take the call and you listen in. Plan for what you're going to say, here in your notebook, okay?' Gavin tapped the pad on the desk and smiled at the young Singaporean perched beside him. 'I'll greet the caller, get their name, find out what they want to know, put them on hold and transfer the call to you. Then I'll listen in so I can see how you're doing. Ready?'

'Will this be another live call?'

'You've already handled some live calls?' Gavin raised an eyebrow.

'Yes, earlier in the week. Mr Carlisle said the customer service department was falling behind, so he pulled a couple of us in to help out for a few hours.'

'He did, did he? That's interesting. What sort of calls did he get you to handle?'

'Mainly complaints. He wanted us to make sure that dissatisfied customers didn't post anything negative online. It's bad for metrics.'

'Did he give you any training before putting you on live calls?'

'Mr Carlisle said the live calls were our training.'

'Really? Okay, well, at least you've got some experience under your belt. What were the complaints about?'
'My first call was a gentleman who spent a week in Italy as a designer with Maserati.'

'That sounds cool. What was his beef?'

'He said he spent all his time in meetings, arguing with accountants over the leather stitching on a new handbrake lever.'

'Well, I guess that's the job,' said Gavin.

'Yes, but at the end of the week, someone from engineering informed him that the new Maserati model he was working on would be getting an automatic braking system. No more handbrake lever.'

'I can see how that would be disappointing.'

'He was also upset he didn't get to have sex with the designer's partner.'

'Was he promised that as part of the deal?'

'It was listed as an option on the rental profile, but the designer was actually a woman, with a husband. The renter was a man, so there was some confusion and disappointment in that regard.'

'I'll bet. Looks like we need to tighten up our profile templates,' Gavin made a note in his Moleskine. 'So how did you solve his complaint?'

'I gave him a discount voucher,' Melvin nodded. 'Fifty per cent off his next ShelfLife rental.'

'What? Fifty per cent? How would we make a profit on that?'

'I'm not sure,' Melvin looked around. 'That's what Mr Carlisle told us to do. Fifty per cent if they promised not to complain. Should I have offered more?'

'Leave that with me but for now, no more discounts, okay?' Gavin closed his notebook and turned to the call routing interface on the screen in front of them. 'All right, headsets on and we'll grab the next call from the general enquiries queue. This one's from Korea, which is in a similar time zone. Here we go.'

Gavin pulled the mic of his headset closer and accepted the call.

'Hello this is ShelfLife, you're speaking with Gavin, how can I help you?' he smiled as he spoke.

'Yes, I want to list my life as rental on your website. I am not sure what category I should be in,' the voice on the line spoke in halting English.

'Okay, no problem, can you tell me a little bit about your life? Let's start with your name.'

'Yes, it Kuen Ho here and I am Olympian. I have bronze medal in fencing.'

'Congratulations Kuen Ho, that's very exciting,' said Gavin, giving Melvin a thumbs-up.

'No, it's not exciting. I give speeches to school kids and tell them they can be anything if they work hard. They touch my medal then they stab me with their wooden rulers. I want to shout at them but I cannot. I need a break, but my contract says I have to visit every school at least three times this year. Your website does not have category for Olympian, why is that?'

'You are right, Kuen Ho, we don't have that as a separate category, but we absolutely can help you,' Gavin nodded as Melvin scribbled notes. 'We'd love to have you list your life with us for rental.'

'But *how*? You don't have Olympian category?' Kuen Ho sounded agitated.

'For exceptional people like yourself, we recommend the category of Sporting Heroes. How does that sound, Kuen Ho? You're a sporting hero, aren't you?' Gavin gave Melvin a wink as he scrolled through the active web log.

'That is correct. I am hero to all of North Korea.'

Gavin paused and stared at Melvin, who shrugged.

'Fabulous, Kuen Ho. Let me transfer you to one of our Sporting Heroes support crew and he'll get you listed on ShelfLife in no time. Thank you for holding.' Gavin clicked to hold the call and swung the mic clear of his mouth. 'Wow, Melvin, this is a first. You think you can handle this one?'

'Are you sure we can send people to North Korea?'

'That's a great question, Melvin, and one that we will have to address, but for now, I want you to talk Kuen Ho through the process and get him signed up.' Gavin tapped

Melvin's monitor. 'Pull up your sign up script and just walk him through it. Okay, here we go.'

Gavin transferred the call and gave Melvin another thumbs-up.

* * *

'Ping's right, you know,' Shanti folded her arms and took a step back from the full-length window. 'This whole thing stinks.'

'Maybe, but these marketing douchelords are paying a stellar day rate to rent her fleet of drones,' said Trent, placing his hands behind his back and balancing against the window with his forehead. 'Rotronica are making their entire quarterly forecast with this job.'

The two founders stood at the window, high above the city streets, looking down onto the unfinished roof of the office tower under construction next door. It had been growing at the rate of three floors per week and was now only about a hundred feet shy of the incubator floor.

'I didn't think profits were Ping's major motivation for Rotronica?' said Shanti.

'Technically, no. But she still has to hit her numbers if she wants to stay part of this incubator program,' said Trent.

'There's no way they're letting Rotronica go anywhere, Trent. The commercial applications for their neural control network alone are huge. Even Charles is sniffing around trying to grab a slice.'

'Charles is making sure there's an economic engine underpinning her business model. You couldn't scale this thing if you were relying on the backing of the big not-for-profits. The lobbying alone would suck up all your time,'

Trent adjusted his cuffs. 'Look, this soft drink thing is not ideal, but it's an opportunity. Ping's smart enough to turn it to her advantage over the long run. If it makes you feel better, the fees from this stunt will cover the vaccines and retrovirals she needs for the field trial she has planned. Not to mention the fuel for the drones.'

'Aren't they supposed to be solar?'

'The prototypes are rechargeable li-ion. But when she scales up for production some of the fleet will have to use fossils for the heavy lifting. Okay, here they come.' Trent pointed out the window where dozens of construction workers in bright yellow hard hats laboured on the exposed topmost floor of the unfinished building opposite.

'I can't watch this,' Shanti mumbled, but made no effort to move away from the window.

A small knot of well-dressed people in red hard hats crouched behind a stack of empty pallets on a corner of the roof, out of sight of the workers in yellow hats. One of the red hats yelled into a megaphone, while another trained a video camera on the construction workers.

A fleet of half a dozen drones swept in from the south, almost level with Trent and Shanti's eyeline. The drones halted in unison and began their short descent to the workers, small red boxes dangling beneath their spider-like frames. The workers cowered, taking half steps backwards as the drones came closer. A man in a red hat started yelling into a megaphone. The men in yellow hats began waving tentatively at the drones.

'Let me get this straight,' Shanti started in.

'Yes, yes, we see the unironic power imbalance of the signifier and the sign. The symbol of white western imperial power controlling brown-skinned people through fear and desire, something hegemony, something something, liberal arts dissertation. Did I get that right?'

'You're such a shit sometimes, Trent, you know?' Shanti narrowed her eyes. 'But I'm not the first person to tell you that, am I?'

'No, my dear, you are not. But for what it's worth, I happen to agree with you.'

'That you're a shit?'

'Funny,' Trent grimaced. 'No, I agree that this drone stunt is appalling. Whoever suggested that a western corporation should drop carbonated sugar water onto poor, immigrant labourers thirty storeys in the air via unmanned helicopter drones and call it a *friendship delivery* is completely retarded.'

'You don't use the word *retarded* when you're giving press interviews, do you Trent?'

'Nope. I'm careful to be politically incorrect only when amongst friends.' Trent smiled and turned back to the window. The drones deposited the boxes onto the unfinished floor of the skyscraper and ascended again, hovering level with Trent and Shanti once more. The men in red hats gestured for the construction workers to open the boxes and remove the cans of drink. More megaphone shouting. The construction workers turned towards the drones, held their cans aloft and waved cautiously.

'What's going on?' Gavin joined them by the window.

'We're watching Ping's fleet of drones,' said Trent. 'She hired them to an ad agency who are using them to drop free sodas on the immigrant labourers who've been building that new office tower across the road.'

'That's the most retarded thing I've seen since I got here,' said Gavin, pulling out his phone to take photos.

'Dude, we talked about this. You cannot say *retarded*,' Trent warned, winking at Shanti. 'Where have you been, man? I haven't seen you the last couple of days.'

'Maybe that's because you were in Bangkok?' said Gavin.

'Jakarta. And yes, I did bag us a whole bunch of press while I was there. So when you see the traffic spike from Indonesia, you'll know who to thank,' Trent took a small bow. 'I spent some time with your latest batch of newbies before I left. How are they settling in?'

'Pretty good. Except for the part where you borrowed them to handle customer complaints and told them to give away massive discounts on our product,' Gavin folded his arms.

'What? I'm in trouble for finding a solution to our complaint backlog? Are you kidding me?'

'At what price? At fifty per cent discount, we'll actually be paying our customers to rent lives,' said Gavin.

'Relax, man. I stole the idea from Shanti's pinhead Swedes who used the same technique at Opod. By the time most of theses complainers get around to choosing another life they like, arranging the time off and getting the money together, the discount has expired. The voucher is only good for sixty days,' Trent put his hand up for a high five. Gavin exhaled, held his notebook up and let Trent slap it. Shanti rolled her eyes.

'Well, I hope none of our complainers has their heart set on becoming an Olympic fencer,' said Gavin. 'Because I just signed one up, if you can believe that.'

'So? Don't we already have a whole bunch of sports stars?' Shanti turned from the window and shrugged. 'They all seem to want to get out of the school tours and receiving keys to cities they have no intention of visiting again. What's so special about this guy?'

'He's from North Korea.'

'Shut. Up,' said Trent grabbing Gavin by the arm and shaking it. 'That is freaking amazing! We absolutely have to have that life on our site. Please tell me you signed him up yourself?'

'I oversaw one of the trainees do it, but he was fine.'

'That life will never work,' said Shanti. 'The logistics alone would be a nightmare. And what if a North Korean official found out their hero was a fake for a week?'

'The guy reckons the government Photoshops all 'national hero' publicity shots to make them look more like the Dear Leader. No-one really expects any of the heroes to look like their propaganda photos. Our fencing guy swaps roles with his handler all the time, just for laughs. Anyone Korean would probably pass.'

'There's no way we'll get our renters into Pyongyang,' said Shanti.

'Way ahead of you. Found three different travel companies that specialise in arranging tours to the hermit kingdom,' said Gavin.

'See if any of these tour companies would be interested in putting a package together with our Kim Jong Rapier,' said Trent, rubbing his hands together.

'Way ahead of you, too. Already got my trainee onto it,' said Gavin with a grin.

'See, that's what I'm talking about, Shanti. Finding an opportunity and working it until it comes round to your advantage,' Trent placed his hands on his hips. 'I need you to stop looking for problems and start finding solutions.'

'That's awesome management advice, Trent.' Shanti turned back to the window. 'You should get that typeset in all caps under a stock photo of an eagle. Frame it, hang it in the conference room.'

'I just might. How are your latest newbies working out, Shanti? Got them through training?' An edge had crept into Trent's voice.

'I sent four of them back, but I'm keeping the other eight. They can code okay, but they need a lot of direction. I wouldn't hire them if I was paying actual cash for them.' Shanti watched the workers on the unfinished tower drink cola and wave at the drones. 'Which reminds me, do you know how much that egghead economics professor wanted to get paid for the privilege of grinding our rentals approval process into the dirt?'

'You met with him? How did it go?' Trent turned from the window.

'He asked me to marry him.'

'Shut up,' said Trent.

'Guy's so desperate to stay in Singapore, he'll marry anyone with an employment pass,' Shanti wrinkled her nose. 'Why did you think it would be a good idea to ask him to work with us?'

'I didn't,' said Trent. 'It was Charles' suggestion. He wants us to show the investors we take risk mitigation seriously.'

'Well ask him if he wants us to take it this seriously.' She handed him the note Jensen had scribbled in the café.

'Holy shit. Is this his asking salary?'

'He says that's what he's paid to consult for the investment co-op.'

'I think that matching algo you were talking about will do us just fine for the moment,' said Trent, crumpling the note into a ball and flinging it towards a wastepaper basket.

'Check it out, the ad guys are taking the unopened cans and branded chiller boxes back from the construction workers,' said Gavin, pointing out the window 'They're taking back the yellow hard hats as well. That's pretty cold.'

Low-key sobbing broke out from the sofa area near the middle of the office. The three founders turned as one to see Ping, face in hands, shoulders shaking.

'I know what that's like,' Trent let out a long sigh. 'You start out just wanting to help people, but it's so hard to stay on track. You make so many compromises along the way, you can end up pretty lost.'

'What on earth are you talking about, Trent?' said Gavin pocketing his phone. 'When were you planning on saving the world?'

'He's romanticising his eighteen months of med school again,' Shanti folded her arms.

'Almost two full years. Transcripts to prove it,' Trent shot back. 'And Gav, don't tag Ping or Rotronica if you post any pictures of this stunt, OK? That wouldn't help anything right now.'

'If you're serious about getting back into the helping business,' Shanti nodded towards the sniffling, 'I think Ping could use some of that world-famous Carlisle cheerleading right about now.'

Trent was already walking, arms held wide as he approached Ping. She looked up briefly before slumping into Trent's embrace.

'You haven't been at the apartment much,' Gavin stepped closer to Shanti. 'Is everything all right in code-land?'

'Yeah, fine. Busy training all the staff the investors sent us. Lots of late nights, I guess,' Shanti took out her phone and started to scroll through her messages. 'There's a gym in the bottom of the building. Showers are nice. Food court across the road. Sometimes it's not worth going home just to turn around and come back to the office again.'

'You know what they say, all work and no play…'

'Makes for a resilient commerce platform with zero latency that's practically impervious to identity theft and DDOS attacks,' Shanti put her hands on her hips and raised her chin. 'That's how the saying goes, isn't it?'

'Yeah, OK. Just saying I haven't seen you much, lately,' Gavin thrust his hands in his pockets. 'Wonder if you're all right, that's all.'

'Don't take it personally, Gavin,' Shanti placed a hand on his upper arm and looked into his eyes. 'I'm just focused, okay? My uncle is getting very suspicious. I can't keep making up stories about why my German employers have transferred me to Singapore. He's going to want me back home and working or I'm going to have to send him some serious coin soon. In case you hadn't noticed, we're still not on salaries, yet.'

Gavin looked down at his arm and back to Shanti. She realised she had been rubbing his bicep and withdrew her hand like it had been bitten. She looked around for a diversion.

'Look at our fearless leader,' said Shanti, pointing to where Trent was holding Ping on a sofa, rocking her back and forth. 'Just when you think he's all Mr Hardcase-startup-billionaire-boys'-club, he does something nice for someone. The way Ping is starting to talk about him, he might be in danger of acquiring an actual girlfriend.'

'He does seem to have a knack for making people feel good about themselves, doesn't he?' said Gavin, jabbing the carpet with the toe of his sneaker.

'That's one of the first things I noticed about him in London,' said Shanti. 'Funny thing is, I don't think he even realises it sometimes.'

Gavin let out a low sigh and rubbed his upper arm. 'A lot of people don't realise how they make other people feel.'

Shanti went to say something, but Gavin had wandered off to his workstation, hands thrust deep in pockets.

'Such a child sometimes,' she muttered to herself.

'My word, did you all see that?' Charles boomed across the office, holding a drone aloft as he played pied piper to a trail of technicians and coders, wilted yet elated. 'That shit, as the kids are fond of saying, is about to go viral. Where's my girl?'

Trent leapt to his feet and intercepted Charles with a high five, giving Ping a moment to compose herself. 'Were you up on that unfinished roof in the heat, you crazy Englishman?'

'Ha! Me? Up there? Come off it, matey,' Charles threw the drone on to the coffee table. 'No, I stayed at ground zero with the Veep of Marketing. Might have just booked another project without those agency muppets taking their cut. Hello, darling. Congratulations, eh?'

Ping offered her hand but Charles grabbed her by the shoulders and kissed her on her forehead.

'Don't forget Tran and his team,' Trent interrupted. 'Perfect formation flying, guys. Very impressive.' He put his hands together and got a round of applause going across the floor. Charles waded into the limelight, high-fiving anyone within reach. Trent turned to see Ping mouth a 'thank you' as she melted away to the back of the crowd.

Technicians started detaching cameras and reviewing footage as they slurped sodas and compared notes.

'He looks bloody terrified, eh?' Charles stood behind a video editor, laughing at the footage of a construction worker smiling and waving nervously at the camera. 'Let's not use that shot in the promo video.'

Trent felt his phone vibrate and moved to a quiet corner of the office floor, pleased to get away from the crowd for a moment. He checked the screen, took a breath and swiped to answer.

'Hey, you must be psychic,' said Trent perching on the edge of an empty desk with a view of the harbour. 'I was just thinking about you.'

'Hello, son. Have I caught you at a bad time?'

'Always have time for you, Dad.'

'If only that were true, Trent. Been trying to reach you these last couple of weeks, had almost given up.'

'I know, Dad, it's just with the time difference and my travel schedule and all the demands of work, I don't even have time for myself anymore,' Trent ran a hand through his hair. 'But that's no excuse, what's up?'

'I'm not supposed to tell you this, Trent, but your mother is not happy that you disposed of your Vandten shares.'

'Appreciate the concern, Dad, but this is old news. She had one of her assistants harass me about it weeks ago when I lodged the paperwork with my broker. Anyway, didn't you tell me to go out in the world and build something for myself? You should be happy for me.'

'Yes, well, I did say something like that, but never intended for you to trade out of the family company. There have been some serious ramifications, I'm afraid. Your mother believes you deliberately sold your parcel to the Onslens. She thinks you're trying to destabilise the ownership structure.'

'Who the hell are the Onslens?'

'I can't really give you any more details. If Susan's counsel finds out I've been talking to you, they could implicate me as well. As far as anyone knows, this was just a friendly father and son chat, checking in to see how you're faring in Malaysia.'

'Singapore, Dad. And I'm doing incredibly well, thanks for asking,' said Trent, getting to his feet. 'Our company is really taking off. Investors are very happy, they've moved us into the top floor of the incubator, we've got about fifty staff, a couple of senior consultants, almost a hundred thousand registered users. It's really exciting, Dad. And I built it all myself.'

James Carlisle sighed into the phone. 'I am proud of you, Trent. I just wish you hadn't used the company money to do it. It's causing problems for all of us.'

'Do you have any idea what it takes to scale up a business from nothing? How else was I supposed to build it?'

'Why didn't you ask us first? We could have arranged an investment loan. I would have given you some money myself.'

'I *did* come to ask you guys for an investment.' Trent started pacing by the window. 'But you know what happened before the meeting even got started? I got fired, Dad. By that fucking slimeball, Jeffrey Small. Then I got thrown out of my apartment. And then he threatened me with criminal charges.'

'Trent, look, I'm sorry but your mother –'

'He threatened to throw me out of the family, Dad. Did Susan tell you that part? He figured he'd already pushed one Carlisle out of the picture, might as well dispose of another one, right?'

There was no answer.

Trent stopped pacing and listened. He could hear his father's breathing, as if he was labouring against a weight that wouldn't budge.

'Dad? Look, I'm sorry, I shouldn't have said that. I was angry at Jeffrey. And at Mom. How she's treating you.'

'I have to go now, Trent.'

'Dad, no, wait.'

'Good luck with everything.'

The line fell silent and Trent clutched the phone as if he were about to snap it. He turned to find a slender girl holding an open folder and wearing a headset.

'So sorry, Mr Carlisle, but I have a message from Mr Archer-Ellis for you,' she handed him a post-it.

It read: *Boardroom in 10 minutes. We have to deal with Mr King.*

'Did he say who this Mr King is?'

'He just said that it was a customer feedback issue,' she closed her folder. 'Something to do with the original Berlin Twofer.'

Trent jogged back to the ShelfLife pod on the far side of the floor to find Gavin wearing his oversized red headphones, and Shanti explaining something to one of her team of young Singaporean coders. He waved his arms in the air to get his co-founders' attention.

'Guys. Is there something I should know about the Berlin Twofer?' Trent glanced at his watch, then back at the meeting room. 'Is that significant in some way?'

'Not to me,' shrugged Gavin, holding his headphones out from his ears.

'C'mon, guys. Charles summoned me into a meeting with some guy called King. Does that mean something?'

'If you're referring to Matt King, the husband of the American woman we sent to Berlin to play dominatrix for a week who came home and set up her own dungeon, then accidentally took some skin off a judge's nutsack and just got deported, then yeah, it probably means something.' Shanti spun her monitor around so Trent could scan the news report. His brows migrated from furrowed to raised and his head started shaking from side to side.

'We did this?' asked Trent as he scrolled through the comments section. It seethed with moral outrage, pious indignation and barely concealed jealousy.

'We haven't been named yet, but it's only a matter of time,' said Shanti.

The sounds of heated argument erupted from the boardroom. The meerkats of the floor rose in unison.

Trent ran along the row of desks, wondering if this was another management test Charles had set for him. If so, Trent was determined to pass. He paused to knock on the door of the boardroom. It flew open and a well-built man in a dark blue suit walked out backwards, yelling, almost banging into Trent.

'Your little startup fuckheads are going to pay for this bullshit, Chuck!'

'Is there something I might be able to help you with?' ventured Trent.

The man whipped around, coming nose to nose with Trent, looking to continue the fight. 'And who the fuck are you?'

Trent held the man's gaze. The office fell silent. Everyone pretended to be absorbed in their work.

'Ah, Trent, glad you could join us.' Charles ambled out of the boardroom, rolling up his sleeves in an exaggerated display of nonchalance. 'It looks like you have another satisfied customer on your hands.'

'I'm pretty fucking far from satisfied right now.' The man's gaze didn't leave Trent's.

'I was referring to Lisa,' Charles snorted.

The man grimaced and closed his eyes, before turning to face Charles. 'One more wisecrack from you and I swear I am going to –'

'Going to what, Matt? Take a swing at me?' Charles gestured around the floor. 'In an office full of people? In the middle of clean-living, law-abiding Singapore? Are you looking to get deported as well?'

The man took a step towards Charles.

Trent moved forward to place a hand on Matt's shoulder, 'I'm sure we can sort out this misunderstanding, Mr King.'

'Take your hand off me, son. You're about to make things a lot worse.'

Trent removed his hand and placed it in the air.

'Don't be afraid of this pillock, Trent,' Charles sneered. 'He's not going to make anything worse. Except for himself.'

'Your dirty little website is wrecking people's lives.' Matt thrust his thumb into his own chest. 'I might lose my job. My wife's about to be deported. The kids are freaking out.'

'Why don't we take a seat? I'll call my co-founders in and we can find a solution together.'

'I'm not interested in talking to you or to your fucking co-founders. Once the cops find out Lisa got the whole idea from one of your life-swap holidays, they're going to shut you down so fast you'll barely have time to catch a cab to Changi.'

'The Singapore government is actually a backer of our not-so-little company, Matt,' Charles folded his arms and rested them on his paunch. 'They're very excited by the number of people coming to our site wanting to change their lives. Though maybe not as dramatically as that little whip-cracker did.'

'For fuck's sake, Charles, that's my wife you're talking about.'

'Oh come on, Matt. You're not going to play the protective husband now, are you? You seemed pretty comfortable with the replacement wife the team arranged for you while Lisa was away.'

Matt balled his fists but let them drop. He turned back to Trent. 'Watch out for this guy. He only knows how to win by making other people lose. Ask anyone who knows him. Been doing it since forever.'

Matt shook his head and walked out of the office. The muffled ding of the elevator rolled through the office, sending dozens of bespectacled faces back to their screens and keyboards.

'And that, my friend, is how you deal with whingers. Now, let's go for a drink, shall we?'

'Fucking hell, Charles, this could look pretty bad for us. The story's all over the local chat boards,' said Trent just as Shanti and Gavin joined them. 'Have we been named in any of the media reports?'

'Nothing so far,' said Shanti.

'We need to fix that,' Charles straightened his sleeves. 'If we wait for the real journalists to find us, the story might blow over.'

'Hang on, you *want* us to be associated with this mess?' asked Trent, eyes widening.

'Now's not the time to play coy, Trent. Your investors are looking for scale. Oh, and they also want some changes to the management structure, get some more oversight and risk mitigation in place,' Charles turned to Shanti. 'Did you have a chat to that economics professor? What did you think? Is he ShelfLife material?'

'Not even remotely. He has no idea how our business runs. Wanted to vet every life rental manually. There's no way it could work,' said Shanti.

'I'm sure you'll figure out a way to get him up to speed. Besides, it's just for a few months. Put on a good show for the investors, make them think we know what we're doing. When can he start?'

'Wait a minute, Charles. You're asking us to dive headfirst into a PR nightmare while also tightening our risk management profile? How's that going to work?'

'I don't see how the two are mutually exclusive, Trent,' Charles raised an eyebrow. 'If you have doubts about your own capabilities, maybe we need to make some more significant management changes?'

'I assure you it's not a problem, Charles. I can manage the publicity,' Trent raised his chin and straightened his jacket. 'But I don't think the prof is the answer to the risk issues. He's on a massive salary package as an investment consultant to the co-op. Our cashflow can't support a hire of that magnitude.'

'Don't worry about any of that, it's all covered by their investment stake in ShelfLife. Just like all the designers and support staff we sent Gavin, and the little army of coders Shanti keeps chained to their desks. They'll throw the professor in as well.'

'He said his contract isn't being renewed,' said Shanti.

'Is that so?' Charles cocked his head, as if listening for something in the wind. 'Well, then, if he's being cut loose, it seems unwise for us to lash him to our mast.'

'I thought you recommended him?' said Shanti.

'There's no way that twerp is getting even a penny of our actual cash,' said Charles. 'Never mind. I'll stay on the hunt for someone to provide some semblance of oversight. Someone the investors can believe in.'

'We have an algorithm in place. It's built on machine learning so it improves every time it evaluates a match. With the heavy traffic that's coming to the site, the accuracy is constantly improving.'

'Yes, well, your hacker tricks are all well and good, Shanti, but we need something more visible. The investors aren't the sharpest tools in the shed, they only understand what they can see,' Charles adjusted his belt as he spoke. 'The professor is hardly unique. I should be able to find another filth like him, kicking around for cents on the dollar.'

'For the record, I never said he was rude or dirty,' said Shanti. 'Just arrogant.'

'No, love, I said FILTH. As in the acronym: Failed In London Try Hong Kong,' Charles gave the group a wink. 'Asia's full of western expats swanning around like they're king shit, but if you got them back home in London or New York they'd be lucky to be tending bar. Whenever there's a recession back home we get another wave of them coming out to the Orient to try their luck. Especially in all the "hot air" businesses. Commercial real estate, advertising, banking, that sort of thing.'

'VC consulting?' Shanti arched an eyebrow.

'Watch yourself, young lady. You're only half as clever as you think you are,' Charles waggled a meaty forefinger at her. 'Now, why don't you get one of the new hires to post something about our dominatrix friend up on that "good neighbour" gossip site, eh? Me and the boys need to work out a strategy to leverage this press coverage into something useful.'

Shanti's mouth fell open, but Trent cautioned her not to continue.

'Right then lads, let's get to the Elbow Room. Happy hour's almost started, eh?' Charles announced as he swaggered towards the lifts.

'I can't fucking believe this,' spat Shanti.

'I know, he can be a bit of a dick sometimes. I'll have a talk with him, get him to tone it down.'

'A bit!' Shanti almost shouted. 'Forgetting his nineteen fifties division of labour for just a second, this dominatrix thing is going to blow up. And not in a good way. I think we should put a lid on it. Gavin, back me up here.'

Gavin took his cap off and scratched his head with the brim, weighing up his options.

'For fuck's sake, Gav. Do you always need someone to tell you what to think?' Shanti snapped.

Gavin's expression hardened and he exhaled through his nose. Trent took the rising tension as his cue to step in.

'Come on guys, this isn't solving anything. Besides, I'm not sure there is a problem here,' said Trent. 'Think of it as an opportunity. One that we can capitalise on.'

'*Seriously?*' demanded Shanti.

'I don't think we're exposed here. Charles doesn't consider this Matt guy to be a significant risk and he's asked us to work out how best to leverage this thing. I don't want him thinking we don't have the leadership skills to pull this off.'

'Sound like you're worried Charles will think *you* don't have the skills,' Shanti put her hands to her hips. 'Have you considered that Charles is getting us to handle this so we take the blame if it all goes wrong?'

'I don't think that's the game he's playing, Shanti. Charles is on our team.'

'At least let's take Lisa's review and Gretchen's dominatrix profile down off the site for a while, okay?' said Shanti.

'That's what I'm looking for. You're making suggestions, you're coming up with ideas, you're being constructive in your criticism.' Trent looked to his other partner. 'Gavin, can you build on Shanti's concept?'

'Concept? Running away is a concept now?' Gavin folded his arms and threw his shoulders back. He challenged Shanti with a sideways glare. 'I didn't come this far to stay on the sidelines. If the investors want scale, I say we give them what they want.'

'Are you saying that just because I'm against it?' asked Shanti.

Trent raised his palms. 'Okay, let's stay focused. We have a majority of management here who want to stir the pot, so let's stir the pot.'

'It's a bad idea,' said Shanti, but it was more complaint than protest.

'Noted. I'll talk to Charles, see if I can find out more about these management changes our investors want. Who's coming?'

Now it was Shanti's turn to fold her arms in protest.

'I'll take that as a no. Gav?'

'Sounds good to me,' Gavin looked at Shanti, who glared back. 'What?'

'I need those designs for the customer save pages.'

'I did them this morning, they're on the server.'

'I can't find them,' said Shanti. 'Trent, can you give me five minutes with Gavin? I promise I'll be quick, then he can join your secret little boys' club meeting.'

'Thank you, Shanti. I appreciate your support,' Trent was already heading for the exit. 'Elbow Room. Cecil Street. OK, Gav?'

'Sure,' he turned to Shanti. 'Do we have to do this right now?'

Shanti watched Trent disappear into the lifts, then grabbed Gavin by the wrist and led him to a quiet corner of the floor.

'I don't care about the designs, Gavin. I'm worried about Trent. Charles is playing some sort of game here and Trent is just going along with everything he says.'

'Why wouldn't we? He got us this far. He found the investors. Put us in the incubator. He's just trying to help us grow ShelfLife, right?'

'Haven't you been paying attention to any of the meetings?'

'Yeah, I have. We've got work to do on our revenue burn and the mezzanine cashflow looks tight, but otherwise the indicators are, y'know, indicating in the right direction. Aren't they?'

Shanti reached up and placed a palm on his cheek. 'Oh my god, you're so adorable when you speak business language.'

Gavin's heart leapt. 'Am I?'

Shanti lifted her palm and struck him smartly on the face. 'No.'

'Fuck. That hurt, Shanti.' Gavin rubbed his cheek as it reddened, only partly from the impact. 'Why'd you do that?'

'Because you can't see what's going on here. I'm working my butt off, Trent's in ego-stroke la-la-land with all these keynote speaking gigs and pressers and parties and nightclubs that Charles is sending him to. Have you seen what his latest round of dilutions has done to our shareholding?'

'I think I saw the email,' said Gavin.

'Our shares are down to ten per cent.'

'But we aren't even listed, yet. How can they be down that far?'

'Not the value, you idiot, our stake. You and I now own ten percent of ShelfLife, each. Trent's down to thirty and now Charles is sitting at twenty.'

'Who's got the rest?

'I didn't recognise the name, but it's probably a holding company the Singapore government is using to fund the co-op that runs the incubator. All the stuff happening here, the neural net drones, the fractional ownership of domestic workers, our life rental platform, we're all too experimental for them to be involved directly. So they hide their investment behind a stack of shelf companies, funds and incubator co-ops,' Shanti looked around to make sure no-one was nearby. 'Point is, when you put Charles and this government holding company together, they have the controlling stake in ShelfLife.'

'How did that happen?'

'Trent's been trading points for all this space, all these people, the servers, the bandwidth, our apartment, all of it. So we've been steadily selling out to another partner, but their investment has not been in cash.'

'You could say the same for us, I suppose,' said Gavin. 'We didn't put in any cash for our stake.'

'Yes, but we're devoted to this thing full-time. Charles has got his fingers in almost every startup in Vertica. I'll bet he's also taking a commission from the Singaporeans for every deal he brings to them.'

'Look, Shanti, are you sure you're not just being paranoid? Trent keeps talking about how good this deal is, how he's such a good negotiator,' Gavin said. 'He told me that we'll always have a majority, as long as we stick together.'

'I think Trent's math assumes that Charles is on our side. By my calculations, that fat fuck is only in it for himself.' She tapped Gavin on the forehead. 'Or can you not see that? Are you stoned or something?'

'What? No. Are you kidding?' Gavin pushed her finger away from his face. 'In Singapore? You can't even find that stuff here.'

Shanti rolled her eyes. 'Jesus, Gavin, wake the fuck up. Charles' friends have been passing around pills every time we've been out with them. I'm sure Trent has been getting on the party train with those guys on a regular basis.'

'Why didn't I get offered any?' Gavin's pitch rose with indignation.

'Maybe they think you're already dopey enough,' she crossed her arms.

Gavin crumpled like an umbrella pointed the wrong way into a monsoon.

'I'm sorry, Gavin,' said Shanti as she reached for his shoulder. 'They never offer any to me, either. They don't talk to me that much at all. It's like they're trying to lure Trent away, isolate him from us.'

'What does Trent say?'

'I haven't asked him. You're the only person I can talk to about it.'

Gavin saw the worry in her eyes. Mainly, he just saw her eyes. They made him think of Austin.

'What about your chakra chick back on Bali? I thought you told her everything.'

'I had to cut her loose.'

'How'd she take that?'

'Amber? She's a little intense. Doesn't cope well with separation.'

'Who does?'

Shanti stared at him a while as if making a decision. 'Maybe you're right. Maybe I'm being paranoid. But I can't help feeling something's going on. It's different from when we started out.'

'You wanted it that way, remember.'

'For god's sake, Gavin, not every conversation we have is about us, OK? I like you, and we enjoy each other's company but we don't have time for anything more. We've got to focus. We need to talk about the business.'

'I don't want to talk about the business,' Gavin thrust his hands in his pockets and looked out the window. 'I want to know when we can talk about us.'

'You make it sound so dramatic,' Shanti let out a sigh and ran her hand through her hair. 'Now's not the best time.'

'When is the best time?'

'Gavin, just. Urgh.' Her eyes moistened. 'I think you should go now.'

'Yeah,' Gavin looked around the floor, avoiding eye contact. 'I reckon that's what I should do, too.'

* * *

Trent was standing on the pavement waving frantically at cabs as they sailed past.

'Why is it that in every city in the world all the cabs change drivers at exactly the same time?' he ranted as Gavin appeared. 'I don't get it. No wonder the taxi industry is getting the shit disrupted out of it. Kind of like what we're going to do to everybody's humdrum little lives.'

'I don't know what's Shanti's problem, man. She's not really getting with the program,' said Gavin.

'It's like people have just been stuck in the same groove for years and we're going to give the turntable a bit of nudge,' Trent checked his watch. 'It's our job to change up the song for them, let them hear some new music. C'mon, let's walk.'

Gavin had to trot to keep pace with Trent.

'She hasn't even been going back to her apartment. She just works all the time or goes to the gym.' Gavin tugged his t-shirt from his torso, trying to generate some airflow. 'It's like she's not even part of the team anymore.'

The lights ahead changed to red and the two stood at the edge of the road as the cars surged past. The crowd swelled around them, impatient for the green man.

'I don't even know where she's going with the code anymore. She just sends me the specs and says "design this page" or "change this dialogue box"' or whatever. It's not really collaboration.' Gavin kept tapping the button to activate the pedestrian crossing.

'Dude, can you not?' snapped Trent.

Gavin froze. 'Sorry, Trent. I was just pressing the button to cross.'

'You were whining incessantly about Shanti is what you were doing,' said Trent. 'Seriously, I've got Ping guilt-tripping over the soda stunt, a mountain of pressure from the investors and Charles with his never-ending dick-swinging competitions. Not to mention all the lawyers popping up everywhere. Now you want me to play counsellor to a high-school romance that doesn't even exist?'

The lights changed and the pedestrians swarmed onto the bitumen carrying Trent and Gavin with them. They reached the other side and stood in the shade of a department store entrance.

'I was just making an observation. About the team dynamics,' offered Gavin.

'Don't waste your time on that stuff. She's not interested right now and I can't afford you to be obsessed with it. Where is this stupid bar?'

'Just down there,' Gavin pointed along the street. 'You go ahead. I'll catch up with you. Got to run a couple of errands first.'

'Fine. But I'm serious, Gavin. Work out what's important to you right now and focus on that. This is a critical time for the business. This is where we go big or we go home.'

'You should lay off the management podcasts for a while, Trent. They're making you sound like Charles.' Gavin pulled his cap down and walked back across the street.

Trent shook his head. He always suspected Gavin might be the weak link in the machine. He'd relied on Shanti to keep Gavin on track. It had worked so far. Now that the pressure was on, maybe it was time to look for a new Head of User Experience for ShelfLife. He'd ask Charles on the best way to unwind the shareholding, if it came to that.

* * *

'I tell you, Trent, I was slightly disappointed with the performance back there,' Charles leaned on a bar table, surrounded by pints. He turned to the circle of bankers in braces. 'Bit of an anticlimax with Matty King in our offices earlier today. I got him all revved up and firing and handed him over to our boy here, but Trent couldn't get him to take a swing. Not like the old days when he was with Barclays.'

'He's gone soft in his middle age is what,' offered a marinated banker.

'Our boy Trent here went all pacifist is what happened,' Charles collected a shot from the table and downed it. 'In case you missed it, that was your moment to flex some muscle, Trent. Hope you won't make the same mistake twice.'

Trent was stung by Charles' assessment and caught a couple of down-the-nose looks from the crowd. It reminded him of a schoolyard. He cleared his throat and mentally arranged some tough-talking of his own. A buzzing sensation in his pocket caught Trent's attention. This was a call he'd been expecting and dreading in equal measures. He went to dismiss it, but the put-down from Charles was still ringing in his ears. Mediation is for wimps, he thought. If you don't want someone taking a swing you, give them an uppercut first. Trent walked to the front door to escape the rabble of Charles' entourage and the blaring of the rugby broadcast that flooded the bar. He stabbed the answer key and steeled himself for the contest.

'Susan, so lovely to hear from you. Are you well?'

'If you must know, Trent, I'm feeling a bit under the weather this morning.'

'Sorry to hear that, mother. Hope it's nothing trivial.'

Pause. He knew he should have kept it cordial.

'It sounds like you're in the middle of something there in Saigon. Would you prefer me to call back later?'

It was tempting to take the exit his mother offered, but it would only postpone the fisticuffs.

'I'm just stepping out of a meeting. Now is fine.' Trent pushed out through the heavy doors of the bar and back onto the street. 'How can I help you?'

'The person you most need to help, Trent, is yourself,' his mother started in with more menace this time.

'Well, the Lord helps those who help themselves.' Trent tried to put a little sing-song in his voice, but it wasn't enough to dull the edge.

'Then let me get straight to it. After your misadventure at General Mercy we offered you a deal that was incredibly generous. We have honoured our side of the agreement and there are no charges pending relating to your attempt to practice medicine without a licence, unauthorised entry of a state medical facility or theft of hospital property.'

'What theft?'

'Doctor Robertson's lab coat. As you may recall, we arranged to have all charges dropped.'

'Dropped? They were never lodged in the first place.'

'You sound disappointed, Trent. Would you like me to see if I can have the charges filed now?'

Trent ran his hand through his hair. He'd overextended himself. Stuck on the ropes, taking body blows. Time to find his footing.

'What's this about, mother?'

'Jeffrey informed me that you recently completed the final disposal of your holding in Mediclinical. You appear to want to remove yourself from all family concerns.'

Trent imagined himself bobbing, waiting for the punch to come. He remained silent.

'He's still running a trace on the transaction but he suspects that you have on-sold your parcel to Exencent Equity Partners,' said Susan. 'Is this correct?'

Time to swing.

'As I am no longer a shareholder in Mediclinical, I believe I have no obligation to discuss my transactions, financial or otherwise, with the directors of that company,'

said Trent, imagining himself stepping forward and connecting glove to jaw. 'Is there anything else you wanted to discuss, mother?'

A brief pause, and the flurry began.

'If you've sold out to the Onslens and their conniving little wrecking crew at Exencent, I am going to fly to Vietnam, find you, drag you back to the US and have you up on charges that you haven't even begun to imagine.' Her voice had moved up an octave and gathered pace. 'Do you have any idea what you've done? In fact, I bet you know exactly what you think you're doing to us. But I can tell you something, Trent, you've got as much chance of hurting us as you have of becoming a real doctor. Forget doctor, you couldn't even make it as a pathetic salesman, could you?'

Trent felt the glove land in the ribs and extract some of his air, but willed himself to lean into it. He heard Charles' voice in his head: one to the jaw.

'Mother, the last thing I wanted to do was cause you trouble,' he said, adding a little syrup to his voice.

'Really?' She sounded genuinely shocked.

'That's because you're the last person I want to think *anything* about.' He imagined himself pushing through his shoulder, putting his full bodyweight behind the throw. 'Why do you think everything is all about you, Mother?'

'You're about to cross a very dangerous line, Trent.'

'Is that supposed to scare me, Mother? You already threw me out of the company, remember? Then you threw me out of the apartment. You even had that little fuckhead Jeffrey threaten to throw me out of the family, for chrissakes.'

'That is absolutely not true.'

'Did he forget to mention that part when he was, what do you call it, *debriefing* you?'

'Do you want me to add slander to the list of charges?'

'Are you going to do that before or after you legally disown me?'

'Trent.'

'Do whatever you want, Susan. It's been a long time since I felt I was part of your family anyway. The only people in your family are your board and your management team and your little suck-hole accountant Jeffrey and your little army of yes-men making their sales targets,' he stopped to take a breath. 'You can't throw me out of something I'm not even part of.'

Trent stabbed the end call button, walked in a small circle and hurled the phone at the pavement. He was expecting it to shatter into pieces, but the screen merely cracked. He put his hands to his face and rubbed his eyes, hearing in his mind the sound of the bell and the crowd roaring. His hands felt wet and he realised he was crying.

'What the fuck, man? Who were you yelling at?'

Trent looked up to see Gavin holding the broken phone.

'Nobody. Just a friend. An ex-friend. Doesn't matter,' Trent looked around as a small crowd of onlookers started to disperse. He rubbed his face and straightened up. 'Let's go in and have a drink. No, wait. Charles is in there with a bunch of douchebankers.'

'Worst.'

'You have no idea. Look, I'm sorry about before. I know Shanti has that effect on some people.' Trent stopped to see the worry in Gavin's face. 'I didn't realise she'd really got to you like that. Don't worry, I'll sort it out.'

'Just forget about it, please,' Gavin gave a grimace. 'She's made her mind up. I need to move on, grow up and focus on this business.'

'Good man. That's the spirit,' Trent smiled and offered Gavin a fist bump. 'But we should do your first idea first.'

'What was my first idea?'

'To forget about it. Let's go find another bar.'

Faux-reign correspondent

'That's not sniper fire, is it?' asked Gavin, pushing himself back into the low brick wall.

'Ees not an invitation to dinner,' said the dusty French photographer as he checked the image on the back of his camera. 'OK, I 'ave what I need. You ready?'

Gavin touched each of his pockets in turn, just as Peter had taught him at the handover. His hand made a final stop at the long pocket stitched onto his thigh but he felt nothing more than his own leg. The fifty millimetre Nikkor lens that was supposed to be in the right thigh pocket of Peter's cargo shorts, wasn't. Gavin peered over the low wall and caught a glimpse of the lens, sitting on a window ledge on the other side of the alleyway. Another volley of shots sent Gavin scurrying to the dirt.

'Oh, fuck, man, what did you lose? Which one ees eet?' asked the Frenchman.

'I dunno. I think it's the fifty,' said Gavin, patting his leg again in an attempt to make the lens reappear.

'*Merde!* Peter fucking loves that lens. You 'ave to get eet.'

Another couple of shots caused Gavin to flinch again. 'I'll buy him another one, Henri. Let's just get the fuck out of here, OK?'

'Not OK. You don't understand. He won eet in a poker game, in Rwanda, years ago. Off a girl who refused to sleep with 'im, even though we all believed we would be dead by morning. She claimed the lens belonged to Eddie Adams. Eet was used to cover Vietnam.'

'Did she win it off Eddie Adams in a poker game, too?' asked Gavin, trying to delay the suggestion he knew was almost certainly coming.

'No. She let him fuck her. 'Ere,' said Henri, handing Gavin a lump of broken concrete. 'Throw thees across the street.'

'Why?'

'Just throw eet,' hissed Henri. His shaven head, patchy beard and wild blue eyes did not invite argument.

'Okay. I'm throwing.' Gavin hurled the lump into the street.

'Jesus, you almost hit zee fucking lens!' said Henri, clapping his forehead. He scrabbled in the dirt for another rock. 'Throw again, but throw better this time.'

The second rock skidded through the gravel and was greeted by several rounds of rifle fire.

'As I thought,' said the Frenchman, pulling up the leg of his fatigues and unclipping a pistol from a leather ankle holster. 'Okay, get ready.'

'Get ready for what? What do you mean get ready?' spluttered Gavin. 'You have a gun? Why do you have a gun?'

'We are not supposed to, but seriously, who is checking?' Henri pulled the firing bolt back. 'I give you cover. You run across, grab the lens and go through that door. Fast as you can.'

Gavin looked at Henri, across to the door and then back at Henri, trying to work out if the Frenchman really knew what he was doing, or was just really crazy. Now that guns were involved, Gavin felt it would be better to know before dashing across the street.

Gavin had met Henri in a bar just a few nights earlier in a meeting arranged by Peter, a no-nonsense German who had been documenting hot spots across the globe since the original invasion of Kuwait in 1990. Peter had made it through his twenty-seventh armed conflict and his third wife, a Filipino singer he'd met in Dubai but had not seen for several months. She had recently sent an email demanding either a visit or a divorce and, not wanting to part with half of his remaining assets for a third time, Peter decided to book a flight home to see her. While searching for cheap flights he came across a banner ad asking him if he wanted to take a short break from his own life while getting paid for it. A few clicks later, he had completed a ShelfLife profile and hit the submit button.

Roughly forty-eight hours later, Peter Hasenberg was training Gavin Mills on the basics of being Peter Hasenberg, freelance combat war photographer. The training started with a thorough tour of Peter's lens kit and collection of battered DSLR bodies. Gavin was a skilled amateur, but had never worked with glass longer than 300 millimetres in a hand-held situation, so they spent a couple of hours working on tripod improvisation in the field. The afternoon consisted of a brisk walk that looped through the centre of Antakya, located on the Turkish–Syrian border, where Peter used the landscape to demonstrate both potential vantage points for getting the shot, and potential sniper points from which to get shot at. Over dinner, Peter rolled out a faded map to explain the layout of the town and the current status of the surrounding countryside.

Although subject to change without notice, it was generally accepted that west of the town square was considered civilian territory, where NGOs, a small corps of embedded press and a growing rabble of freelance journalists were allowed to rest and re-fuel between assignments. East of the town square was generally considered the start of the combat zone, although it had been relatively quiet in recent weeks. After dinner, Peter took Gavin to meet with Henri, a fellow freelancer who had agreed to take Gavin under his wing for the week, in return for a split of Peter's ShelfLife earnings. The evening comprised heavy drinking and war stories that led to a chorus of moaning about the complications brought upon their respective lives from their obsession with women.

'We spend our lives in the most dangerous places known to man, but is still safer than being under their spell,' said Peter, raising another glass.

'At least here, we know for sure when we are in trouble,' said Henri before throwing his head back.

'And I guess no-one blames you when you run and hide, right?' said Gavin, wiping the back of his mouth.

The photographers laughed and nodded.

'I think you will be just fine in this life, Gavin Mills,' said Peter, signalling for another round.

Gavin turned out to be a natural at being Peter. Perhaps it was the whiskey, but by the time he put Peter in a cab for the airport the following morning, still drunk, Gavin felt he'd found not only a life he could inhabit for a week, but one he could relate to. His relationship with Henri was more strained. The added pressure of live gunfire wasn't helping.

'OK, so once I get through that door, should I wait for you to come and get me?' asked Gavin, still trying to delay Henri from firing his weapon.

'You really are a fucking tourist, aren't you?' Henri stared at him. 'No, I am not coming to get you. I am staying out 'ere, with the people trying to shoot you, so you can rescue that fucking lens you left behind because you were too stupid to keep it in your pocket.'

Gavin stared back, silently willing the people trying to shoot Henri to try harder. He took a deep breath. 'I mean, what do I do once I go through that door?'

'I am sorry. Ees good question,' Henri tapped his helmet as if trying to wake an answer. 'That house has been abandoned for a while. Go through to the other side then turn left, follow the lane up the hill until you get to the market. We still have a little daylight left, so you should get there in time, if you hurry. Then find a taxi to take you to Hotel Gungor. When you get there, you will buy me many drinks.'

Henri pulled back the mechanism on his pistol once more, winked at Gavin and started to rise slowly above the edge of the stone wall.

Gavin had been hoping to keep the Frenchman talking for another half an hour, at least until sunset, but Henri was now taking aim at a nest of rebel snipers hidden in an upstairs apartment less than a block away.

'Hey mister!'

Gavin looked at Henri but saw the Frenchman's jaw was clenched in fierce concentration, adding new veins to his temple.

'Hey mister!' the voice said again. Gavin turned to see a young boy standing in the doorway across the street. His hair unkempt but his smile was immaculate. He held the Nikkor lens aloft. 'This you photo?'

'*Trois... deux...*' Henri's voice was almost trembling with excitement.

'Wait, Henri –'

'*Un.*'

Henri began pulling the trigger with one hand while the other shoved Gavin out into the laneway. The snipers returned fire.

Gavin rolled through the dirt, holding his head and scrabbling hard with his legs. He glanced up but saw only dust. He heard swearing, in French, but not as close as before. More shots rang out, but he couldn't tell where they were coming from or at whom they were directed. A tug on his collar brought Gavin the final couple of feet to the shallow doorway. Gavin looked up and saw the boy, still smiling and still holding the lens.

'Mister, get up. Dangerous for you.'

Understatement of the week, Gavin thought. He looked back across the laneway but Henri had vanished. So much for providing cover. Gavin steadied himself against the door frame and slid himself upright, trying to stay as flat as possible. He wondered if the snipers could hear his frantic breathing and were using it to train their scopes onto his heaving chest. A single bullet whistled past, kicking up stones and dust as it connected with the street.

Panic. He wrestled with the door handle but it merely spun in his hands. He slammed the panel with his open palms but it brought only more gunfire. Backing up as far as he dared, he launched his shoulder into the timber. White pain flooded his arm, ringing through the nerve endings of his fingertips and drawing tears. It took a moment to register the tugging on his sleeve.

The boy was still smiling. Gavin wondered if it was his only expression. A slender brown hand snaked inside his collar and fished out a single bronze key on a string necklace. He ducked into a half crouch and slid the key into the barrel. The door swung open, catching Gavin off balance. A fresh wave of pain crashed through his shoulder as he landed heavily on the dirt floor. The door swung shut and stole the light away before Gavin could take in any detail. A woman's voice, cracked with age, began to yell from somewhere in the darkness.

Gavin rolled off his throbbing arm and onto his back, looking up at the boy who was now pleading for the woman, presumably, to be quiet. The woman shuffled into the edge of Gavin's frame of vision, still yelling at the boy in Arabic. She buttressed her side of the argument by poking the boy in the chest with a walking stick that looked as if it had been fashioned in Mordor. The argument ricocheted between the two as the boy tried to calm the woman, but progress was slow. Gavin pushed himself up to get a better look at the room but was returned swiftly to earth by the woman who placed her entire body weight on his shoulder, via her walking stick. The pain warped Gavin's vision, and he closed his eyes for a moment.

*   *   *

Gavin awoke to find the business end of a shotgun pointed directly at him. It wandered, as if trying to find target lock on a drowsy housefly, but never strayed far from Gavin's forehead. The woman's face, lined by decades of mistrust, appeared at the other end of the firearm.

'Hello mister, you okay?' said the boy. 'You want tea?'

Gavin shifted his gaze, being careful not to move his body. He cleared his throat. The barrel jerked then held steady, trained on his mouth. Target lock achieved.

'My auntie does not trust strangers. Please forgive.' The boy turned and spoke gently to the woman, then reached into his pocket and pulled out Peter's battered lens. 'You will buy this photo from me?'

Gavin nodded and the boy spoke to his auntie. After some negotiation, she lowered the gun in disappointment and the boy rushed forward to shake Gavin's hand.

'Why you come here, mister?' the boy's mouth smiled but his eyes telegraphed confusion. 'Everybody else want to leave.'

'I had to come,' Gavin winced as he rubbed his shoulder. The sniper fire had subsided to a few random cracks in the middle distance, but it still rendered the task of acting nonchalant a challenge. 'I'm a photographer.'

'You look more like tourist. Maybe you should go home.'

Gavin smiled thinly. The kid's face was stuck on mindless grin, but his smarts were in overdrive. 'What about you?'

'This is my home. Where is yours?'

'I live in Singapore.' The words had fallen out of his mouth before he remembered that, as Peter Hasenberg, he would have a basic level of combat immunity and a more comprehensive insurance policy. As Gavin Higgs, he'd be toast. 'No, wait, I used to live in Singapore. But I'm from Berlin, Germany. My name is Peter. Peter Hasenberg.'

'German?' the boy's smile shrank a fraction.

'Yes. Cherman.'

'*Du bist wirklich nur ein dummer Tourist, der keine Ahnung hat, was ich Sie fragen, nicht wahr?*'

Not for the first time, he wished Shanti were with him.

'Look, I need to get back to my hotel and send these pictures to my editor.'

'One thousand.'

'What?'

'One thousand dollars American. I take you to hotel, no problem.'

'No way, kid. For that kind of money I could buy myself a hotel.'

'OK, time for you to go now.' The kid trotted to the door and began unfastening the deadbolt.

'Whoah. OK, OK. How about a hundred?' Gavin started to fish inside his vest.

'No hundred. Thousand,' said the kid. The snick of a rifle bolt recaptured Gavin's attention. The old woman smiled from across the room where she had been watching the negotiations. Her smile had the same slightly demented quality as the kid's. Clearly they were related.

'Two hundred.'

'Seven.'

'Three.'

'Five hundred. Last offer.'

Shanti's lessons in roadside bargaining in Bali had paid off. 'Okay. Five.'

Gavin removed his vest and laid it on the concrete floor. He took a leatherman from one of the pockets and sliced open a seam to reveal a handful of banknotes. The boy started forward but Gavin held up a palm.

'What's your name?'

'Amir.'

'Okay, Amir, you get half now.' He drew the blade through the notes, picked up one stack and handed it over. 'The other half when I get to the hotel.'

The boy's smile froze, but his eyes betrayed a hint of admiration for a fellow negotiator.

Amir led Gavin on a snakes and ladders route through the neighbourhood, turning into tiny laneways and doubling back through peoples' homes to avoid the main streets. Amir slid through gaps in fences and rock walls as if he were water. Several times Gavin lost his young guide in an alley full of doorways and felt that he was truly lost, indisputably alone in a city that no-one appeared to understand or wanted to trust. His Boys' Own adventure was now more a dangerous blunder. His breathing became ragged and his heart rate skidded like a stone on a lake as he imagined the windows above him sprouting rifle barrels. Amir's smiling face appeared from an alcove up ahead and Gavin scrambled through the dust to join him, not because he trusted the boy, but because he had no other option.

Gavin and Amir found themselves boxed in behind a series of DIY roadblocks installed by the gangs of militia who emerged to patrol the streets as night fell. They banded together in gangs of a dozen or so, wearing military colours of various shades, but it was impossible to tell which side they were on or, indeed, how many sides there were. Many didn't appear to know themselves.

The good news, said Amir, was that roadblocks meant they were getting closer to the hotel. The bad news: it was now too dangerous to keep going. The dark made the militia jumpy, and jumpy militia made people dead.

The boy took a few notes of local currency from Gavin to purchase a night's worth of relative security on the bare floor of a front room in a modest family home. Gavin spent the night wrestling with sleep in between the sounds of random gunfire and the throbbing of his shoulder. The bulk of his waking moments were spent wishing he had simply told Shanti that she meant far more than a little crush, instead of choosing to run and sulk.

* * *

'Where the fuck is Gavin?'

Shanti spun her office chair to find Charles, uncharacteristically unkempt and fuming.

'His customer experience team is behind on vetting and approving the new listings. Our investors were promised fifteen hundred new listings this week, with a stretch target of two thousand. And I'm tired of telling you kids that the stretch target is the real target. Trent is going to be in a world of pain if we miss that number.'

'Why Trent?'

Charles blinked as if to reset himself. 'I know you're supposed to be a whizz with the code, Shanti, but you should pay more attention to how this business functions. Trent is the CEO. If the investors get upset with the performance of the business, ipso facto they get upset with him. My job right now is to protect the CEO. If we could get Gavin to come into the office and do his fucking job, it would make that small part of my very difficult job significantly easier.'

'Did Trent promise the investors fifteen hundred additional listings this week?' Shanti folded her arms. 'Or did you?'

'I think you should concentrate on finding Gavin.'

'Didn't you just say I should to pay more attention to how this business functions?'

'And right now, this business will function much more smoothly when that moody little hipster gets his bunch of brain-dead keyboard monkeys to load up those fucking listings on the fucking website.' Charles rolled his cuffs up and smoothed his hair. 'If you kids aren't interested in putting in the effort required to take this company to the next level I'll have no hesitation in replacing you with talent that are. I trust I've made my position clear?'

Then he was gone. Charles was a best-in-class douchebag, but he did have a point. Gavin *was* a moody little hipster who hadn't really been doing his job, even before he went AWOL. She took a quick tour through the row of ShelfLife staff on the other side of the office floor, but no-one had seen or heard from Gavin in the last few days. She'd assumed he was sulking, perhaps working from his apartment or a café. Truthfully, she'd been ignoring him with extreme prejudice. The little-boy-hurt routine was wearing thin. If he couldn't understand the importance of her no-fraternising-with-colleagues rule, at least he could have the decency to accept it with stoicism. And if he couldn't have decency, he could at least have a little discipline. Just because you want something, doesn't mean you should automatically have it, right? She hadn't got to where she was today by simply giving in to every impulse that struck, had she?

'Miss Shanti, please. I was responding to this request for information and I think I found a mistake in the listings. There's a whole category that's live in the database on the server, but it's hidden on the website, like a restricted access section.'

A slim Chinese girl in jeggings and t-shirt thrust a printout at Shanti and scurried back to her desk. Shanti looked around at the incubator floor. This was where her years of toil and self-denial and rule-abiding had got her: thirty-three storeys in the sky, in the middle of a manufactured Asian metropolis, taking abuse from ignorant managers, making money for anonymous investors and cleaning up after the sloppy work of inherited coders barely out of their teens. Maybe her self-imposed rules had passed their use-by date.

The printout was of an email sent from an address administered by an arm of the Singapore Government Investment Oversight Committee. The body of the message contained a lot of all caps. The author wanted to know why the managers of ShelfLife continued to approve listings that were outside the extensive and detailed guidance for morally and socially acceptable content as specified by the board (and subsequently enshrined as a central tenet of the terms of agreements between aforementioned board and the specified shareholders in ShelfLife, the company); wanted to know if the company's standard indemnities and policy notes would cover them (the board, not the shareholders) for damages, injuries or fatalities sustained while renting these off-limits ShelfLives; and could they (the author, personally, not the board nor the shareholders), be informed immediately should any listings become available for a coach of a professional cheerleading squad.

Shanti rolled her eyes, stuffed the printout into the back pocket of her jeans and logged back on to investigate this alleged cache of 'restricted access' listings.

* * *

The crow of roosters and the smell of frying onion suggested they were close to the city markets. The morning call to prayer suggested it might be wise to lie low until the streets quietened. Gavin hadn't eaten for over a day and a half, which could well have been a new personal record. Amir had insisted they wait until the midday prayers before moving out. It was only then the militia left their roadblocks for the day, significantly reducing the chances of being shot. Even snipers needed to pray.

'There. You hotel,' Amir pointed through the slow-moving crowd of traders at the end of the street. A white, semi-colonial building stood out among the row of slab-sided concrete structures, but all were similarly pockmarked.

'How did you know that was my hotel?' Gavin asked, rubbing his stubbled head.

'This. In your vest,' the boy held up a matchbook bearing the logo of The Gungor.

Gavin reached for the internal pocket of his vest and found it empty.

'I already take my pay,' the boy held a wad of half-banknotes in each hand. 'Thank you mister and good luck.'

Gavin began to protest but Amir had already melted into the markets and was gone. At least he hadn't taken the lens.

Gavin shuffled through the foyer of the hotel like a weekend jogger crossing the finish line of a professional marathon. He rested against a wall and weighed the effort of ordering something from the kitchen against his overwhelming desire for sleep.

A collective groan welled from the dining hall, followed by agitated chatter that unravelled into several simultaneous arguments. Gavin recognised the group from his first day in the city. A couple of the journalists were from heavyweights like *The Times* and *Le Monde*, but most were stringers and freelancers, hoping their coverage of the Syrian conflict would be the break they needed to land one of the last remaining salaried correspondent gigs in the international press corps.

They jostled for position around a laptop, pointing at the screen. A few were holding hands over their mouths, heads slowly shaking. Gavin craned his neck over the small crowd to see a grainy video of a figure, kneeling at the rear of a bare concrete room, head covered by a black cloth bag. A masked gunman yelled as he entered the frame and held a small book directly up to the lens. The autofocus struggled to keep pace with the shift in scene but eventually the image sharpened to reveal the photo page of a French passport. The watching journalists fell silent.

'Oh god,' the words escaped from Gavin as he stumbled backwards. The journalists turned as a group to stare at him as he slumped to the floor. A flash of recognition lit up the face of a Korean reporter, who pointed and stammered at Gavin. More talking, all at once. A Frenchwoman leapt up, grabbed Gavin by the shirt collar and went nose to nose, demanding to know why he had abandoned Henri to die in the streets of Antakya.

There was a frenzy of pacing, shouting and finger pointing, and it took more than an hour of interrogation before the reporters were satisfied Gavin had not delivered Henri personally to the jihadis who were now threatening, via YouTube, to separate Henri from his head. The Frenchwoman promised to do the same to Gavin, possibly in Gavin's sleep. It made for an exhausting afternoon.

* * *

The mechanical ring of the Bakelite telephone jolted Gavin awake.

'Hello?'

'Mister Hasenberg?'

'No. Who?'

The other end of the line gave him another chance.

'Oh, right, yes. Hasenberg here. Who's this?'

'Reception. You have a visitor. Can I send them up to your room?'

Gavin realised he had been sleeping in the same clothes for several days. 'What time is it?'

'Eleven-thirty.'

It couldn't be good news to have a visitor this late at night. He'd retreated to his room to hide from the thousands of questions everyone fired at him about Henri. No-one cared

238

that Gavin himself had been shot at by snipers, slept in the dirt and had to bribe his way back to the hotel. And all to rescue a camera lens.

'Did you want to order breakfast, Mr Hasenberg? Kitchen is closing.'

Gavin looked up and saw shafts of light stealing in past the edges of the blackout drapes. He must have passed out and slept the clock completely around. God, he was hungry.

'Yes. Eggs. Toast. Coffee. Thanks.'

'Very good. And your visitor?'

'Did they say who they were?'

'Yes, Mr Hasenberg. It's you.'

Gavin almost cried when he saw the German through the spyglass of his hotel door.

'Jesus, Peter, I'm so fucking glad to see you, man. Come in, before you get shot or something.'

The two men shared a fierce bro hug.

'You're the one who's been getting shot at,' Peter made a pistol with his fingers. 'You spent the night out there in the streets because of a lens?'

'It's right here, mate. I wasn't going to let you down,' Gavin retrieved the fifty millimetre from the shabby bedclothes. 'Not after Henri told me how much it meant to you.'

'What are you talking about?' Peter briefly examined the lens before dumping it in one of his pockets. 'Piece of shit. Bought it in Kabul. Chinese copy.'

'No! Henri told me it belonged to Eddie Adams,' Gavin sank onto the bed. 'You won it off a girl? In Rwanda?'

'That's Henri. Always telling stories,' Peter sat on a wicker chair opposite Gavin and lit a cigarette. 'Only the story he's in now might not have such a good ending for him.'

'Fuck. I'm so sorry.'

'Tell me, Gavin, how did this happen? Were you with him when he was captured by those dogs?'

Gavin shook his head. 'It must have happened after.'

'After what?' Peter's eye narrowed against the smoke.

'We had lunch by the market, it was a slow day, he got talking with some locals who said there were rumours of an attack being planned on the east side of town, close to the centre. Henri wanted to check it out.'

'You went with him?'

'He wanted me to stay here at the hotel, but I guess I was being stubborn,' Gavin looked down at his fingers. 'I told him that you had said to always go in a pair if it looked like it could be trouble. Safer that way. Besides, I wanted to see it for myself. That's why I rented your life.'

'What did you want to see for yourself?' Peter studied the lit cigarette between his fingers.

Gavin looked around the small room, the peeling walls and the mismatched furniture from another century. 'War, I guess.'

'So, Gavin, what was war like for you?' Peter's eyes locked onto Gavin's.

'It was awful. I just wanted to get out of there. To make it stop, or go home, or anything. I really thought I was going to die,' Gavin looked to the ceiling, jiggling his clasped hands back and forth, as if in epileptic prayer. 'I still do.'

'People think we do this because it is exciting. That's bullshit,' Peter took a long drag. 'War is terror, nothing more.'

'Then why do you do it? It can't be for the money?'

'Of course not,' Peter gave a small laugh. 'There was not much money in this job before, even when we did have regular jobs with the newspapers. But now we are all contractors, freelancers. It is almost charity. Once the newspapers learn to fly drones properly, they won't need us at all. No, we do it because people forget that war is terror. Our job is to try to remind them. Otherwise, it can become very easy for people to get used to war.'

'How can you get used to this?'

'You'd be surprised what humans will adapt to when they have no choice. Look at this city. Almost a battlefield, but still every day people wake up to sell meat at the markets, to drive taxis, to clean this hotel, to take photographs,' Peter stubbed his cigarette on the sole of his boot. 'It's madness.'

'Henri and I got separated when the snipers were shooting at us,' Gavin's voice broke at the recollection of the sound of the air being split by metal.

'Don't take it personally, Gavin. Those fuckers shoot at everyone. Even each other,' Peter smiled.

Gavin blinked hard. 'He told me to run for a door across the alleyway while he was shooting back at them, to give me cover. That's the last I time I saw him.'

'He had a gun?' Peter raised an eyebrow.

Gavin nodded.

'I'm sorry. He's been getting mixed up with one of the local factions. I heard some militia were after him. It's tempting to get involved, to take sides, but it never does any good. For any of us.' Peter pushed himself off his thighs and stood. 'He should never have taken you to the eastern side. Better for you to go home now. This is no place for you.'

'I think you're right, Peter,' Gavin rubbed his face with both hands and exhaled. 'I told myself I came here to see something real, something exciting. Truth is, I did it to impress a girl.'

'It must have worked,' Peter smiled. 'She sent me to come get you.'

'Seriously?' Gavin's mood brightened.

'This is the girl you moaned about when you first got here, yes?' Peter asked. 'Tracked me down to my wife's house in Dubai. Told me I had to extract you or she'd tell my wife how much money I have in my other accounts. I don't know how she knows this stuff.'

'This girl usually finds a way to get what she wants,' Gavin sat back on the bed. 'I just wanted her to want me.'

'That's funny, my wife said something very similar. Told me that if I really wanted her, I had to stop running away. This girl at your company? Shansi?'

'Shanti.'

'Maybe she wants to tell you the same thing?' Peter patted his pockets and extracted a crumpled piece of paper. 'She also told me to give you a copy of my flight costs. She says that you'll cover them out of your part of the exit deal. Does that sound right?'

'It does. Thank you, Peter, for letting me be you for a few days,' Gavin smiled and took the paper. 'Now I just want to get back to my own life.'

'How lucky you are to have a life you want to get back to. So many people in this shithole don't,' Peter said. 'Pack your stuff, you're waitlisted on the next Lufthansa flight.'

* * *

Gavin sat on the front steps of the hotel, roasting in the afternoon sun as Peter scanned both ends of the street for a taxi. A few children played in the shade opposite and a couple of small shops had rolled back the shutters to start trading again.

'What are you going to do?' asked Gavin.

'About what?'

'About your wife?'

Peter blew his cheeks out and squinted into the glare. 'I told her I'd come home, try a normal life with her for a while.'

'Really? In Dubai? What are you going to do there?'

'Oh, there's plenty of commercial work. I can shoot for tourism, for property, all sorts. Just not weddings. I never shoot weddings. Too dangerous.' Peter swung to check the other end of the street. 'And what are you going to do when you get home to Singapore?'

'Get straight back to work. The company's gone off the rails a bit. We need to tidy things up and get our exit sorted.'

'Commendable, but I was talking about the girl,' Peter looked down at Gavin. 'I see myself, chasing after so many girls because I don't want to be on my own. But I see you, chasing just one because you don't want to be with anyone else. I think you should chase a little harder when you get back home. OK, this might be your ride.'

Peter waved at an asthmatic old Mercedes as it lumbered up the dusty street. It wasn't marked as a taxi, but most car-owners in Antakya were happy to put their vehicles to work. The Mercedes saw them and picked up speed. Gavin saw the figures rise in the back seat, but wasn't able to move fast enough. He heard Peter shout in his ear and felt a hand plant itself in his back. A burst of gunfire spat through the heavy sunlight, far louder than the sniper fire he'd heard a couple of days before.

He rolled in the dirt and pressed himself behind some crates left in the street, covering his head as the shots continued. Angry voices shouted. The Mercedes bellowed as the driver sped past.

Gavin opened his eyes but saw only dust, kicked up by the gunmen's car. The street had fallen quiet just as quickly as it had been engulfed in violence. He rolled on to his belly and crawled through the dirt, staying close to the crates, back towards the steps.

'Peter?' he whispered.

There was no sound on the street. No sirens, no screams, no calls for help and no assistance. Only Gavin's harsh, shallow breathing rushing through his own ears. It was as if the sound of gunfire had chased away the entire population.

After a few moments, Gavin pushed himself around to the end of the crates, to where he could see the hotel steps.

Peter stared back at him, his body splayed awkwardly on the concrete steps. His eyes did not move.

Cancel all my meetings

A genuinely relieved Trent pocketed his mobile as he leaned into the frosted glass door of the incubator, protecting his takeaway coffee: Gavin had been located and would be on a flight back to Singapore by the end of the day. The downside was that the episode had heightened the Singapore investors' angst. Charles had recommended Trent cut short the promotional tour of north Asia and return to HQ: 'Nothing major – just show your face and help me calm the horses.' Whatever happened, Trent was determined not to miss his speaking slot at StartSlam Taipei, a three-day mosh pit of investors, dreamers, coders and hustlers, now being scrutinised by the likes of Bloomberg, AWSJ and Fast Company.

He should have prepared something a little more formal in the way of a debrief for Charles, but then again Charles had advised against spending too much energy on reporting success when your primary job was to generate it. Trent was sure he'd done plenty of that. Charles' connections had opened doors almost everywhere and the continued rise of ShelfLife guaranteed Trent was invited to step inside.

'Ready for you now, Mr Carlisle.' A sharply-dressed young man carrying a tablet and wearing a headset intercepted Trent before he could get to his desk. Clearly someone had been hiring in his absence. And purchasing headsets. He hoped the costs were covered by incubator management. ShelfLife's costs were continuing to outpace revenues, but Charles said this was standard for a hot startup and absolutely necessary for the Private Equity market to consider them a legitimate IPO candidate.

Swinging open the conference room door, Trent was met by a row of executives wearing tailored suits in variations of navy, seated at the opposite side of the conference table. There was no sign of Charles.

'Good of you to join us finally, Mr Carlisle. Perhaps now we can begin.'

It was the woman he had met on his first trip to Singapore, Ms Lim, the one who had fashioned the original investment deal.

'Mr Shaw, pass a copy of the agreement to Mr Carlisle, please.'

A younger man – perhaps the same young man at the initial meeting, Trent couldn't be certain – slid a stack of papers across the table.

'I think I might be in the wrong meeting,' Trent gestured outside. 'My apologies.'

'Take a seat, Mr Carlisle. You are exactly where you need to be,' Ms Lim said.

'But not where *we* need you to be,' added an older Singaporean man, peering over his wireframe glasses.

Trent took a sip of his coffee and surveyed the room. He guessed these were heavyweights from the investment co-op, or maybe even higher up in the government itself. Trent had met dozens of these types at presentations and cocktail parties, but most of the upper-level government relationship management stuff had been left to Charles. Which is what he thought Charles should be doing right now.

'I was expecting to have a private conversation with my business partner,' said Trent unhitching his carry-on from his shoulder and taking a seat.

'Which is exactly what you are doing now, Mr Carlisle,' said Ms Lim. 'As representatives of the organisation that has acquired a significant stake in your firm, we naturally consider ourselves to be your business partners here in Singapore. And we have serious reservations about your ability to manage this business and deliver continued growth.'

Wire-rims cleared his throat. 'We are most concerned with your ability, or rather your inability, to follow simple instructions: you continue to offer an array of dangerous, immoral and, frankly, distasteful life-rental options to our citizens. This is unacceptable.'

Trent gave tight smile and a small nod. This must be blowback from Gavin's little Syrian adventure. Some initial media reports had mentioned a so-called a 'job-swap app', but then the world's attention had swung to a second video the Jihadis had released claiming they would strap the French reporter to an anti aircraft missile.

'I can assure you the incident in Syria was completely unrelated to our business,' Trent smiled warmly.

The senior representatives exchanged glances. A few of the juniors began flicking through stacks of documents, murmuring to each other and shaking their heads.

'An incident in Syria?' Ms Lim adjusted her eyeglasses. 'Would you care to elaborate?'

Trent reached for his coffee cup and took another sip to buy some time and hide his reaction. Fuck. If they didn't even know about Gavin's little Middle Eastern flame-out, then what was their grievance? And where the hell was Charles? Stall them, Trent reasoned with himself, just buy the fat man a little more time and he'll straighten things out, surely.

'My apologies. I had assumed you were referring to rumours that had surfaced recently. I assure you, none of our operations are garnering negative publicity. Quite the opposite.' Trent reached into his bag for his laptop. 'I'd like to give you an update on my press tour of our major growth markets in north Asia,'

Wire-rims cut Trent off, shaking a sheaf of papers. 'You are currently offering a week as a drug dealer in Los Angeles, several dominatrixes – dominatrices? Dom? What are they called?'

'I think we decided on dominatrii,' a junior offered.

'So did we,' Trent brightened.

'Your input is not currently required, Mr Carlisle,' said Wire-rims. 'At least a dozen listings for dominatrii; a…a "dole bludger" in Perth; a hydroponics grower in the Netherlands; a police officer on the east coast of Malaysia –'

'I thought we decided that one was OK?' The junior was quickly shushed.

'A breast health technician at a clinic in Toronto, a stunt driver in Bollywood, a race car driver in Santiago and a tank driver with the Ukraine army.'

Trent made a mental note to ask Gavin to ask his team of interns to please do their fucking jobs. He made another note to get them to package up those last three as 'the Ultimate Driver Experience.' He placed a finger in the air to start, but was mown down by Ms Lim.

'Also of growing concern is your list of creditors. It appears you have arranged to pay many of your vendors in kind, promising to deliver services you cannot hope to provide,' she flipped open a ring binder. 'Your hosting company claims you owe them a week as an engineer with NASA's Jet Propulsion Lab. A coding company in Bangladesh claims a week as a Development Lead in Silicon Valley for ten individuals…'

'And we have received several requests, via diplomatic back channels, from a senior Cambodian Ministry official,' added the junior without looking up from his paperwork, 'who believes he is owed either a week as a ranch-hand in Colorado or a new Harley Davidson Fatboy.'

'You appear to be in breach of several clauses of both your shareholder's agreement and director's contract,' said Wire-rims as he stood and straightened his tie. The other executives also rose, straightening their clothing in sartorial support. 'Make a swift and silent exit, Mr Carlisle, and we may decide not to prosecute these breaches. If we do pursue, it will be as a criminal suit, not a civil matter.'

Wire-rims strode from the boardroom, shadowed by his entourage of suits.

The air-conditioning hummed in the empty room. Trent exhaled. It had to be a mistake. Or maybe a bluff. The investors were probably jockeying for a lower valuation prior to the IPO, which would increase the intra-day gain on listing. Charles had warned him of this.

Where was the pudgy old Brit? Trent wondered. He reached for his phone just as the main door crept open and the young man wearing a headset peered in.

'Ah, Mr Carlisle, there is someone here looking for you.'

'If it's Mr Archer-Ellis, send him in,' Trent said, leaning back in his chair and placing his feet on the boardroom table. Headset Boy winced.

'Ah, no. He says he is from a business publication in Taipei and he would very much like to interview you.'

Trent sprang forward and checked his watch. 'I wasn't planning on doing any media before lunch, but you can send him in.'

The man who pushed past Headset Boy did not fit Trent's expectations of a Taiwanese business journalist. He didn't fit Trent's expectations of a Taiwanese anything.

'I understand you're pressed for time so let's get started,' the journalist lowered his solid frame into a chair and slicked back his blond hair. 'I'd love to get your profile in the weekend edition.'

Trent waved Headset Boy away and smoothed his fringe. 'Well, of course, that would be great. Can I just ask which publication you're from? My assistant neglected to tell me.'

'Just let me get set up here,' the reporter placed a small black recorder on the table. 'I want to get this straight from the horse's mouth.'

Trent nodded. He had several new sound-bites ready.

'Okay, if you could just state your name, your title and your area of responsibility.'

Trent leaned in towards the recorder and spoke from his diaphragm, just as the media trainer had advised. 'I am Trent Carlisle and I am the CEO and founder of ShelfLife,' he said with the bravura of a weekend anchorman. 'My role is to help people change their lives, one week at a time.'

'Mr Carlisle,' said the reporter as he scooped up the recorder and replaced it with a manila envelope. 'You are hereby served with notice to appear in court in the state of Connecticut within thirty days.'

'What?'

'You heard me. You've been served.' The journalist tapped the envelope to underline his point.

'Seriously? Is that even a thing anymore?' Trent grabbed the envelope and shook it as if it were covered in wasps.

'Apparently so.' The fake reporter had pushed himself out of his seat and was now looming over Trent. 'Unless we serve you with US papers, we'd have to file our claim here in the local court. And Susan Carlisle has no intention of travelling to this fake sweaty Manhattan-in-the-tropics to attend a court case.'

Trent looked down at the envelope. 'This is from my mother?'

'She's seeking the total proceeds of the Vandten Corporation shares you sold, while in breach of your employment contract with Mediclinical.'

'She's wasting her time. The money's gone,' Trent folded his arms.

The fake reporter wiped his brow with the back of his hand. 'She's not after the cash, she's after what you spent it on. She now considers herself the owner of a significant stake in a hot new interweb startup, which I assume is what these flash offices are all about.'

Trent exhaled. 'I can't believe my mother would come after me like this.'

'I've only been working her for a few weeks,' said the fake reporter as he made for the door. 'And I can definitely believe it.'

The door closed behind him and the boardroom was silent once again. Now the walls seemed much closer, the door much further away. Trent cradled the envelope in his lap for a while but didn't open it, fearing it might trigger some sort of automatic extradition. Or firing squad.

'Mr Carlisle?' it was Headset Boy again.

'What now?' Trent said without looking up.

A deep clearing of the throat. 'Sorry I'm late, old chap. Mind if I step in for a quick chat?' Charles lingered in the doorway like a vampire angling for a formal invitation.

Trent sat up with a start, fumbling with the unopened document.

'Pressing matters?' Charles asked, gesturing to the envelope.

Trent wanted Charles to iron out this morning's wrinkle with the investors before tackling the issue of a litigious parent.

'Minor issue with the family firm. Where were you this morning?' Trent reached for the stack of papers left on the table. 'I could have done with a bit of Archer-Ellis muscle to keep our investor friends in check. They got a bit snotty. They appear to have forgotten who's actually running this company.'

Charles walked to the far end of the table but made no move to be seated. 'Yes, look, about that …'

Trent started leafing through the pages. 'They were a little rude – but if you get them to calm down, I promise I'm not going to hold a grudge. After all, it's just business,' said Trent, the pace of his page-leafing subsiding as he took in more of the document. 'They're kind of over-reacting with these demands, aren't they?'

'They're not demands, old chap, they're instructions,' said Charles. 'And it is expected you will follow them.'

'They're asking me to sign over almost my entire stake in the company,' Trent slapped the pages with the back of his hand. 'Why do they think I would do that?'

'Because I told them you would,' said Charles.

Trent stopped reading and looked up, hoping to find Charles' familiar sly grin, the one that indicated an utterly brilliant and completely unexpected strategy was about to unfurl. There was no grin.

'You had a great idea, sunshine, but the ideas market is in surplus. Execution is the only thing in demand and yours has been flawed from the get-go,' Charles shot his arms out and adjusted his cufflinks. 'I told you to get some oversight on board, demonstrate you were serious about addressing the investors' concerns. The grown-ups will take it from here.'

Was Charles role-playing here? Practising a speech for another meeting? Trent had seen Charles pursue the hard line before, but to find himself on the receiving end was disconcerting.

'I know I wasn't keen about getting someone senior in to handle operations when we talked about it the first time, but now with the scale we're achieving, it's starting to make a lot more sense.'

'For fuck's sake, Carlisle, give yourself an uppercut.' Charles gripped the back of the chair with both hands. 'I told you to put a psychologist on retainer to prevent these high-risk life rentals from sneaking through and you ignored my advice.'

'You told me not spend a cent on those guys, that we didn't need them.'

'If you'd listened, you would have heard me tell you that you couldn't *afford* them. If you'd spent less time making promises and more time delivering results, you would've had the revenue to cover your basic opex requirements.'

'I can't believe you're saying this,' said Trent.

'And I can't believe how quickly you've become the handbrake on this business, Trent. I'm here to take back the wheel.'

Trent sank back into his chair, gripping the arms for support.

'Did you even listen to what the investors were saying to you this morning? You kids are giving people all sorts of ideas, telling them that they can be anything. This country can't handle that sort of social instability,' Charles pointed his finger at Trent. 'Not everybody gets everything they want. Including you.'

Trent had admired Charles' chameleon-like ability to fit any situation, which he'd always done with a wink and a nod. This transformation was complete and unnerving.

'The offer you've just been handed is a very good one, Trent. You walk away and get one point one mil in cash, local currency, which is nothing to sneeze at. Plus, you keep a small parcel of shares, almost a half a per cent, which is a nice souvenir for you. It's also an insurance policy for us, in case you want to use your last fifteen minutes of startup fame to say something stupid in public.'

Trent's throat constricted. This seemed like the part where he was getting kicked out of his own company.

'Don't look so glum, Carlisle. Most founders get shown the exit long before this,' Charles stepped closer and lowered his voice. 'You've actually hung in reasonably well, for a novice.'

Trent had admired Charles for his ruthlessness, had even sought to emulate it on occasion, so it was a shock to realise Charles had always regarded him as disposable. It embarrassed him that he hadn't seen it until now.

'Not signing.'

'What's that, old chap? Didn't catch that one,' said Charles.

'I said I'm not signing,' Trent placed the documents on the boardroom table. 'I'm not giving up my own company.'

'I've got a lab test says you will,' Charles took a small screwtop jar from his suit pocket and placed it on the document stack. 'Try not to miss, eh?'

Trent looked up, open-mouthed.

'You think you were invited to all those parties for your sparkling personality?' Charles snarled. 'I recommend you read the section of your Director's agreement that pertains to drug-testing.'

'Drug testing?'

'Doesn't anyone from your generation do their fucking homework?' Charles straightened his back and folded his arms across his chest. 'You kids think you're so smart when you discover a shortcut, then you complain when it takes you right back to where you started. So have a little think and a good, long read of your contract this time. It's your only way out.'

Trent clenched his fists under the table. 'What happens to Gavin and Shanti?'

'I told you to keep a closer watch on those two. Letting your hipster go missing was a bad idea,' Charles walked towards the main door. 'And as for your little coder friend, you might want to ask her how a bunch of rich kids from São Paulo with no technical experience launched an exact copy of our site in just a few weeks. I'm told even the code is identical.'

Trent glared at Charles, his urge to choke the older man stayed by the realisation Charles was expecting it. An assault charge would be an even cleaner way to remove him from the company.

'You can either sign the fucking papers, or piss in this jar and hope the lab somehow screws up the results.' Charles pushed open the double doors of the boardroom. 'I know which one I'd rather do.'

Trent sat and stared at the pile of documents from the investors, the envelope from his mother and the sample jar from Charles.

'Fuck me,' he said, running both hands through his hair. He was at zero from three. He wondered if the boardroom was jinxed. The explanation appealed to his 'why me?' gene.

He'd known his mother was angry, pretty much since birth, and the investors always seemed hard to please, but he couldn't understand why Charles had turned on him. Should he call a lawyer? Get the documents looked over, their weaknesses exposed? Maybe he could use Charles' own gambit to oust *him* from the company, regain a majority stake and put the investors back in their box. Trent reached for the document, knocking over the empty sample jar. It spun lazily on the glossy black table.

'Fuck,' he said to himself, again, in the empty room.

Initially, he'd been hesitant to indulge, mindful of the signs and posters and leaflets and forms that had spelled out Singapore's intolerance of all recreational substances except booze. But soon it seemed like a rule that only applied to other people. Sure, if you weren't connected, you'd be a fool to tempt the laws of the state, but Charles had connected Trent to 'the right people' from the moment he landed.

And there it was. Charles' connections. Charles' investors. Charles' party friends. And now, Charles' sample jar.

'Fuck, I'm such an idiot,' he said, again to no-one.

'Sometimes.' Ping had slipped in through the gap between the double doors, sat next to Trent and took his hands. 'But not all of the time.'

Trent managed a weak smile as he slumped back in his chair. His hands slid from hers.

'What is it? You look so worried.'

His face had betrayed him. 'Oh, a tough meeting with the investors.'

'For the whole morning?'

Trent checked his watch. 'It felt longer, to be honest. But hey, what's happening with you? I haven't seen you in a week.'

'It's been almost two. I thought you were in Taipei for a few more days, whipping up more press coverage for yourself?'

'For ShelfLife. Every time I get on stage, it's for the company,' he countered. 'But we had a thing in Syria that was looking serious for us, so Charles called me back.'

'It's looking serious for the French journalist,' she shot back.

'Oh god, look, I'm sorry. That sounded stupid,' Trent offered.

'Gavin's the stupid one. What did he think would happen in a civil war?'

'How did you know Gavin was involved?' Trent's eyes narrowed. What if Ping was part of Charles' plan to infiltrate the company? Is that why she had been spending more time with him over the last month or so?

'Shanti asked me to help track him down. One of the new hires stumbled across a whole stash of secret listings,' she took Trent's hands again. 'We found the life Gavin had rented, completely off the books. When the news broke about the kidnapped journalist, we tracked him down and got him out, just in case he was mixed up in it.'

'But that guy's an actual war photographer. Gavin is just some designer from Melbourne who likes taking photos. I mean, why did he even go over there?'

'Is it because you're so focused on your work,' Ping brushed Trent's fringe from his eyes, 'or are you really that oblivious to the human condition?'

Trent shook his head, unable to follow the logic.

'Can't you see it, Trent? Gavin was trying to get her attention.'

'Get her attention? But they work together. We all live in the same apartment block. Couldn't he just talk to her?'

'Oh boy, you're in your own little world right now, aren't you?'

Trent exhaled and realised he most definitely was: a family out to sue him, a mentor out to frame him and business partners trying to desert him. At this point, he couldn't decide if Ping was his soul-mate or part of Charles' set-up. He'd have to make a choice fairly quickly.

'I came to tell you I'm thinking of leaving,' said Ping before Trent could make the mental coin toss. She took some papers from her satchel and laid them out on the table. 'I wanted your opinion on a couple of things first. Charles is pushing me to take another round of funding from a panel of investors he has lined up.'

Trent sucked in his breath. It was bad enough he might be losing her, the fact that it was Charles stealing her away pushed it into the realm of horrible. Was this another part of Charles' plan?

'Don't worry, I don't like it either,' Ping quickly leafed through the document. 'Their valuation is based on us becoming a white-label courier drone service, aimed mainly at marketers.'

'Like that thing with the soda on the building site?'

'So limited, right? Plus, I can't stand Charles because he's a stupid inbred sack of meat.' She blew a stray hair from her face. 'I know he's your mentor but don't expect me say nice things about him.'

Trent leaned over and kissed Ping.

'That was a strange response,' she said. 'I thought we weren't supposed to kiss in the office. Or are you changing the rules again without telling me?'

'It's been a strange day. I think lots of rules are changing right now,' he tucked a lock of hair behind her ear and smiled gamely. 'What's the other interesting development? Who else wants to take you away?'

'Wow, possessive too,' she smiled as she shuffled the papers. 'Next thing you'll be wanting to tell me your life story and introduce me to your parents.'

'Trust me, you don't want anything to do with my parents,' Trent shook his head. 'What's this other thing?'

'Another offer, looks more promising. It's a fund that invests in technology to support medical industries in developing countries. The kind of partner I've been looking for.'

'That's great news,' Trent lied. 'Where are they based?'
'The offer is from their Hong Kong office. They've just opened there, but their HQ is in New York, so I figured you might know them. Didn't you tell me you worked in med tech back home?'

Trent scanned the pages, pretending to take in the detail, but froze when he flipped back to the cover. The funding proposal was from Bioma Ventures, the innovation arm of Mediclinical.

'Unbelievable,' he said, shaking his head and letting the document fall to the table.

'I know,' said Ping. 'It seems like a low offer but I'm going to accept if they're legitimate.'

'Oh they're legitimate, all right,' said Trent. 'They're actually kind of a big deal.'

'So you have heard of them?' her eyes narrowed.

'You could say that,' he smiled weakly, gripping the envelope in his lap. 'But you should move fast if you're going to do it. They get their R & D funding from a big corporation that's, well, entering a period of instability. Let's leave it at that.'

'How can I leave it at that, Trent? Clearly you know these people, why wouldn't you tell me about them?'

'Because these people are connected to my parents.'

'Oh, so the no-talking-about-family rule is still in effect, is it?'

'Ping, I'm trying to do something without my parents' involvement, so I prefer not to talk about them. I know family means more to you than it does for me but I'm not trying to hide anything. I'm just doing things my own way. Like you leaving the incubator, getting your own investors.'

'Investors you have information on, but won't share with me,' Ping slapped the papers. 'If you won't tell me as your kinda-sorta-maybe girlfriend, then at tell me as a fellow entrepreneur. C'mon, founder to founder.'

Trent exhaled and looked her in the eye. If he couldn't bring himself to tell her he had started think of her as his girlfriend, he could at least tell her who she was getting into bed with financially.

'It's my dad.'

'Your dad works for Bioma?'

'He's on the board. He didn't write the offer, but he would have approved it. They'd be a good partner for Rotronica.'

'The father you won't tell me anything about would make a great investor in my company?'

'Dad's okay. My mother's the problem. My dad is just, y'know, married to her. So they come as a set. Which is why I've been trying to have as little to do with them as possible. But if you like this deal, then do it. Bioma is a good firm and they have connections everywhere.'

'Not that I need your blessing,' Ping smiled.

'You don't need anyone's blessing.'

'But I want you to understand that it means moving the project out into the field,' she took his wrists. He found her intensity unnerving at times. 'This is my chance to take

Rotronica into the real world. See if we can help change people's lives. So maybe we should stop this while it's still just a casual thing.'

'Casual? It's not *completely* casual, is it?'

'Isn't it?' She didn't sound angry.

A knock sounded at the boardroom door. Ping let go of Trent's wrists, but he continued to cling.

'I don't want to see anyone else,' he said.

'Maybe they have the boardroom booked. You've had it for hours.'

'No. I mean you. I only want to see you. I *am* only seeing you. I work, I travel, I do meetings, I do interviews and I see you. That's it. I don't want you to go anywhere. I want you to...' Trent trailed off, realising he wasn't sure what he wanted.

'You're not very good at this, are you?' said Ping.

Trent shook his head. 'There's a lot of things I thought I was good at, turns out I'm not.'

Ping pulled Trent towards her and kissed him. He pulled back for a moment and searched her face. 'I'm sorry, I'm just...'

'It's OK. I've just not seen you look like you need anyone before,' she slipped a wrist free and snaked her hand around the back of his neck, stroking it. 'It's nice. You should try it more often.'

A knock on the conference door again, more forceful this time.

'I don't think I can handle any more surprises today,' Trent blew a lungful of apprehension out through a nervous laugh. 'If it's Charles again, can you make sure I don't stab the fat fucker in the face? Apparently Singapore has laws against that.'

She smiled at Trent and called to the door. 'Come in.'

'Oh, I'm so sorry. I didn't know you two were together,' Shanti stopped in the doorway. 'I mean, I didn't know you were together in here. Wait. Are you two together?'

'Funny, that's just what I was asking him,' said Ping, removing her hand from Trent's neck. 'I'm not sure he knows either.'

'Gavin's flight is landing soon. I don't know what state he's going to be in, so I sent a car to collect him. I'm going to wait for him at the apartments, see if he's okay.'

'Now I'm the one who's interrupting. I'll be around if you need me,' said Ping, as she collected up her investment proposals, giving Trent a look as she left.

'Is Ping angry at you?' said Shanti, taking a seat.

'One of the few who isn't,' said Trent. 'Look, before we talk about Gav, I have to ask you about something Charles told me earlier today.'

'Is that who you were in the boardroom with all morning?'

'Among others. This is crazy, but he seemed to be suggesting you sold our source code to some Brazilians. The crew who launched Lifeswappr last week.'

'Oh Jesus,' Shanti put her hands to her mouth. 'Trent, I'm so sorry. I should have told you about that.'

Trent almost leapt out his chair. 'What the? I was about to tell Charles to go fuck himself. Now you're saying it's true?'

'No, no. I never sold it. I never even gave it to them. Truly.'

'Then what? How the fuck did they launch a site identical to ours in a matter of weeks? Did they steal it?'

'They found it,' Shanti mumbled.

'Found it? What do you mean found it?'

'Or maybe someone found it and sold it to them.'

'How is that even possible?'

'Remember when we first got to Singapore and I was hassling you to upgrade all our laptops?'

'Kinda. Not really. No. Why?'

'That's because I lost mine.'

'I can't imagine you losing anything, ever. How'd you lose a laptop?'

'I was at an airport. It was charging. I was tired and got distracted while I was on a call. I picked up the wrong laptop by mistake. By the time I landed, the tracer had been disabled. They probably pulled the drive from the case and did a hard transfer.'

'Was it me, calling you? Was I hassling you about the site or something? I know I push you pretty hard sometimes.'

'No,' Shanti looked down and fiddled with her watch. 'It was Amber calling me.'

'What's an Amber?'

'Yoga instructor. Bali.'

'Why was *she* calling you? Did you forget to cancel your meditation class or something?'

'Something,' Shanti mumbled.

'Something? What something?' Trent leaned in, eyes wide. 'Like a relationship something?'

Shanti nodded but didn't look up.

'What ever happened to the ice queen of hard code?' Trent slumped into his chair and interrogated his hair with his fingers. 'What is wrong with everyone today? Why is nothing making sense any more?'

Shanti bit her lip and stared at the wall.

'Oh Shanti, you've got a lot more going on that I give you credit for, don't you?'

Trent looked on in horror as Shanti's face crumpled and she began to sob. 'Oh Jesus, was it *that* serious?'

'Not for me,' Shanti wiped her eyes with the back of her sleeve. 'She got a bit attached, I suppose, and I didn't want to just ditch her like she was some stupid boy. I couldn't tell her she was just a distraction.'

'A distraction? From what?'

'From Gavin, you idiot!' Shanti slammed her fists down on her thighs. 'Okay, I said it. You happy now? I screwed this whole thing up because I fell in love with Gavin even though I wasn't supposed to.'

Shanti resumed sobbing, her face in her hands.

'The only one who has screwed anything up here is me.' Trent placed a hand on his own chest. 'Is it awesome that you lost your laptop and someone stole all your code off it? No. Also not awesome is Gavin running off to a warzone, presumably to get away from you. Oh, and we should also add "getting sued by my mother" to the list of things that are not awesome, now that we're making one.'

'What is wrong with that generation?' Shanti shook her face out of her hands to look at Trent. 'Your mother. My uncle. They're supposed to be family but they treat everyone like a box on an org chart.'

Trent laughed a little. 'Hard to believe, but we've got more than just family issues to deal with right now.'

'Who else is lining up to screw us out of our future?'

'Charles.' Trent reached for the termination contract and handed it to Shanti.

Shanti's eyes narrowed as she scanned the document. 'What is that fat shit up to now?'

'Looks like he's trying to take us out of our own org chart.'

* * *

Gavin shuffled through the front door of the apartment and let his duffel drop to the floor.

'I'm so sorry,' he whispered.

'You're so stupid,' Shanti unfolded her arms and flung them around his neck. He leant into her as if she were a lifejacket and he were drowning. She grabbed a fistful of his collar, and waited for him to surface.

'Hey,' she shook him to try and make a connection. 'It's not your fault. You couldn't have known.'

'It was a fucking war zone, Shanti.' Gavin's jaw trembled as he fought off more tears. 'That's what happens. People shoot, people die and no-one knows what the fuck any of it means. I don't even know what happened to the body.'

'What do you mean?'

'I got bundled into a van, hustled on to a plane and given a couple of tablets. I woke up over Myanmar. When I landed back in Singapore they just scanned my passport and said "welcome home" like I'd been golfing in Phuket. I've screwed the company, haven't I?' Gavin rubbed his eye with his palm.

'I think it's screwed us, to be honest,' said Shanti.

'I don't follow.'

'We need to talk to Trent, but he seems to think it's all over for us anyway. We're getting kicked out.'

'Kicked out? By who?'

'The investors. And that sack of cholesterol, Charles.'

'It's because of me, isn't it?' Gavin took a step back. 'Shanti, I'm really so sorry.'

'And you should be. But the investors didn't even know about you being in the Middle East, so there's something else at play.' Shanti crossed her arms. 'Why did you go to Syria, anyway?' She knew the answer, she just wanted to hear Gavin admit it.

'Technically, it's in Turkey. I was testing a new ShelfLife listing to see if it was legit.' Gavin swallowed and looked around his bare apartment, avoiding her eyes. 'You were always bugging me about quality assurance, so I was doing something about it.'

'Gavin, I know you went because of me.'

'You do?' Gavin looked directly at Shanti.

'And I love you for it.' She reached behind his head and pulled him towards her. 'I'm the one who should be sorry.' Their kiss seemed to last for days, or at least until there was a knock on the door.

'Are you done with running away?' Shanti whispered, lingering to assess his response.

He blinked a few times, eyes moist.

'I think so. It's a lot to take in. Wait here,' he said and returned to the front door.

Gavin began to smile at the sight of Trent but caught himself, memories of the last few days flooding back. 'Mate, I'm sorry. I just wanted to, y'know.'

Trent grabbed him for a fierce bro hug. 'It's okay, man. You're alive, you're here and you finally got Shanti to act like a human. We should be celebrating.'

'I don't feel a whole lot like celebrating, to be honest.'

'Then let's commiserate instead,' said Trent, placing a wrapped bottle on the kitchen counter. 'Do you have glasses?'

'Four tumblers. Same as your place. Same as my place,' said Shanti reaching into a cupboard.

'Ladies and gentlemen, as the original co-founders of ShelfLife, I believe it is time for us to speak freely. I'll go first,' said Trent as he arranged the tumblers, cloudy from a thousand dishwasher cycles. 'It is my professional opinion that we are well and truly fucked.'

'Pour one for Peter,' said Gavin staring at the glasses. 'He loved his vodka.'

'You weren't responsible,' Trent raised a hand.

'No. I am. He's about as fucked as you can get, because of me.'

'We don't know that for sure,' said Trent.

'Well, he looked pretty fucked lying in the dirt in Antakya.'

Shanti placed an arm around Gavin's shoulder. He shrugged, but made no attempt to move away.

'Trent's right. There have been no reports of Peter, nothing in the media. And not just in the local press. It's weird, like you were never even there.'

Gavin looked up at Trent. 'So then where is he?'

'Who knows? But someone bundled you out of Syria or Turkey or wherever you reckon you were and got you back to Singapore in a real hurry. So maybe they got Peter out as well,' reasoned Shanti.

'Why would anyone do that?' Gavin looked around the apartment, as if he might find the answer written in the corner of one of the anonymous corporate artworks.

'I'm starting to think someone wanted to get you back here, with us,' said Trent, lifting his glass, 'They didn't want any loose ends. They want to get rid of us as a box set.'

'If anyone should get fired, it's me,' Shanti volunteered. 'I'm the one who lost the laptop with all our code.'

'They're not playing favourites. We're all getting the axe,' Trent threw his drink back and grimaced. 'Charles is throwing us out of the company. He convinced the investment board that we should all be replaced. He's blackmailing me into agreeing with them and signing over our stake.'

'Serious?' said Gavin.

'Completely. Oh, and my mother wants to throw me in jail for a period of not less than seven years.'

'I made friends with a member of the Syrian Resistance Army. Or one of the Syrian Resistance Armies. He's like ten years old,' Gavin stared into his glass and took a slug. 'Saved my life.'

'Cute. What's his name?' asked Trent.

'Trent, can we just cut the fucking banter and work out what's going on here?' Shanti slapped the benchtop. 'Gavin's been shot at, there's still one photographer missing, maybe dead, you've been gone for a week, then you spend the day locked in secret meetings only to announce we're getting kicked out of our own company? What the actual fuck?'

'You forgot the part about his mother trying to put him in jail.' Gavin looked up at Shanti, the fatigue visible on his face.

'We'll get to family issues soon enough,' said Shanti. 'Let's start with Charles. How is he going to kick us out?'

'He's setting our island on fire and then offering us a boat.'

'I handed him the match, didn't I?' Gavin's chin sank to his chest.

'If we don't sell our shares to him for his specified price, he'll trigger the Dereliction of Duty clause in our agreement with Vertica.'

'He gets to keep the company's reputation intact and all the risks disappear with us. He knows the company's about to go ballistic so he's trying to take it all for himself,' Shanti clenched her fists.

'What's his specified price?' asked Gavin.

'Works out to just over a mil, Sing dollars.'

'Are you fucking crazy? A million dollars? Why are we even discussing this?' asked Gavin. 'I'm done. I don't know if you've ever been shot at, but it kinda changes your perspective on things. Let's take the money and go home.'

'Wait a minute Gav,' Trent motioned for him to calm down. 'After we split it and tax it and pay fees and withholding and god knows what else they have up their contractual sleeves,

I reckon each of us would be lucky to walk with less than a hundred gee once we convert it into real money. I put more than that into the company in the first place.'

'Hundred gee more than I have right now,' said Gavin. 'And a hundred more than anyone I met in Syria.'

'With ShelfLife at the scale it is now, it could go on to make hundreds of millions,' said Shanti, toying with her glass. 'No wonder they kept a lid on your trip to the warzone.'

'And on Peter,' said Gavin.

'You might have been right all along, Shanti. Charles has been playing this game the whole time, acting as the middle man between our idea and the real investors,' said Trent. 'If we fail, he washes his hands and moves on. Not his money, not his problem.'

'Didn't he put cash in as well?' said Shanti.

'You know, I always assumed he did, but I think he just pledged that villa in Bali as equity instead,' said Trent.

'That's bullshit. Marty told me foreigners can't own land outright in Bali anyway. You need to partner with a local,' Gavin rubbed his chin. 'Some poor villager thought he was going into property development, but the land was actually collateral for a startup he didn't even know about. That Charles is a slimy fucker, eh?'

'It doesn't even matter anymore. Now that they're positioning ShelfLife for an IPO all he has to do is push us out, take our share and leverage a buyout from the Singaporeans.'

'And he's using the lost code as evidence we can't be trusted to run the company,' Shanti with a note of resignation. 'That's how he'll cut us out.'

'He doesn't need to use that. I handed him the hatchet when I went off to Antakya.'

'I appreciate you falling on your respective katanas, but it was actually me,' said Trent. 'I fucked it up. For all of us.'

'You? How?'

'If we don't take the deal - all three of us - Charles is going to make me take a drugs test,' Trent stared into his empty tumbler. 'He wants a goddamn urine sample.'

'How does he even know you'd test positive?' Gavin asked.

'All those party people I've been hanging with, they're Charles' friends. He introduced me to them. He set it up. Just like he set this whole thing up, all the way down the line. We did all the work, the investors took all the risk and he's about to make all the money.'

'So what do we do?' asked Shanti.

'I still say we take the settlement cash. Shanti can pay out her uncle,' said Gavin, refilling their glasses. 'Peter said he had to downgrade his insurance coverage when he was forced to go freelance. I want to find his wife in Dubai, give my share to her.'

'Love the sentiment, Gav, but even if we wanted to, we couldn't. My mother just unleashed a pack of lawyers on me. If she wins, any entitlements I am owed by ShelfLife, be they cash, shares, high fives or whatever, all go straight to her.' Trent pushed himself upright. 'And because your shares were issued by me before we incorporated, she'll claim those too. Sorry to say.'

'I must have missed this part when I was in a war.' Gavin wiped his mouth with the back of his hand. 'How does your mother become entitled to the profits that Charles is blackmailing you out of?'

'It was her cash that started this thing.'

'I thought it was your money that started us up,' said Shanti.

'It was, in the beginning. Then we ran out, so I sold my shares in The Vandten Corporation.'

'Who the fuck are The Vandten Corporation?' asked Gavin.

'My parents' holding company. A private equity firm has been angling to buy Vandten and break it up for the underlying assets. That's why they paid so much for my shares.'

'That's like out of *Wall Street* or something. Nice move,' said Gavin.

'Except for the part where I'm apparently in direct violation of my shareholder's agreement for selling my shares to a hostile private equity firm.'

'When did we run out of money? I thought that's why we moved to Singapore, so we could take on the funding from the investment co-op?' said Shanti.

'It was just after Saigon,' said Trent.

'You sold shares in your parents' company to bail me out of that mess?' Gavin looked aghast.

'No, that money came from when I got fired for impersonating a surgeon.' Trent lifted his glass. 'I sold the stock mainly for me. I wanted to get out of the family business. Start afresh. I used the money to prop up our balance sheet so Charles could get us a better valuation from the investors. Which is how he's going to make an absolute fortune from a minority stake he didn't even pay for.'

'He's a lot better at this game than we are, right?' Shanti shook her head.

'Impersonating a surgeon?' said Gavin.

'Story for another time. Charles has me on the drugs thing, but if it wasn't that it would be something else. That's just the icing. He always planned to steal the entire cake.' Trent looked to Gavin then Shanti. 'I'm sorry I convinced both of you to give up your real lives for nothing.'

'It was better than pushing pixels around for an ad agency,' said Gavin. 'And you saved Shanti from becoming a waitress.'

'You'd make a lousy waitress,' said Trent.

Shanti waved his joke away. 'It wasn't for nothing, Trent. Look at what we created. We found a way to let people change their lives, even if just for a little while.'

'We've started up a mini-industry, y'know? There's a whole ecosystem popping up around it. Companies that produce custom ShelfLife video profiles. You can buy specialised insurance packages,' said Gavin. 'There's a consultant in LA who assesses your current lifestyle and then recommends the perfect ShelfLife rental to help you feel better about yourself.'

'Better how?'

'He books you into a life that's way more challenging or boring than your real one, so after a week you come home grateful for what you've got.' Gavin took a sip and shrugged. 'I see the appeal.'

'All the more reason Charles wants to steal it all, right now,' said Trent.

'At least we'll be able to say we were running ShelfLife when it was cool,' said Gavin. 'Charles is going to be the guy who ran it during the lame period.'

'What do you mean lame period?' said Trent.

'The government wants it all safe and sanitised and not very interesting anymore. People will get bored with it. That's partly why I went to Syria. Partly,' said Gavin, shooting Shanti a look. 'I wanted to be able to say I rented one of the cool lives before ShelfLife jumped the shark.'

'That's right, in a way,' said Shanti. 'I mean, all the interesting stuff, the challenging part of the build, is all done. We should be proud of what we've made.'

'I love that you're still jazzed by how cool it is and you're proud of the code, but I promised you guys a big exit and we were really, really close,' Trent placed his palms together under his chin. 'What if I go talk to the investors?'

'And tell them Charles tricked you into taking ecstasy? Or that I lost their IP? Or Gavin flew to a warzone and impersonated a press photographer?' said Shanti. 'We all love that never-say-die Carlisle attitude, Trent. But it's not enough this time.'

'I guess you're right,' Trent's shoulders dropped. 'There's nothing I can do except sign the papers, take the cash from Charles and hand it straight over to my mother.'

'Why be a middleman? Get Charles to take it to her directly,' said Gavin.

'Fuck, I could just imagine those two together,' Trent placed his hands behind his head as he walked a slow circle. 'They almost deserve each other.'

Shanti's eyes went wide. 'Hang on, so why don't we give him what he deserves?'

'I'd love to, but the bell's rung. Once he dilutes our holdings, he controls the whole thing. The fight's over.'

'Hold up,' started Shanti, rubbing her palms together, 'what if the thing he takes control of turns out to take control of him?'

Trent stared at Shanti, waiting for an explanation.

'I need the name of that Finance Minister Charles was always fawning over. The one from Eastern Europe,' said Shanti as she rummaged in her backpack for her laptop. 'And what's your wifi password, Gavin?'

'Do you know what she's talking about?' Trent turned to Gavin.

'About my password?'

'About the Finance Minister.'

'No, but I think Charles is about to find out what happens when a pissed-off coder decides to rewrite the rules,' said Gavin, grinning as he watched Shanti punish her keyboard. 'How can you not love this girl?'

Everything works in theory

Two soldiers stormed into the Minister's office, rifles raised. They were followed by a heavyset man in a dark grey suit.

'Where is the money?' The suited man appeared to be absent of a neck, and his eyes were unnervingly close-set.

'That's exactly what we're trying to figure out,' said The Professor, gesturing at the piles of paper spread across the table. 'There are many discrepancies but, at the risk of repeating myself, I am not an accountant. I am a professor of behavioural economics.'

The scrum of advisors and translators seated around the table began to inch backwards, as if trying to distance themselves from the matter.

'Either you return the one point two billion,' said the official, 'or you go to jail. All of you.' The soldiers raised their rifles slightly higher and swept the room with their barrels. 'I come back at four pm. You better have some answers, Slizhevsky.'

'I told you, I'm not Slizhevsky,' the Professor protested.

'You very happy running around all week, telling us to treat you the same as Slizhevsky. But now you don't want us to do that any more.' He signalled for the armed officers to take up positions by the door. 'Too late. While in my country, you *are* Slizhevsky.'

The Professor waited for the official to close the heavy wooden door behind him before whispering to his working committee. 'What is he talking about? What is this one point two billion?'

The group sat in awkward silence, none of them daring to make eye contact with The Professor. Or each other.

'One of you must know what's going on?' The Professor scanned the group, stopping at a tall, gaunt official from the treasury who had been the most helpful of the bureaucrats so far. 'Yuri, has this got anything to do with the figures we've been looking at?'

'I. It's not. There have been...'

Yuri was shushed by several of his co-workers and a heated exchange broke out in a dialect The Professor couldn't quite place. After some discussion, Yuri prevailed.

'There were rumours. None of us knows for sure...' Yuri glanced around the table and then to the soldiers by the door, one of whom had already started playing with his phone. 'They were about special deals, secret contracts, shelf companies, tech startups and tax breaks all set up by Slizhevsky. The funds were from many programs – tourism, mining, innovation – they all went to these special companies.'

'That no-one has ever seen! They don't even *exist*!' hissed a young woman in severe horn-rimmed spectacles, stabbing the piles of printouts with her finger.

'Calm down, we know all this,' Yuri motioned for the woman to sit. 'So the Minister, he ask us to move all this money into these nothing companies, tells us it is all approved and then...'

'Then what?' asked the Professor.

'Then now you are the Minister,' a portly official in a rumpled suit fixed the Professor with a stare. 'You are Slizhevsky.'

'What? Me? You can't possibly suspect that I had anything to do with this? I came here to try to help fix your economy, introduce some new stimulus measures, suggest some reforms, that sort of thing.' The Professor pushed the papers off the desk in frustration. 'This has gone quite far enough –'

The re-snicking of rifle bolts brought the macroeconomic discussion to an abrupt halt.

'I think we can clear this up relatively easily,' The Professor made a calming motion with his hands then pointed at the phone on his desk. 'Just a phone call, that's all.'

The Professor pressed the yellow button on the phone and spoke slowly into the intercom. 'Yulia, can you get Minister Slizhevsky on the line please?'

After a pause, Yulia's voice emerged from the speakerphone. 'You are already on the line Mr Slizhevsky. You want speak with someone?'

'Slizhevsky. Get the real Slizhevsky on the line.'

'The real Slizhevsky?'

'Yes, the man who normally sits in this office. He was here last week.'

'I am sorry, but I don't know who was here last week. I am temporary replacement,' Yulia's voice brightened, 'Is someone else you would like for me to speak with you?'

'Never mind. Thank you,' The Professor looked up to find the entire room watching him.

Years of teaching – decades, when he added them all up – had won him a respectable standing within the theoretical economics community, tenure and even a few admiring glances from impressionable sophomores. One had even slipped him a love note, just before the final semester exams. All he had wanted, however, was the chance to test his theories in the real world. He'd taken on a few international consulting engagements during semester breaks, but the consulting fees proved to be only a temporary balm. It frustrated him greatly to be asked for his expert advice only to have it ignored. The stint in Singapore had been particularly bittersweet. His behavioural economics modelling had recommended against almost all of the 'innovative proposals' the Singaporeans were considering. As a counter, he put forward his own scheme to re-balance income tax brackets and reform the import duty regime. The government thanked him, paid him and ignored him. To add injury to insult, they had cancelled his contract just as he was beginning to build a rapport with a fetching young admin assistant by the name of Christina. They had bonded over his admiration of her extensive collection of high-heeled shoes.

Professor Jensen had almost resigned himself to a life of teaching economic theory (with a sideline in theoretical economics consulting), until the afternoon he got a call from one of the founders of a startup in Singapore he'd almost managed to land a job with. She'd started with a half-apology, explaining their investors had prevented them from offering him the role that they believed he would have been perfectly suited to, before moving swiftly along to the heart of the enquiry: would the Professor be interested in running a small eastern European economy for a week or two?

She explained that the post of Finance Minister of Vitebsk, a small but growing region in the northeast of Belarus, was a life-rental opportunity marked as strictly 'expert level' and that he, the Professor, was easily the most expert of all the macroeconomics experts they were considering. It occurred to him now that he should probably have asked exactly how many other macroeconomics experts they were considering.

Once she assured him that he would have most of the same powers and responsibilities as the actual Minister, he agreed to help at a substantially discounted rate. The fact that he was using the Singapore Government's own frivolous investment vehicle to demonstrate the effectiveness of the theories they had paid handsomely to ignore was the icing on the cake. He spent the short flight studying economic data and scribbling in his notebook – he didn't want to waste his week at the helm of a real-life Finance Ministry by being underprepared.

Upon landing, the Professor was ushered into a tired old stretch Mercedes, the driver either unwilling or unable to make small talk. At the Ministry, he was made to wait several hours before Finance Minister Vasily Slizhevsky appeared, their hurried greetings interrupted by an awkward pause as the two men realised they bore more than a passing resemblance to one another.

Jensen was crestfallen to learn the Minister had not read any of his published theories but he pressed on regardless, eager to present his plans for the coming week. The meeting moved in fits and starts as the Minister took calls on his bluetooth headset without warning, while his aides scuttled about, presenting documents for him to sign. When Jensen tried to engage in some macroeconomic chit-chat, the Minister didn't appear overly interested, or even that familiar with the topic. What the Minister did appear overly interested in were the ample breasts of his blonde companion, who was introduced only as the 'special executive assistant to the Minister'. She smiled politely, adjusted her blouse ineffectually and fluttered her eyelids incessantly. The blue light on the Minister's earpiece flashed and the aides scuttled about, bringing folder after folder of documents to be signed. A moment later, the Minister rose, shook the Professor's hand and brought the meeting to a close.

'I think you'll find everything has been prepared for your tenure. I oversaw the paperwork myself,' the minister smirked and was gone.

Unwilling to waste even a minute, Jensen began sorting through piles of documents on the elaborate timber desk in the Minister's office and taking briefings from a variety of aides and officials. On the second day a herd of high school students on a study tour ambled through and he was also asked to approve a banquet menu for an upcoming state dinner but, generally, he was allowed to concentrate on the task at hand. He found a few kindred economic spirits among the bureaucrats, happy to talk into the night, nodding their heads at his ideas then shaking them as an indication of their suitability in Vitebsk. 'The money,' they would whisper, glancing around the empty office and taking a long, guilty pull of ministerial scotch, 'it is gone.'

By the third day the Professor had constructed a wall of cross-referenced printouts worthy of the under-lit Swedish detective series he was fond of binge-watching. He had barely noticed that the assistance, so freely flowing in his first couple of days as Minister, had begun to ebb once the bureaucrats cottoned on to what he was doing. Which was at about the same time the military officials cottoned on to what he was doing.

* * *

'What do you mean no longer with the company?' Jensen bleated down the per-minute international mobile line. He realised now he should have purchased one of those pre-paid calling cards at the airport but, at the time, it seemed a bit of a scam.

'That's correct, sir. Is there anything else I can help you with today?' asked the cheery voice with the lilting Filipino accent.

'Quite a bit, actually. I'm having a misunderstanding with my hosts and I wonder if you could get your manager to have a chat with them.'

'So you are on a ShelfLife rental right now is it?'

'Yes I am, as a matter of fact.'

'Okay sir, and do you have a booking reference number?'

'A booking reference? I'm not sure. Just let me check,' Jensen scrambled over to the big wooden desk and opened his laptop.

'Take your time, sir,' said the call centre representative, implying the opposite.

'I'm awfully sorry, I don't seem to be able to find my booking details.'

'That's not a problem, sir. Can I have your last name please.'

Heavy knocking on the office door startled the Professor.

'My surname is Jensen.'

'Just for security purposes, can I just ask you to confirm your current billing address and your date of birth please?'

'Oh, yes, certainly.' He always felt a little awkward that his current billing address had always been his billing address. The awkward was tinged with sadness as he reeled off the date. So many years, so few adventures.

'Thank you Mr Jensen, I'm just –'

'Professor.'

'I'm sorry, Mr Jensen, what was that?'

'It's actually Professor.'

'Oh, I'm so sorry, Mr Professor, I do apologise.'

'No, not Mr Professor. It's Professor Jensen.'

'Okay, certainly, sir, I mean, Professor.'

The line filled with the sound of a keyboard being punished.

'Okay, I am having some difficulty retrieving your booking. Can you give me the name and location city of your Host?'

'It's Vasily Slizhevsky, in the city of Vitebsk, in the province of Vitebsk, in the country known as Belarus,' said Jensen, closing his eyes to try and block out the banging on the door. 'And I do need you to hurry.'

'Of course sir, and while I'm looking for your booking can I ask you if you'd be interested in staying on the line after we're done to answer a short three-minute survey about the service you received today?'

'Okay, fine, but please just put me through to someone who can help me. There's been an awful misunderstanding and I am concerned that –'

The door left its hinges at the same moment the phone line dropped out. The Professor never did get the opportunity to take that short three-minute survey about the service he received.

* * *

The camera flashes made it difficult for The Professor to find his footing. The battered Kalashnikov wedged in the small of his back only compounded the problem. There was none of the sassy repartee reminiscent of the TV series' White House pressers he enjoyed. After a short statement, in Belarussian, from a bloated military official, questions were asked and answered without much input from Jensen. He looked about for his translator, without success.

There was a long pause and he looked up to find the entire room staring at him, with the exception of the military official, who was, in addition to staring, pointing. Jensen was lifted by the elbows and transported from the room as it began to seethe with whirring motordrives and shouted questions. A heavy door closed behind him and he found himself in a much smaller, much less comfortable office, surrounded by the team of assistants and advisors he'd been working with over the last couple of days.

'What did you tell them?' hissed a small, mousey bureaucrat.

'Well, actually, nothing. Nobody spoke to me at all,' Jensen straightened his sleeves and checked his pockets methodically - a high school excursion to Spain had left him with a life-long fear of pickpockets. 'At least not in a language I could understand.'

Muffled shouting drew everyone to the grimy window. In the square below, a few hundred citizens had gathered, brandishing placards. A bearded man holding a megaphone led them in a series of chants. A small group of police hovered nearby, observing the crowd as if it were a mild rash.

Taking advantage of the distraction, Jensen opened the door, only to be met by a wall of khaki and submachineguns. He paused for a moment to compose his thoughts, but the feeling of steel on forehead persuaded him to retreat into the office where, once again, he was the centre of attention.

'Professor, you have to tell them what you've found,' said one of the assistants, clasping her hands together.

'I rather wish I had the opportunity to do so, but no-one in your government seems to want to listen. It's something of a recurring theme for me, I'm afraid,' said Jensen, adjusting his glasses. 'But I'm sure we'll get our chance to explain what we've found so far. Why don't you tell them about the progress we've made? They'll listen to one of their own, don't you think?'

The room was split evenly between gentle nodding and scathing eye-rolls, but genuine support for Jensen's plan was not forthcoming. The shouts and chanting from the crowd outside grew steadily as night fell. The advisors and bureaucrats shuffled about in small groups, whispering, arguing, darting glances at Jensen and making hurried calls. Jensen found a vacant section of wall to slide down and rest his head against.

He woke some time later to find the last of the bureaucrats in fevered negotiation with the guards by the door. They shook hands with their captors and were ushered out. Looking about the dimly-lit room, Jensen noted that his sole companion was the temporary receptionist. She was engrossed in a tile game on her mobile. He rubbed his legs as he got up and hobbled to the window. It was hard to see in the darkness, but the crowd appeared to have swollen substantially. Several armoured vehicles had been called in to support the police. Jensen felt the woman's breath by his ear.

'It looks like a lot of people want to talk to you,' she nodded out the window.

'Yes, but no-one seems to want to listen to me,' he rubbed the back of his neck. 'Do you have any idea what is going on down there?'

'The people. They think this government very bad for taking all the money. Now the people want the money back.' She turned to look into his eyes. 'But you have the money, don't you?' She shifted closer.

'What do you mean?'

'It must be very lonely when you cannot trust anybody.' She pressed herself against him. 'But you can trust my body, Professor, because I am your assistant, yes?'

'I suppose you are.'

'So when the guards come back, let me help you. We can choose somewhere sunny. Somewhere with not so many people.' She looked down at the crowd as the first light of dawn began filling the grey square. 'I think Portugal would be perfect.'

'Why will they ask me to choose a country?' Jensen tried to wriggle from her embrace.

'Why, my love, for the exile, of course.' She closed the distance between them once more.

'Exile? Who is being exiled?'

'Oh my wonderfully mad Professor,' she ran a hand through what was left of his hair, 'you don't need to play games with me now. We'll have plenty of time for that in Portugal, yes?'

'It's not a game. I need to know what's going on. Please.'

She stopped mid stroke and her smile fell. 'Seriously?'

'Yes.'

'Oh my gott!' She blew a stray lock of hair from her face. 'They will come and ask you where the money is. You will tell them. They let you keep a little bit, but not too little, then put you in a helicopter and fly you wherever you want to go. You promise never to come back. They will hold press conference, telling everyone you escaped, but the clever police found out where you hid the money. Then the police will split the money between themselves and the military. They buy some big guns and some shiny planes. Then everyone make a big party and we start again.'

'A party?'

'Why you don't know anything about this? This happens every time,' the assistant placed her hands on her hips. 'You are the Finance Minister, no?'

'Not exactly.'

'But at least you know where the money is, yes?'

He was ashamed at how fond he had become of having his hair stroked by his assistant. 'Not really.'

The assistant gave a snort, turned and stamped over to the door, rapping it violently. After a brief, flirtatious conversation with the guard, she disappeared without a backward glance.

The sound of breaking glass drew the Professor back to the window. The crowd was chanting with renewed enthusiasm at the line of soldiers protecting the parliamentary building. An armoured truck nudged its way to the front of the crowd while a news van nudged its way to the back.

On the one hand, the protestors seemed like everyday citizens, unfamiliar with violence and posing no real physical threat to the soldiers. On the other hand, there were an awful lot of them, with thousands more pouring into the square as the sun rose higher. On a theoretical third hand, The Professor was not sure what the protestors had been told of his involvement. It would probably be wise to explain the situation before the mob reached their own, possibly violent conclusion.

It took several minutes of pummelling on the heavy wooden door to get the guard to open up.

'Vot?'

'I was wondering if I could have a word with the protestors?'

'*Nyet.*'

'It would only take a minute, I just want to make sure they understand everything correctly.'

'*Nyet.*'

'Well, can I talk to someone from the government, to find out what's going on?'

'*Nyet.*'

'How about your boss?'

'*Nyet.*'

'What about you?'

'What about me?'

'Can you tell me what's going on?'

'*Nyet.*'

Jensen sighed. 'Well, can I have something to eat, please?'

'*Nyet.*'

'At least let me use the bathroom.'

'You want bath?'

'Well, I wouldn't mind, but no, I need the toilet. For God's sake man, I've been in here all night. Please.'

The guard looked along the long hallway in each direction and nodded tersely.

* * *

Jensen stood on the lid of the toilet seat, the narrow window offering a glimpse of the square below. He could just make out the soldier on the roof of the armoured truck, but he appeared to be facing away from the crowd. A couple of protestors climbed onto the roof of the truck, dancing around the soldier, waving banners. Soldiers then moved through the crowd, smiling and receiving slaps on the back and open bottles of wine from the protestors. The Professor rubbed his eyes and strained his neck, trying to make the scene make sense.

A loud cheer broke out as the crowd surged towards the building, lifting bottles into the air, pumping fists and taking selfies. Drones hovered overhead and reporters walked along backwards with the surge, addressing their cameras and adjusting their hair as they went. Brutal thumping on the stall door startled the professor and a foot slipped into the bowl.

'Out, Professor. Back to room. Now!' the guard shouted through the thin plywood door. 'You make big trouble for me, understand?'

A quick blow with the butt of the rifle splintered the lock before Jensen could reply. The guard grabbed a handful of jacket and dragged the Professor back down the corridor, slinging him into the office with the grace of an airline baggage handler. The door slammed shut and Jensen sat, pondering his sodden shoe.

A moment later the door flung open again. The guard walked backwards into the room, hands raised, staring at a thicket of rifles held by a mixed dozen of protestors and soldiers. They started shouting and pointing. Jensen cowered in the back of the room.

'Enough!' The cry silenced the group and a small woman in camouflage stepped forward. 'You are the Minister?'

'No. Well, sort of.'

'You know where is the money?'

'I found some records of funds transfers but it's not entirely clear –'

'The hostage is not co-operative,' the camouflaged woman announced to her walkie talkie.

'Let's take him upstairs, present him to the comrades,' one wild-eyed protestor proclaimed, reaching down to grab Jensen by the sleeve. 'They will see what we have achieved together, using the will of the people as a collective force for meaningful political change.'

'Just take him upstairs, Jako. Leave the slogans to someone more qualified.'

Jensen was escorted up several flights of stairs, past offices filled with fluttering papers and gently burning desks. Protestors and militia ran giddily through the corridors, pausing to tear framed paintings from the walls, topple filing cabinets and pose for selfies. Jensen was marched into a grand office, littered with debris and manned by a group of about twenty rebels working a bank of laptops and barking into cell phones. The room came to a standstill as the soldiers announced their cargo.

'Put him in that office,' said one of the rebel leaders, pointing at a glass cubicle across the room. 'Nastya and I will deal with him.'

The door swung shut and Jensen pushed himself back into the office chair. The student leader wore a red beret and a goatee. Jensen could smell his garlicky breath as he and the camouflaged woman hovered in front of his face.

'Do we need to restrain you, Minister?' said Nastya.

'I'm not the minister,' said Jensen. 'I'm just a professor.'

'Bullshit, you are Slizhevsky. Look,' said the student leader, holding a printout of the Minister. 'He's lost some weight, but it is him.'

'He also lost the people's money. Our money,' said Nastya, drawing a pistol from its holster.

'Yes, the resemblance is remarkable, but I assure you I'm not the minister. You have to believe me,' Jensen's voice trembled. 'I'm a professor. Of behavioural economics.'

'Then what are you doing here, pretending to be Slizhevsky? Your assistant said you know where the money is but you refused to share it with her.'

'She's just as bad as those greedy dogs in the Ministry,' said Nastya. 'You should not have let her go, Danik.'

'She was just a temp, Nastya. She doesn't know anything,' he said, adjusting his belt. 'I have her phone number if I need to get more proper debriefing.'

'I'm the same. Just a temp,' said Jensen. 'I'm not Slizhevsky, I was just renting his life for a week.'

'That makes no sense to me, I think,' Nastya crossed her arms and squinted at Jensen like he was an experiment. 'Why would anyone want to do such a thing?'

'Answer her,' said Danik, poking Jensen in the chest. 'Why do you want to be this scum? Even for a week?'

'I wanted to test my economic theories. In the real world,' said Jensen, his eyes darting around the small office, confirming only one door. 'Really, you've no idea how frustrating it is when no-one wants to listen to your advice.'

'And how did you trick Slizhevsky into letting you impersonate him? Did you have him killed? Did you get plastic surgery for your face? Who's funding you?' Nastya raised her pistol. 'We want some answers we can believe in.'

'It was a website, a portal, they let you rent other people's lives,' Jensen sputtered, squirming back into the chair and raising his hands to cover his face. 'They called me, asking if I wanted to be a Finance Minister for a week. It was Slizhevsky who tricked me. He stole the money, got me to take his place and then disappeared. You have to believe me.'

'I say we shoot him now,' Nastya clicked the safety on her pistol.

'Wait! Wait! Let's think about this,' Danik stepped between Jensen and the pistol. 'Listen to the people outside. They are united. The students, the workers, even our brothers in uniform. They have seen the truth. They all want change. But first, they want someone to blame.'

'Then they should blame Slizhevsky,' said Jensen, peering around Danik's shoulder.

'No-one is talking to you,' Nastya levelled the pistol at Jensen's forehead.

'Nastya, please.' Danik reached for her arm and guided it gently to her side. He leaned in close and whispered. 'What happens if we go out there and tell our comrades their money is gone and the thief has escaped? We'll look like fools. Maybe they even blame us. The protest is peaceful, for now. That could change very quickly.'

'We promised them a revolution,' hissed Nastya. 'And all we have is an imposter and his economic theories.'

'My theories would have worked. They would have given you what you want.'

'What?' Nastya barked at Jensen.

'Redistribution of wealth. That's what you want, right?' said Jensen.

'Yes. For a start,' said Danik.

'Don't forget collective bargaining, the emancipation of the workers, the right to artistic freedom,' Nastya's speech gained momentum. 'These are the legitimate aspirations of the people.'

'Well, yes, the artistic stuff generally comes later, but with a simple recalibration of your taxation regime, a more progressive application of a bracketed framework and fiscal stimulus in areas of the economy that flow to the sectors where your demographics are strong,' Jensen paused to take a breath and check his audience were still with him, 'I can install a policy platform that will achieve those goals.'

'What the fuck are you talking about?' Nastya shook her head.

'Economic reform,' Jensen started to smile. 'The invisible hand, but guided by a new understanding of personal motivation in a societal framework. It's behavioural economics. Very advanced, very exciting. I'm surprised you haven't heard of it.'

'I'm only in second year of business school. We're still covering the basics,' said Danik, turning to keep an eye on the group of militants in the main office, most of whom had drifted back to their laptops and phones. 'This theory of yours, how quickly will it emancipate the workers?'

'I'd need better access to official economic data. My models are based on what I could gather before I came here. But from what I've seen of your records so far…' Jensen gave a little laugh.

'How long?' Nastya raised her pistol again.

'Three to five years,' Jensen swallowed hard.

'We could all be dead by then!' yelled Nastya. A few of the militants looked up from their screens.

'Calm down, Nastya. Revolutions are fast, but change is slow,' said Danik as he coaxed her arm lower, smiling and nodding out to the main office. 'We just need to buy some time. Explain to the people that change is coming. Professor, how confident are you that your theories will work?'

'I've devoted my life to the study of economics and psychology,' said Jensen, straightening in his chair. 'I assure you there is almost zero possibility my policies would not have the desired effect on your economy. But I'd need ministerial-level access to data and policy-making apparatus.'

Danik led Nastya to a corner of the office, whispering in her ear. Eventually, she nodded and he kissed her. Danik stood beside Jensen's chair, placing a hand on the professor's shoulder.

'How would you like to be doing job for us?'

* * *

'Wake up,' a boot tapped Jensen on the shin. 'It's for you.'

He blinked at his laptop screen, filled with random letters. Jensen rubbed his forehead where the keys had left an impression. By the orange glow coming through the balcony doors, Jensen guessed evening was approaching. He could still hear the chanting and singing from the crowd in the square below, but it sounded more upbeat, less demanding.

He rubbed his neck and tried to stand up, but his legs were numb. A military officer handed him a satellite phone.

'I need to know if you have been harmed in any way.'

'What? Who is this?'

'If you have been harmed or are in any physical danger, just say the words, "My hosts have been treating me very well."'

'Well, they weren't at first, but we seem to be getting along much better now,' said Jensen.

'So you are physically unharmed?'

'I've got a bad case of pins and needles,' said Jensen, rubbing his thigh. 'Otherwise I think I'm okay. I haven't eaten anything since morning, though, and I've been working all day.'

'What do you mean working?'

'Economic policy doesn't write itself, you know. Now, who is this? Who am I speaking to?'

'I'm from the Home Office. Before our team attempts the extraction, I need you to listen very carefully and follow my instructions.'

'Extraction?' Jensen, gripped the arms of his office chair.

'We think there's a very real possibility of an invasion. Perhaps armed conflict. You may be in some danger.'

'If you'd said that to me earlier today, I might have agreed with you. A lot of people have pointed guns at me over the last twenty-four hours,' said Jensen. 'But I think we've sorted things out now. We've got some alignment on our short-term goals and the public seem in favour, so we're putting together a hundred-day plan to get some quick wins on the board. I'm working on it now. They've given me an office.'

'Professor, this is a secure satellite uplink, so if there's nobody in the room with you, you can talk freely now.'

'I have been,' said Jensen. 'Why would I do otherwise?'

'It's a bit soon for Stockholm syndrome, but you may be suffering post-traumatic stress disorder.' The voice spoke in calm, measured tones. 'Your appearance on the balcony earlier today, along with the rebel leaders, was a very high-risk situation. You did well to play along with your captors, but it can sometimes provoke a violent response when they realise you've betrayed them. So I need you to sit tight. Neutral behaviour from now on. As I said, our extraction team is en route.'

'I'm *not* playing along, sir,' Jensen stabbed his desk with his forefinger. 'I've been asked to construct a new economic policy framework and that's what I intend to do.'

'Professor. I need you to try and focus. The situation is escalating rapidly. It is possible that Latvian forces are marshalling on the border, just a few hundred kilometres from your current location. We believe they may mount a hostile invasion within hours, to exploit the political instability you've caused.'

'That I caused? What do you mean I caused?'

'You recently purchased the right to assume the identity of the Finance Minister of Vitebsk. Is that correct, Mr Jensen?'

'Well, yes,' Jensen took a deep breath. 'But that was just a rental from some online startup. Now the protest leaders want me to stay. They want me to help them re-design their economy, it's a very exciting opportunity. You can't extract me now, we're just getting started.'

'Stay calm, Jensen. Keep away from windows and balconies. Try not to let them move you out of the room that you are in now.'

'All I wanted to do was test some economic theories,' a note of disappointment crept into his voice.

'Yes, professor. Now hand the phone back to the rebel leader in the beret.'

'You want to speak to Danik?'

'You're in dialogue with them?'

'Well, you can't draft someone's economic policy framework if you're not on speaking terms, can you?'

'And they understand you're not the real minister?'

'A couple of the leaders are aware. It was actually their idea. I think they told the crowd that I've joined the protest. Well, not me. Slizhevsky has. They explained a couple of my new theories, asked for some time to draft some new policies. It's gone down remarkably well.'

The line buzzed and made a squelching sound, as if the receiver was muffled by a hand.

'Excuse me? Hello? Are you still there?' said Jensen, rising from his seat.

'Jensen. Stand-by for further instructions,' said the voice on the phone. 'We're going to need you to be the minister for a little while longer.'

We can be heroes, just for one day

'Are you paying for this room or am I?'

'I just gave most of my money away,' said Gavin, turning out his pockets like a street mime. 'Besides, you're the one who chose this ridiculous confection.'

'When in Rome,' said Shanti, fishing her wallet out of her shoulder bag.

'That's for two nights is it, Ms Menon?' the hotel receptionist gave a slight bow as he took her credit card with both hands.

'Yes. We'll take the buffet breakfast and your deluxe spa package as well.'

'I'm glad this is coming out of your payout,' said Gavin, taking in the ornate hotel lobby. 'Or what's left of it.'

Sheikhs swept past, engrossed in their iPhones and trailing whole families of women in their wake, like sets of babushka dolls in burkas. Bellhops strained under stratified layers of LV luggage, and western businessmen compared sweat rates while adjusting their belts. The entire lobby looked to be finished in gold-plated gold.

Shanti collected their room key and beckoned for Gavin to follow. The glass bubble of an elevator swept them skywards at a dizzying pace.

'She seemed nice. Not what I was expecting,' said Shanti as the gridlocked streets of Dubai fell away beneath them, becoming smaller, engulfed by the surrounding desert.

'What were you expecting?'

'I don't know. Something a little more...'

'Slutty?'

'Okay, yes, I was.'

'That's not very charitable of you, Shanti.'

'It was more a judgement of him. Older white European man in the Middle East, marries a Filipina lounge singer he barely knows and then spends his time in warzones a thousand miles away,' she pushed her sunglasses up onto her head. 'But it seems like they really were in love. Or at least she was.'

The elevator came to a halt and the doors opened.

'He was a decent guy. She seems genuinely sad that he's gone,' said Gavin as they searched the parade of doors for their room number. 'She wanted to know everything about that last day.'

'I think she's grateful, Gavin. Not just for the money, but the fact that you came to see her yourself,' Shanti paused in front of their room door. 'You did a good thing. I'm proud of you.'

* * *

The package fell from the sky and landed with a thud. The tiny helicopter arced away with a high-pitched snarl and a small scrum of children hoisted the parcel aloft like a football team with a trophy. They brought it to the front of a small tin building and placed it on a dusty plastic table. The noise of the rotor blades faded and the tin roof cracked occasionally, expanding in the mid-morning heat. An old man in a chair poked the package with his walking stick. A woman emerged from the doorway and took the package inside, where half a dozen hospital gurneys, jammed side-by-side, consumed almost all of the space.

Each bed was occupied, some by more than one patient, and the concrete floor was littered with cardboard boxes, battered suitcases and small piles of clothes. The woman opened the package carefully while a nurse typed on a battered laptop and fiddled with a cell phone. She initiated the video conference and a couple of male faces, one white and one dark, appeared on the screen. Each time the nurses held up a small box or bottle, the young doctor on the screen spoke quietly to the local boy, who translated for the two nurses. Package by package, the doctor and the local boy described the contents, listed the symptoms they were to treat and explained their application. One of the nurses took notes in a small notebook.

Ping watched from over the shoulder of the local boy as the two nurses on screen smiled and gave a thumbs-up sign. Another local boy tugged her sleeve and led her out through the open doors of the warehouse, where an ancient lorry had juddered to standstill, bringing with it a cloud of red dust.

'Wait. Don't unload anything,' Ping yelled as the young men swarmed from the cabin of the lorry to loosen the spiderweb of ropes securing the tarpaulins. 'First we check the manifest. Then you unload the medicine. Same as last time.' She muttered under her breath. 'And the time before that.'

* * *

The flap of the tent snapped in the breeze. Trent looked up from his textbook, but the high sun had whited out the landscape beyond the open doorway. He underlined a section of the text and closed the book, tossing it amongst a pile on the floor next to his low camp bed. He rolled onto his back and rubbed his eyes, watching the patterns momentarily swirl and melt into the roof of the tent.

'No wonder I dropped out the first time,' he said to the empty tent. 'Too many big words.'

The tent was a boxy canvas affair in a drab camouflage, a cast-off from one of the dozens of conflicts that had scarred the landscape and haunted the population over the last decade or so. A small card table sat in one corner heaped with books. Two stylish leather duffels struggled to contain a small mountain of clothes. A set of shelves, made from planks and cinderblocks, held a modest collection of liquor and glassware, watched over by a framed photograph of Trent, Shanti and Gavin, beaming, arms draped across each other's shoulders, indifferent to the crush of revellers at a beachside nightclub somewhere in Bali. Trent smiled, pushed himself up off the bed and checked his watch. He'd almost forgotten the time.

Flipping open the laptop, Trent pivoted on the corner of the bed to lock onto a stronger signal. He hit the call button on the video conference software.

'I thought you'd forgotten about us,' said a pixelated Shanti. She was dressed in a bathrobe, a white towel making her head appear twice its regular size.

'Holy shit, where are you guys?' said Trent, peering intently at the screen.

'Marriott Dubai. It's pretty killer,' said an equally pixelated Gavin, bouncing into frame and landing beside Shanti on the bed.

'Who the fuck is picking up the tab?'

'She is,' said Gavin, arranging a forest of pillows behind his head. 'I tried to warn her that she won't have much left after she pays off her uncle. But the lady wants a little luxury before we go back to a life of ramen profitable and I'm not one to argue.'

'Bullshit, Gav. You love arguing,' Trent smiled into his webcam. 'How did it go with Peter's widow?'

'It went okay,' said Gavin, rubbing his upper arms. 'Wasn't easy man, but I'm glad I did it.'

'He did great,' said Shanti, also rubbing Gavin's arm. 'Good to see some of our payout going to a good cause. Unlike mine.'

'But you'll never have to waitress again,' said Gavin. 'At least not for your uncle.'

'Hey, did you see the Belarussians dropped the charges against Jensen?' said Trent. 'They've invited him back to consult on economic policy, for real this time.'

'See. We really can help people change their lives,' said Shanti. 'What about your charges? Is your mother still pressing ahead?'

'I guess so, but she's got bigger issues now.'

'I honestly didn't think it would go that far, Trent. I'm really sorry.'

'God, don't be. Belarus is blaming Singapore for meddling in internal affairs, Jensen is blaming ShelfLife for sending him to take the fall for Slizhevsky, Singapore is blaming Charles for criminal mismanagement of ShelfLife. Now Charles is claiming Susan Carlisle owns the majority of ShelfLife and should be held liable for any damages caused by Jensen's life rental. It's like a merry-go-round for assholes.'

'Why doesn't your mother just cut and run?' said Gavin.

'She's trying, but her legal action against me was already in train. The Singapore Government has the opportunity to make a listed US firm the fall-guy for the whole mess. They're also dragging Vandten into a series of competing claims from hosting providers, data security firms and a certain mid-level official at the Vietnamese Ministry of Home Affairs. It'll keep lawyers fed for years.'

'Sounds like a complete trainwreck,' said Shanti, shaking her head.

'My dad maintains the whole thing has been orchestrated by Singapore to distract from their secret role in destabilising the regime in Vitebsk. I thought that was just a wacko conspiracy theory, but now it's running as a serial investigation in The Guardian, so you never know.'

'Didn't you make friends with someone there on one of your press tours?' asked Gavin.

'Like I said, you just never know,' said Trent, grinning. 'Anyway, what's the plan for you two?'

'We're going to use those tickets to SouthBy you bought months ago. It's coming up in a couple of weeks,' said Shanti, rearranging her bathrobe. 'We've had some offers from startups and investors so we're going to Texas to meet them, see if there's anything we want to be a part of.'

'I had a cool idea for an app that helps people find their doppelgangers,' said Gavin. 'But we don't really have any money anymore, so I have to put my own startup dreams on hold again.'

'Would you believe he also wanted to build a nerf gun that shoots tiny little facepalms made of latex?' said Shanti, rolling her eyes.

'I would believe that, yes,' said Trent. 'You've gotta back yourself, Gav. No matter what she says, OK?'

'I dunno, man. Things have been going a lot better for me since I started listening to her,' said Gavin as Shanti punched him in the shoulder. 'I might just keep doing that for a while. I'll let you know how it goes.'

'You do that. I have to go. Miss you guys,' said Trent.

'Are you getting emotional, Trent? I can't tell if it's the student poverty or the desert that's affecting you most,' said Shanti, smirking. 'Let us know if you need us to send in a chopper.'

'Shut up,' said Trent, smiling as he closed the laptop.

Trent's gaze drifted back to the stack of textbooks by his camp bed, appearing like a mountain seen from the savannah.

'At least someone believes I'm going to finish all this,' said Trent to himself, rubbing his hand across the stubble of his chin.

'Stop whining, you big baby.'

He looked up to see Ping standing at the tent's opening, cradling a package on one hip.

'Was that the delivery truck I heard before?'

Ping let out a long sigh. 'Every time they make a delivery, they unpack it before I can check the manifest. This time, I made them wait while I counted all the packages. There's like a dozen items missing. I tell the driver there was supposed to be a hundred packages and you know what he says to me?'

Trent shook his head.

'He says that's normal. If I want a hundred boxes delivered, I should order a hundred and ten. Then he laughs at me!'

'I guess everybody's looking to get paid.'

'For doing what?'

'For not stealing all of it? I don't know. It's human nature. Everybody's looking for a shortcut.'

'Haven't you heard? Shortcuts don't work anymore,' Ping laughed gently and tossed the package on to Trent's lap.

'Ooof,' Trent buckled a little under the heft. He spun the package around to find the shipper's address label and let out a groan. 'Why didn't you let the driver steal this one?'

'Baby, you need these. Your exams are coming up, right?'

'You're right. I might have to go into the village and use the connection at the hospital. The online exam is timed and I can't have the signal drop out halfway through. I only got to talk to Gav and Shanti for a few minutes before the connection went spotty.'

'Well, I've got a crazy idea. I have to go to Paris at the end of the month and present our progress to the investor panel. Why don't you come with me, sit your exams from there, then go and hang out with your friends?'

'I don't think I can,' Trent reached under his pillow, retrieved a small black Moleskine and leafed through the pages. 'Yep, I'm supposed to run clinic that week, so I really can't go.'

'Oh, come on. You're behaving like a doctor already,' said Ping, taking a seat beside him. 'You've got years more study before you get to act all self-important, call yourself Dr Carlisle and flirt with young nurses. You sure you don't want to come to Paris with me?'

Trent put his hand in hers.

'Of course I do. But I can help these people. They actually need me. Besides, I'm behind on my coursework as it is.'

'Plenty of people need you, Trent. Just don't forget that maybe you need people, too.' She stood up and kissed him on the forehead. 'I'll ask Herve to run clinic that week. Now quit your moaning and start your studying. Work hard, get it done and come with me to Paris.'

Trent smiled as she pushed her way out of the tent. He made a few notes in his Moleskine and returned it to the spot under his pillow.

'She's right, again,' Trent said to himself as he opened the new delivery of textbooks, 'Shortcuts are for suckers.'